Jack D'Arc

G. P. Taylor lives in North Yorkshire overlooking the cold Oceanus Germanicus. He has spent most of his life in search of the eternal truths and finally believes he has found the reason why he inhabits a tiny space on this planet. He can be contacted @gptaylorbooks on Twitter and Instagram.

Content Warning: Due to the period that it was set and the occurrence of Jack the Ripper, this novel contains graphic depictions of violent acts, along with language and attitudes prevalent at the time, that some may find upsetting.

First published in 2024
by Markosia Enterprises, Ltd
PO BOX 3477, Barnet,
Hertfordshire, EN5 9HN

Paperback: ISBN 978-1-916968-32-5
eBook: ISBN 978-1-916968-33-2

Editor: Alexia Markos

Book design by: Ian Sharman
Cover art by: sarahphotogirl.com

www.markosia.com

Jack D'Arc

G. P. Taylor

[1]
SOHO, LONDON. 1923.

The smog in Old Compton Street was thicker than Alicia Pringle had ever known. It was a mixture of exhaust fumes, chimney smoke and the dank air that came in from the river, bringing with it the swirling mist. It hung to the high bars of the streetlights like the web of a spider and damped the sounds of the juddering motors as they rattled over the broken roads. As she walked, Alice could feel the rainwater slowly seep through the thin leather of her flat shoes. It had come in a sudden brief shower that she thought would clear the air. As soon as the squall had stopped, the smog thickened even more than before. It covered London like a cowl and had entombed the city for all of that week.

She had woken up at four in the afternoon and had dressed later that day. Opening the window of her apartment, the smog had crept over the sill and filled the room. Alice took the bus from Chelsea that had crawled through the evening streets and dropped her at Leicester Square. From there she had walked in the road and then cut through the back alleyways to Old Compton Street, it was quicker that way.

Looking down at the pavement, she jostled through the crowded street of office workers hoping to get drunk to make their journey home bearable. She had been back in London for two years and hated it more than Paris. With each step she tried to avoid the deep puddles that dimly reflected the lights from the shops and bars. They filled the sides of the road, the water held back by the discarded newspapers and show cards that filled the street. Alice didn't want to see anyone; Soho made her feel that way. She kept her eyes down to avoid the faces of the men who pressed against her in the crowds. They smelled of beer and cigarettes. It mixed with the dirt of the street and the sour odour that came from the back of the restaurants.

'You doing business?' a man in a shabby jacket asked as he stopped her with a pointed finger pressed into her chest.

She shook her head and felt the drip of water splash from the brim of her hat onto her face. Alice looked at him briefly. He was old, with dark hair and a worn Homburg hat. She thought he looked like a bank clerk. The grubby finger that pressed against her was ink-stained.

'No,' she answered flatly, looking away before pushing him out of the way to walk by.

'Pity. I like them young...' she heard the man trail off above the noise of the street as she continued on, stepping into the road to avoid the men gathered in the doorway of a cinema. 'If you change your mind...' the man hollered after her.

Alice didn't look back as she fought the urge to roll her eyes. She slipped through a narrow alleyway lit only by the light from the high back windows of a restaurant, as she made her way to Dean Street. It was a passageway she knew well and even in the half-light it held no fear for her. Far behind she could hear the voices and dulled conversation from the drinkers outside the pub. Even on smog-filled nights they preferred to stand under the striped canopy and drink beer than sit inside. She saw the same faces most nights, old men with thick jowls, others much younger, fresh-faced and hopeful. Their voices soon faded as she walked briskly into the darkness.

In her head she tried to arrange the words she wanted to say, repeating them again and again, hoping they would make sense. Alice rehearsed the lines knowing she had to tell him tonight; she was late and prayed he would wait for her.

On the corner of the alleyway she turned left. Dean Street was busy as usual for that time of night. The peanut vendor with his handcart smiled as she walked by. Her eyes darted to his bright grin that spread across broken teeth. He screwed up his broad face as if he would laugh.

'You coming back later, Alice?' he called out after her, as if they were old friends.

'Already eaten,' she answered with a wave of the hand that she had taken from her pocket to wipe the last drops of rain from her face. 'Besides, they are making me fat.'

Alice turned back to glance at the man–he spoke to her every night and yet she didn't know his name, though he had known hers from the first time he had given Alice free food. She remembered him telling

6

her in broken English that whenever she felt sad she should come to him and that he would make her laugh. He seemed different from the other men she knew in Soho. There were no strings, no extras, no talk of sex. That was so unlike the two doormen outside the Jazz Club. They stopped their conversation momentarily as she came closer. She could feel them staring at her, as if they were wondering what was underneath the khaki coat.

'Coming with me, girl?' one of them spoke up as he reached out a hand.

She ignored the words, shrugged her shoulders and kept on, her eyes staring at the road. She knew they would not follow. It was a skill Alice had quickly learnt. Don't look, don't speak and keep on walking.

In twenty strides she could see the doorway. Above were the flickering lights and the sign that read 'PRIVATE CLUB'.

Alice stopped for a moment and checked her reflection in the window of the music shop. Taking a pressed handkerchief from her pocket, she slipped a pointed edge under the rim of her eye to take away any trace of smudged makeup. With a rehearsed hand, she clicked the hasp on her purse and took out a small silver tube. Alice twisted the base and quickly smoothed the rouge across her lips. She checked herself in the glass, pulling up the gabardine so she could see the reflection of her legs that stuck out from under the tasselled skirt.

'Dandy,' she said to herself as if pleasantly surprised, then slipped the gabardine coat from her shoulders and took off the hat to check the fall of her bobbed hair. She looked thinner than ever before. The bones on her cheeks pulled the skin tight, her white teeth filled her mouth and pushed out her red lips. It was what she wanted, how she needed to look. When Alice had arrived in London, she had felt like a pig. A band of flesh had hung under her chin, prompting her to straighten her neck and look up when she walked. Now all that was different, nothing felt like this. It had been a long two years and she was about to get all she ever wanted. For the last time she checked herself in the glass. 'Looking good, Babe,' she spoke to herself as she shook her head and turned her profile.

Alice checked the street; it was as if she was looking for someone she knew. A sigh left her painted lips as she pushed on the door of the club. It gave way easily and opened out onto a wide stairway. Looking up, she saw two young women on the stairs. They sat close together, arms entwined, mouths moving in a lengthy kiss guarded by locks of hair that fell across their faces.

'Thought you would be working?' Alice asked as she climbed the steps and peered up at the man in the dinner suit on the landing above.

The girls didn't answer. The smaller, dark-haired girl raised her hand as if to greet her, but didn't take her lips away from her friend.

'Been like that the last hour...' the doorman joked with a smile at Alice and lifted the velvet rope from the hook on the dingy, unpainted wall. 'Not natural. Wouldn't see that in Billericay,' his thick Essex voice rasped. 'Still, it's a modern world. Country has changed since the war– just look at London. We got motor cars, lights, you name it.'

'Is he here?' Alice asked, ignoring what the doorman said.

'Miss Pringle, if you would go on through. He is at the bar. Asked me to give you this.'

The man pressed a small envelope into her hand. Alice squeezed it tightly, almost as if she could count the money from gripping the thickness of the envelope. She smiled at him as the door opened. 'That's kind,' she answered.

Laughter and cigarette smoke spilled through the open door. The noise of a jazz band echoed along the short passageway. Alice walked on, coat over her arm, hand still clutching the envelope. Her shoulders brushed against the fabric walls that swirled in a pattern of flock roses, her feet sinking into the soft carpet. The passageway grew darker. Alice pressed against the red, buttoned leather door. It opened into a large room. Another doorman, with a snake tattoo on his neck, looked at her. The man stroked his moustache and then nodded to the bar. The room was crowded, noisy and swirling. Dimmed chandeliers hung down from a high ceiling. Alice looked around. She always tried to find someone she recognised. It was a force of habit. In a booth on the far side of the room, she glimpsed an old man. He had a face looking like it was made of papier-mâché and thick eyebrows. She knew he was a politician. He was married, yet his arm gripped a girl half his age. The girl drank from the same glass and slipped her hand inside his shirt. Alice didn't know his name but had seen his picture in the *Evening Standard*.

He was there most nights and had once bought her a drink. The man had then asked her back to an apartment overlooking the Thames, along with two other girls. She had refused politely and he had never spoken to her again.

Alice walked quickly across the room. She could feel the pulse beating in her neck. Her stomach churned as she walked in and out of the crowded tables and caught glimpses of half-laughed conversations. It was just the excitement. She knew that. It never changed. The music, the cigarettes and the smell of perfume made her tingle and feel alive. Like a child on Christmas Eve, she was filled with anticipation.

She smiled, catching a glimpse of herself in the long mirror on the far wall. It was then the music stopped. The crowd applauded. A woman in a black, beaded dress got up from a table and waved her purse in the air. Alice walked over to the tall man at the bar who stared at the wall. He had short-cropped hair and a neat, black suit and tie. As she got nearer, he instinctively turned.

'I thought you would never come,' he said as he touched her bare shoulder and fingered the thin strap of her dress, slipping it down her arm.

'I have been working,' Alice answered with a smile as she sighed and picked a strand of hair from his jacket. 'You've been talking to a blonde–she left the debris behind.'

'She wasn't as beautiful as you and far too expensive.'

'Does that mean I come cheap?' Alice shot back, sipping his drink as she counted the lines on his forehead.

'Do you have what I want?' the man proceeded to ask as he took back his glass.

'I don't want to talk about it here,' she stated with finality as she looked about the room and then pointed to a door guarded by an older woman wearing a black dress and a scowling face. 'I know a place upstairs where we can talk.'

Alice took his hand and led him to a small door at the end of the room. She handed the woman a white five-pound note. The woman held it to the light above her head and smirked earnestly. With a quick tilt of the head, she nodded. It was as if the payment was only just enough.

'Twenty-three,' the woman said. 'Leave it as you find it. Break it and you pay for it...'

Neither the man nor Alice spoke. A narrow, dark staircase led to a corridor above. Several gloss, black doors with silver handles lined the dim passageway. The man counted the numbers of the doors in a loud whisper. His breaths were staccato and short. As Alice walked ahead, he touched her shoulders.

'Nineteen... twenty-one... twenty-three...'

Alice glanced up at him. He put his hands on her waist as he pulled her towards him to kiss her.

'Can't you wait?' she teased as she pushed him back. 'Open the door.'

The man leant on the handle and pushed the door open. The room was lit with faint candlelight. Alice stepped inside. It was a small room, filled with a low bed covered in wrinkled satin sheets. By the door was a washstand. A half-filled ashtray and two dirty glasses were pushed against the flocked wallpaper. On the table by the bed was the candle. It had been roughly forced into an old holder covered in wax. Next to the table on the wall behind the bed was a gilt-framed mirror with cracked glass from side to side.

'Not much for your money,' the man said as he began to unbutton his starched, white shirt.

'We have an hour, how else do you expect them to make a living?'

'On the watered-down gin?' he laughed as he slipped the straps from her black tasselled dress and watched it slide to the floor. 'You have dyed your hair. I can see it in the candlelight. I liked it before.'

He smoothed back a strand of her hair as he pushed her onto the bed and began to bite her neck.

'Who said you could...' Alice tried to breathe as he roughly took her, forcing himself within as his hands gripped her wrists until she could feel them bruise. 'Slowly... slowly,' she whispered.

He breathed hard. Alice looked at the sweat on his face. He was older than she was by at least twenty years, possibly more. His hair was grey at the temple and the skin around his eyes was dull. She could feel the nails of his manicured fingers dig into her skin.

'I thought this is how you wanted it?' he questioned, pressing against her as he pushed harder.

Alice slipped her arm from his hand and twisted her fingers in the hair of his chest.

'Whatever way you want it, Mister,' she said as she reached over to the bedside table.

The man closed his eyes. He smiled and groaned. Alice grabbed the candlestick. She stabbed it swiftly into his back, pushing the burning flame against the skin until it was snuffed out. The man moaned hard, opened his eyes and stared for a moment. He stopped moving as if he waited for some inner voice to tell him what to do.

'You shouldn't have done that,' he whispered.

No one in the room downstairs could hear the sound of screaming in the corridor above their heads. The man tossed Alice around the room. He held her against the wall and smashed her against the door. She let out a desperate scream as he held her to the silk-covered mattress and laughed. Before she could move, he gagged her tightly and tied her to the bed. Then all was silent. He lay next to her in the dark and lit a cigarette. Time and time again he rested the burning tip against her skin.

It was an hour later when Alice left the room. The knocking of the woman at the door had woken her. The man had gone. Another envelope of money had been left on the table. The candle had been relit and placed back in the holder. Before the woman could knock again, Alice dressed. She opened the door and pushed past the woman.

'It's another fiver. You were late leaving,' the woman spoke before noticing the fresh burn marks on her arm. 'You alright?' she asked, her voice concerned.

'I get what he pays for,' she tried to laugh as she slipped on her twill-woven coat.

[2]
DEAN STREET

Alice thought about having a drink of gin as she walked through the bar towards the stairway. The bartender looked away as if he didn't want to catch her eye. He straightened his tie and picked up a glass. It was late and the room had emptied. The old man sat in the booth, chancing his time with the young girl. She was obviously trying to pry the wallet from his aged fingers. No one noticed her leave. The gabardine coat covered her burnt and blistered skin. It was worth the money. She wondered if anyone could guess. How many people knew what had just happened? How many actually cared? It made her feel invisible and alone.

In the corridor, Alice stopped and drew her breath. The burns on her arm seared in pain like bursting ulcers. She knew they would scar, but then that was what he had wanted. It was as if it was his mark. Five burns in the pattern of a star. It was a sign of possession, like a dog pissing on a streetlight. For one hour she had earned a hundred pounds. More than some did in a year, and for that she thought the pain was worth it.

Alice checked her purse as she walked. The money was there, in two envelopes, as usual, half before and half after. The man would see her again, a letter would arrive at her apartment giving a time and date. Alice would just turn up, give him an hour of her life and another morsel of her soul and he would be gone for another week. She didn't know what he did nor did she really care. He was not the man she loved and never would be.

'Goodnight, Miss Pringle,' the doorman said as she walked down the stairs.

Alice nodded and smiled. 'Goodnight,' she answered.

'If you don't mind me saying, you may need to check your makeup.'

She stopped on the stairway, turning and glimpsing at the man. He was gesturing to his eyes. Alice thought that he looked kind, like a bear in a suit. His hands were big with thick fingers, his accent strong and words jagged. A short-cropped, black beard covered his face and his head was shaved close to the scalp. The collar of the shirt dug into his skin. As he turned his head, she could see the deep scar on his cheek.

'Thanks. That is so kind of you.'

'Don't want you going out not looking your best. You are a beautiful woman.'

'Appreciated,' she spoke softly as she turned away. She knew what he meant–the man pitied her. He thought she could do better than being a whore, regardless of what money she made. It was the look she had seen before. 'Thanks, Harry, you are a gem.' Alice wanted to cry–perhaps he was right.

Outside the club she checked her face in the glass of the shop window. Alice had done this a hundred times before. Her stare took her through her reflection and into the dimly lit shop. For the first time she noticed the man sat in the back office, scribbling away at a desk with a long pen. His shirtsleeves were tied with silver braces. On the desk was a steaming cup and a plate of biscuits. The man looked happy, content in what he was. For a moment he looked up, aware he was being stared at, so Alice turned away and shrugged her shoulders.

The night was still misty and full of fog. A wall of dark grey smog hung as a curtain across Old Compton Street. She could see the faint lamps edged in mist. People seemed to appear and then disappear as if they crossed into another world.

Alice walked in the other direction to what she had planned. One moment in time had changed everything. Instead of strolling towards Old Compton Street, she set off at a pace towards Soho Square. She remembered there was a coffee vendor in the park and some tables. Alice had the idea of sitting there a while before she took a taxicab back to her apartment. She tried not to cry as she forced her way through the crowds of people on the pavement. Her stomach twisted with the urge to take all of the money in her purse and throw it in the street and see which of those around her would dive for the crisp, white five-pound notes.

As she walked further, the street beyond Richmond Mews emptied. Alice pulled up the collar of her coat then slipped her hand inside to soothe the burn with her fingers. It was as she turned into Carlisle Street that she knew she had to look back.

The man was hard to notice at first. She could see the tip of his cigarette as he stood on the corner of the street, lingering in the shadow of a doorway. His black fedora hat was pulled down and his long trench coat came almost to the ground. It didn't seem out of place. Soho was a place of men who stood in doorways and smoked cigarettes, waiting for the night to pass.

As Alice peered back again, the man stepped from the shadows. With the click of his steel-toe boots, he began to walk behind her. His pace increased. With each step he got closer. She prayed someone would turn the corner from Soho Square and she would not be alone. Alice could hear the footsteps of the man on the cold slabs. Trying to stop the shudder running down her spine, she walked faster. Turning into Soho Square, Alice laughed nervously. It was ridiculous, but she thought that the man was waiting for her. The street gave way to the tree-filled square. It was brighter here, the fog quite sparse. She pulled the belt of her coat tighter as she crossed the road to the park, following the string of Chinese lanterns. They led from the gate through the trees then to the coffee vendor and three tables under a span of branches.

An old man played a small accordion by the iron gates. He leant against the painted supports as his fingers pressed the keys. A cigarette hung from his bottom lip and danced in time with the music–it reminded her of Paris. Alice asked for coffee, and it came quickly in a neat, white cup. She sat by the brazier and gazed down at the embers.

'Anything else?' the man asked as he wiped his hands on the starched apron.

'That's fine,' Alice said as she sipped the coffee. It was bitter and burnt her tongue.

There was no sign of the man in the fedora. He had vanished into the smog. She scolded herself for even imagining that she was being followed.

'Are you sure?' the waiter asked, almost as if he knew something. 'It is late and you are alone. Perhaps we could…'

Alice understood what he meant. She had seen him looking at her face and then to her legs.

'I don't think so,' she answered as she stood from the chair, dropping three coins onto the plate as she walked away.

'Next time?' the waiter said. 'And I'll give you the coffee for free.'

At the gate, Alice dropped the last coin from her purse into the hat at the feet of the accordionist. He nodded and smiled as he watched her disappear into the smog of Frith Street.

Soon she was back amongst the crowds of people that hung around the doorways of the bars and clubs. The music rolled across the pavement like the fog. Alice looked in. Under the bright light, a woman sat at a desk, her neck wrapped in an old fox skin. The head of the long dead creature hung limply across her chest. The man next to her held out tickets and shouted out the price.

She moved on, walking quickly towards Old Compton Street. It was the best place to find a taxicab. Alice knew some of the drivers. They would always laugh and joke, never asking too many questions. They were the kind of company she needed.

She looked ahead, counting the echoes of her steps. A newspaper boy was folding up his stand on the corner of the crossroads. He tied bundles of unsold papers together and stacked them in the doorway of a shop. Alice walked by and then looked back. She was alone. A sigh came from within her. It was unexpected.

Suddenly, she was pulled from her feet. A hand grabbed her coat and then smothered her mouth. In an instant, she was dragged from the street. The alleyway was no wider than a doorway. It was dark and cold. With one hand, he held her tightly across her mouth so she couldn't speak. The man dragged her deeper, then pushed her against the wall. Her feet could hardly touch the ground. She stood on the tips of her toes, praying she would not slip.

'Don't scream or I will kill you,' the man said.

'It's you. Why are you following me?' Alice asked instinctively, as if she knew who it was. 'How did you find me?'

'I thought that would be obvious,' the man answered as he dragged her further into the darkness.

'What do you want?'

'Everything that a woman like you can give me,' he muttered the words close to her face.

'I'm not working. I'm going home,' she said, hoping he would ease the grip on her throat.

'I've been watching you, Alice. That's what you're called now, isn't it? Watching you and your friends for days... weeks... I know what you have for me,' he said softly as he stroked her face.

'This isn't the place. Maybe later–for old times' sake?' she begged.

The man laughed. She could feel him groping in the pocket of his long coat.

'This is the place, Alice. I never thought I would see you again. This is the night.'

The man released his grip on her throat. She could feel the bricks pressing into her back. Alice slid slowly down the wall.

'What do you want from me? I have nothing to give you. If it's money... here, take what I have,' she said as she held out the purse and tried to hold back the tears. 'Look, whatever you want. Take it. Just don't hurt me. I told you before.'

'Open your coat,' he said coldly. 'Open your coat. I want to see.'

Alice could see the knife in his hand. It was silver with a thin blade, more a scalpel than a knife. It glinted in the half-light of the alleyway. She thought of screaming and then changed her mind. With a shaking hand, she pulled open her coat. The tasselled dress shook as her body shuddered with fear.

The man looked at her for several moments. He stroked her neck and then slid his hand lower until his fingers fleetingly touched her breast.

'Do you know what I am going to do to you, Alice?' he asked as he swallowed back the excitement.

'Please... not like this...' she pleaded as she saw the hand come forward, felt the blade slip under the straps of her dress and then felt it begin to slip from her as he cut the straps one by one.

Alice shivered as the dress fell to the floor. Taking the knife, he cut her underwear from her with great care. Alice could hear him breathing. He sighed as if with each cut of the knife he took more of her.

'You're beautiful, thin and fragile. Fine, white skin–milky white, almost pure. I have thought about this moment for a long time, wondering what it would be like if you would scream or try to run away.'

'Why are you doing this?' she asked, having no choice but to watch in dread as he pulled her severed pants from between her thighs.

'What you know can often kill you. Who have you told, Alice? Where is it?'

'They all know. All my friends–every one of them,' Alice lied, hoping it would stop him. 'What have I got?'

The man didn't speak. He took hold of her jaw with one hand as he forced her harder against the wall. Pressing his mouth to hers, he kissed her, nibbling on her lips.

Alice could feel the knife slide down her thigh. He held her tightly as he unbuttoned his trousers.

'Please… please…' Alice pleaded as tears rolled down her cheeks.

'Don't cry,' he insisted, as he jerked himself roughly inside her. 'Just stay still.'

'No,' Alice answered as she was shoved back and forth against the wall with each of his thrusts. She twisted her fingers in the collar of his coat. He reeked of gin and cigarettes. Alice held on tightly as her coat slipped from her shoulders and the wet bricks and lime mortar cut her skin.

The man stopped. Alice could feel him shiver as he gripped her shoulders and bit hard on her neck. He groaned, shuddering as he emptied himself deep within.

It was then that he slowly stepped away like a drunk. Leaning back against the wall, he buttoned his trousers. She could see the gold clasps of the braces glint in the night. The man looked at her, eyeing her from head to foot. She stood there naked. The dress was around her ankles, coat in the gutter. Instinctively she lifted her hands to cover her breasts.

'I want to see what you look like,' he insisted.

'Why are you doing this? I thought it was over between us?'

'Take your hands away, I want to see you.'

Alice lowered her hands. She stood naked and afraid. The pulse beat in her neck faster and faster.

The man looked at her. He took in the colour of her skin and every contour of her slight frame. Spit dripped slowly from his mouth as he rolled the knife in the palm of his hand.

'Just let me go,' Alice said as she bent to pick up her dress from the ground.

It was without warning that his fist jumped forward like a swift punch. The blow hit Alice in the chest and she was suddenly gasping for breath. He punched her again. Alice could feel the blood but no pain. With rising panic, she realised that she had been stabbed. The knife impaled her again and again. She couldn't scream. Her fingers gripped the wall. They clutched the cement pointing that encased each brick. The man stabbed her again, the blade now jammed in her ribs. With both hands, he yanked the knife from her body. Her lung was punctured. The blood gurgled in her throat then flowed from her mouth. Wide-eyed, she stared at him, unable to move. Again and again he stabbed at her. The knife cut through her heart. Alice slipped slowly down the wall as he held her by the hair to stop her falling. She hung like a rag doll in his hand as he frantically sliced her skin.

[3]
OXFORD STREET

The open-top London omnibus rattled as it waited at the stop. Its glass-plated windows juddered as the conductor swung on the bar of the open rear doorway and pushed people inside. He called for more room upstairs, wanting every seat to be filled before the omnibus moved away from Oxford Street. The passengers on the cramped open-top deck looked down onto the people that filled the pavement outside Selfridges department store. It was three in the afternoon. The smog had thinned in the morning sunlight and a chill breeze blew the first sign of autumn from Highgate Hill.

Jack D'Arc crossed the junction of Orchard Street. He could feel the change in the air. The old bullet wound in his right leg acted as a barometer. It could tell him quite clearly that the rain was an hour away. The pain would grow more intense as if the splinters of the casing that the surgeon could not find dug deeper to the bone. It had been six years since he had been shot. It was June of 1917, eleven days before his twenty-fifth birthday. It had been a last charge across the fields of Messines Ridge, as he ran ahead of the Battalion, pistol in hand. The corporal who had dragged him back to the lines had told him it had been a sniper. D'Arc could only feel the burning in his leg.

'You're lucky he shot you in the leg. They only do that to the officers and then try to kill the enlisted men when they are sent to bring them back. Lucky you're not dead, Governor.'

D'Arc had heard those words often. They had echoed in the long nights in the French hospital, on the troop ship across the channel and in the sanatorium in Yorkshire. He remembered again and again the moment when he was cut down. There was the smell of the blood-soaked mud, the smoke and the sound of the machine gun fire. All around was death. It was soaked in the stench of cordite and vomit. There were the screams of those falling around him as they marched towards the German trenches. Then he fell. For three hours, he had lain in the mire. He had listened to the screams of dying men. Some of them sobbed, others shouted for their mother. A boy in a shell hole next to him had reached out as he cried. D'Arc thought he looked no older than fifteen. The boy had touched the tips of his fingers as blood trickled from his mouth. It was as if he was trying to hold onto life. In his eyes was the fear of death, death that crept through his stiffening body and took him within the hour.

As night fell, D'Arc had heard the taunting shouts from the German trenches. As the sun had set, he wondered if they would come and kill him. He waited, slept and dreamt of London. Later in the night, star shells had exploded high in the sky above him. They lit the night, casting long shadows. Then, as he thought he would be left alone to die, he heard the thunder of the land mines. Buried deep within the Messines Ridge, they exploded. Like the shudder of an earthquake, the vast explosions lifted the ground. They burst through the sodden soil like the opening mouths of ruptured volcanoes. Clods of mud exploded through the air. Surrounded by a falling mist, he waited to die. Hell opened up beneath him. The cries of fear were all around. D'Arc could hear the screams from the German trenches as the soldiers were pulled deep within the earth. It became like quicksand. Thick, black Belgian soil turned to dust by a thousand tonnes of explosives buried deep within. Then all was silent. An hour later the corporal found him choking on the sludge. D'Arc was dragged back under the barbed wire and machine gun fire, loaded on a cart and taken away.

Each day he had the wound to remind him. Each night he had tremors and the memories came storming back.

As the omnibus drove away, Jack D'Arc stepped into the doorway of Selfridges. He picked a strand of thread from the wide lapels of his double-breasted jacket. Instinctively, he studied the people around him, his gaze trailing over his surroundings. In the bus queue, a pickpocket dipped the wallet of an old man stopped by a flower seller. D'Arc watched as he palmed his prize to a companion before the old man had realised it had vanished. D'Arc said nothing as he watched the pocket-dipper calmly pick up the shopping bags of a distracted passenger and walk away.

By the streetlight, a woman stood waiting for the Clapham bus. She wore a blue gabardine coat, a faded hat, old shoes and stockings rolled down to her ankles. Her legs were covered in red sores that trickled mucus across her skin. From where he stood, he could see that the face powder was applied thickly. Red lipstick was daubed on crusted lips.

It was the rouge lipstick that Jack D'Arc noticed about her more than anything. To him it looked out of place, obviously given to her as a gift and something she would never choose for herself. She was a study in human life, an open book to be read, understood and analysed. Everything of her inner self was displayed for the world to see, and yet no one would ever notice unless they really looked.

For Jack D'Arc, this was everyday London. He would walk the streets looking at the world as it passed him by. In every face, in every street, there was another story. Villains, pickpockets and prostitutes filled his life. Jack D'Arc was a private detective; he had seen it day in and day out in the time before the war. In all the years since, it had not changed. People were just people–fallen, frail and waiting for death. They may never know it, but the Grim Reaper loomed throughout their lives. All of their comings and goings, trivia and melancholy led to the same place.

It was in that place that D'Arc held great fascination. He was intrigued by the human condition. Those around him were more than just people; they were windows to understanding, whirling maelstroms of motive, emotion and story. In the mud of the Messines Ridge, D'Arc had come close to death. Now, filled with life, he had to understand the reason for every pulse of his beating heart.

The bus to Clapham arrived, bursting through the growing smog as the sun faded. The woman stooped to pick up her forgotten bags. She looked bewildered, checking again and again until she realised that they had gone. For D'Arc, this was his most precious time. He waited expectantly to see how she would react. His eyes searched her face for the telltale inner thoughts. The widening of the eyes, trembling lips, unsteady hand. He lingered for a moment. The woman sighed as her hands shook. She leant back against the streetlight and cried. Tears trickled down her face as she sobbed as if she had lost the world. The woman looked down again as if she expected the bags to reappear.

Those around her either didn't see her strife or chose to ignore it. They shouldered by her and fought their way onto the bus to get to the last empty seats. The woman licked her dry lips and rubbed her lined face. D'Arc thought she must be younger than the crow's feet and harrowed brow implied. He could see that her hands were blistered, worn and tinged with a faint blue dye. There was a smudge of wax on her shoe and her hand was bandaged.

'Madame?' he began as he stepped from the doorway. 'You have had your bags stolen?'

'Everything, purse as well–bits of savings, week's wages, all gone,' she answered as her lip quivered. 'Twenty-four shillings in all.'

D'Arc reached into the inner pocket of his jacket. He took out a crocodile skin wallet and from within a large, white five-pound note.

'Then take this as compensation for your loss,' D'Arc said as the woman clutched the note in disbelief. 'And from that, take a taxicab to York Road, Battersea.'

'How do you know I live there?' she asked.

'You work at the candle factory, do you not? Recently you have been burnt with wax. It was a severe accident from which you are recovering? Isn't that why you are on Oxford Street at this time of day?'

'Well yes…' she answered warily, as she quickly folded the note and held it in her hand. 'And you want nothing from me?'

'Madame, I would have paid more to learn about the human condition. What I have seen today was well worth five pounds.'

Without warning, the doors of Selfridges suddenly burst open. Women ran into the street as the alarm within the store sounded. There were the shouts of the guards, the bleat of a police whistle. The crowds surged forward as a man in a white shirt dragged a woman to the ground.

'Stop her!' he shouted as another woman kicked at him. 'Thieves… thieves!'

The crowd fell back, reluctant to intervene. They watched as twenty women dressed quite elegantly pushed through them and ran off.

The woman on the floor got to her feet, but the man grabbed her by the leg. She turned quickly and stamped the short heel of her shoe into his face.

'Men pay to touch me!' she shouted as she grabbed the bag of clothes and disappeared into the crowd.

Jack D'Arc stood back, folding his arms as he smiled. One woman in particular had drawn his attention. She stood by the door as if an onlooker to the catastrophe. Her red hair was pinned under an expensive hat that sat on the side of her head. It was flat like a French beret and edged with jewel stones. Everything about her was elegant. She had neat, manicured nails, a finely-cut trouser suit and a ruby ring on each finger of her right hand. The woman breathed deeply, turning her head from left to right as if a spectator to what was happening. She held herself gracefully as she clutched the shopping bags in her hands.

D'Arc watched her, intrigued by her manner. She eyed the crowd like a cornered lioness looking to escape. A constable broke through the mob and picked the guard up from the floor.

'What happened here?' he asked as the man wiped his bleeding face.

'Robbed… robbed… they did it again,' the man answered.

The constable blew seven short blasts on his whistle as he looked around.

'Where are they now?' he asked the man.

D'Arc edged closer to the woman. He saw a slight shudder run down her spine–it was quite indistinct but he knew what it meant.

'If you run now, they will realise you are one of the thieves,' D'Arc whispered as he stepped even closer to her.

'You the police?' she asked, her quiet voice from south of the river.

'I am the man who will save you from prison. Do as I say,' D'Arc answered softly as he gripped her by the wrist.

'Take your hand off of me or you will regret this day for the rest of your life,' she seethed through gritted teeth as she tried to cover her disgust with a smile.

'That's one of them,' the guard stated, pointing to her. D'Arc turned quickly. He pulled the woman to him and kissed her.

'You… you are one of them,' the guard spoke again.

The constable stepped forward.

'This is my fiancée. How dare you speak to her like that?' D'Arc answered, as he looked the copper in the face.

'This man said she is a thief. What's in the bags?'

'Didn't you hear? This is my fiancée, I have been waiting for her to come out of the store. Surely you know what women are like when they are in Selfridges?' he said as he looked down on the man.

'Then you won't mind if I search her bags, will you?' the copper asked as if he would not be stopped.

'I am Jack D'Arc. The commissioner can vouch for who I am.'

The constable stepped back. He looked him up and down as if he searched for some clue. It was then that the expression of recognition swept across his pock-marked face.

'Mister D'Arc... I am sorry, sir. I didn't realise,' he murmured, embarrassment coating his words as he turned to the woman. 'Madame, I am so sorry.'

The copper backed away, chuntering as he pushed the guard into the department store. The crowd turned as if the show was now over.

'You a magician?' the woman asked.

'Why?'

'Because I have never seen anyone make a copper disappear that quick before,' the woman continued as she looked at him.

'That remains to be seen,' D'Arc answered as he looked in the bags and saw they were filled with clothes, the price tags still attached and obviously not paid for.

'Are you a copper?' she whispered.

'Are you a thief?' he answered quickly, licking the remnants of her cherry rouge from his lips.

'Why did you stop him from searching me?'

'We should walk. Before the constable realises who you are.'

'And who might that be?' the woman snapped.

'I suspect you are Ruby Alder–the leader of the Forty Elephants.'

'A strange name,' she answered cordially. 'What might it be?'

'A street gang that has taken to mobbing shops and is now the scourge of Oxford Street,' D'Arc answered abruptly.

'So you are a copper. What do you want?'

'Coffee... perhaps tea? From the stains on your fingers, you may possibly need a cigarette.'

'Are you a detective?'

[4]
JERMYN STREET

From the window of the café at 113 Jermyn Street, Ruby Alder looked into the street and then back to the man opposite her. She had sat for the last hour and listened to the soft, deep voice that spoke to her of his life. Jack D'Arc had ordered coffee. It was something that she would never usually drink, but this time she was glad she had. It tasted pleasantly bitter and somehow lifted the tiredness of the afternoon. Ruby had watched his eyes. She could tell they were searching her face. It became a growing realisation that Jack D'Arc did not just look at you when he spoke. With every word, he stared. His eyes flickered across her face and she knew he was looking at her as if he were inspecting a corpse. He had just finished talking of a murder where the body had told him everything about its short and brutal life. Now she felt the same. Even though he took up most of the conversation, Ruby knew that with every second of her silence she was giving more and more of herself away. This could be seen by the growing smile on his face. In return, she stared back and tried not to let him know that she found his cute angular features, all framed in a mop of thick, dark hair, most appealing.

'So after the war, I had nothing to do,' D'Arc said. He broke off the conversation to take a sip of coffee as Ruby stubbed out another cigarette. 'I was unfit to return to the Metropolitan Police Force and my commission as a captain finished when I was wounded at Passchendaele. I tried writing as a journalist and then became a private detective.'

'So why do that?' she asked, genuinely intrigued that someone should choose to investigate the indiscretions of bored Hampstead housewives.

'A family business,' he answered, his words strangely abrupt. D'Arc realised that he needed to give her a full explanation as he tapped his long fingers rhythmically on the table. 'My father was a police inspector and my grandfather was a detective before he left France. It seemed right for me to do the same,' D'Arc tried to smile at her. He could see the line appear above her right eye as if she doubted what he said was the truth. 'And you... what brought you to this place?'

'Is this some kind of interrogation?' Ruby asked as she stirred the brown embers at the bottom of her cup.

'I am not that kind of detective,' he answered. 'In the cases I investigate, I hope to have the answers before I even speak to the suspect.'

'The only private detective I knew spent all his time looking through curtains to see who was sleeping with the husband of his employer. Are you that kind of detective?'

D'Arc sat back in the chair and looked at her. The suit she was wearing was neatly cut, and the cuffs were edged in fine leather. Around her neck was a gold chain on which hung a love heart brooch. On both wrists were gold bracelets, her right hand still glistening with the ruby rings adorning each of her fingers.

'I am the kind of detective that tries to earn his living as honestly as he can.'

'Then you are one in a million. Every one that I have met seems to be on the take. They either want to have a cut of what you are stealing or a bite of what is under your skirt,' she answered quickly as she eyed the waiter and, with a flick of a finger, ordered more coffee. 'How come I've never heard of you when you were in the police? I've heard of most of the coppers around here, why not you?'

D'Arc laughed to himself. He remembered the first day he had walked through the door of Scotland Yard. He had stood in the uniform line with three other men in their early twenties. The door had opened. A man with a monocle and moustache read out the names of the other men and then looked at him.

'Are you D'Arc?' the man asked. He had nodded in response. 'Then you won't be needing one of these. Not where you are going.'

'I was never in uniform. Not even at the beginning,' D'Arc said. 'I was drafted into the Detective Branch. For the first year I made the tea and then was in fingerprints and criminal intelligence. I joined the army a year after the war broke out. When I told them of my job, I was made an officer.'

'I knew a copper who spent all his life walking Battersea Park Road. I would see him every day from my window. He always said he wanted to be a detective,' Ruby answered as the waiter brought fresh coffee.

The man looked at D'Arc as if he needed permission to pour the cup. D'Arc nodded. 'Perhaps he didn't have a father in the job. I think they kept me off the streets on purpose, protected from every villain my father arrested.'

'Do you look like your dad? I remember a copper just like you,' she said glibly, wondering why this man wanted to spend such time with her.

'He died in 1907, when I was fifteen.' D'Arc could see Ruby trying to calculate his age. 'I am thirty-one. You would have been eleven.'

Ruby thought for a moment. 'I was nine.'

'And you lived in Battersea?' he asked.

Ruby looked out of the window. For the first time in the conversation she had started to feel uncomfortable. She knew enough about D'Arc to understand that this time was not just for pleasantries. He had already known her name and that she was a thief. Ruby leant forward.

'What do you really want from me, Jack D'Arc?' she whispered.

'I am in need of a friend, a friend just like you. A friend with contacts and connections,' he answered.

'A grass?' Ruby asked as she lit another cigarette and blew the smoke across the table.

'More of an advisor. Someone who knows what is going on,' D'Arc answered.

'How did you know who I was? Was it a coincidence you were outside Selfridges just as we mobbed it?'

'I have been following your career with interest. From what I hear, you are holding on to the Forty Elephants by the skin of your teeth. The youngest woman to run the gang and there are others who want to take your place.'

'Who told you?' Ruby asked. 'Someone talking out of place?'

'You took over the gang in 1920 and for the last three years have made a lot of money. Some of that money has come from the houses of my clients that you have robbed. Now I need your help,' D'Arc answered as he reached across the table and held her by the hand.

Ruby didn't move. She could feel the warmth of his fingers.

'I don't help the law–private or not, you are still a copper. My girls would never follow me if they thought I was a grass,' Ruby answered as she slipped her leg forward under the table making ready to run.

'Then I am mistaken. I thought I saw a morsel of goodness in you,' D'Arc replied, his right eyebrow raised in annoyance.

'Just because I take things from rich people doesn't make me bad. Keeps my girls off the streets. Anyway, your clients can afford it.'

'My clients would like to see you locked up in Holloway Prison for a very long time.'

'Is that why you came after me?' she asked as she licked her drying lips.

Ruby looked out of the window to the street. On the corner was a fat copper, his stomach held back by his leather belt. He leant against the wall of the alleyway with his hands behind his back. It was then that a black police van pulled up in the road. The driver got out, walked back and spoke to the copper.

D'Arc felt her beating pulse with the tip of his finger as he gripped her hand.

'That is the first thought of every creature when they are backed into a corner,' he said. 'Do they fight or take flight?'

'What do you mean?' Ruby asked as her gaze darted back to the police van in the street.

'As soon as you saw the officer across the road, your heart began to race. I saw you lick your lips and felt your body stiffen.'

'Is this some kind of a game? You had them waiting all along whilst we were talking? Are you going to turn me in, is that why they are here?' Ruby asked.

'What do you think?' D'Arc said as he let go of her hand. 'Is this an elaborate trap?' he whispered.

Ruby looked outside–the van and the copper were gone.

'You bastard,' she shot, venom coating her words.

'A coincidence, Miss Alder... a coincidence...' he said as he reached into the pocket of his jacket. 'I take it that you have my wallet? I thought I felt your hand slip inside my pocket on Oxford Street.'

Ruby slowly opened her purse and handed D'Arc the wallet. She tried not to look like a schoolgirl caught pinching sweets.

'You see, Mister D'Arc, I just cannot resist temptation. You looked like a man who could afford a few quid. I see blokes dressed like you all the time. Fine jacket, brushed shoes, leather gloves, wife at home, a servant perhaps?'

'Then, as you are obviously far wealthier than I am, you will be able to pay for the coffee, no?' D'Arc finished as he got to his feet and looked across the café to the waiter. 'The lady has insisted she will pay, and why should I resist temptation?' he remarked as he walked towards the door. 'Until next time, Miss Alder.'

The bell above the door jangled as it slammed shut. A sharp gust of cold air rushed in from Jermyn Street. A thin woman in a whalebone corset and long skirt looked around. When she saw Ruby, she grimaced. Ruby knew that look. She had seen it many times before. It was the glare of condescension, dislike and arrogance. The woman eyed her clothes as if she was working out the prices. Her eyes narrowed as she stared at Ruby.

Looking away, Ruby watched D'Arc walk along Jermyn Street. She hoped he would turn back. There was something about him that she found fascinating. Even though he was a detective, there was something about him that she liked. He smelled of cologne and soap. There was no dirt on the collar of his shirt and, more than that, he had a bright smile. It wrinkled the lines around his eyes.

D'Arc was quickly out of sight, covered in swirls of London haze that filled the empty pavement. He disappeared towards Duke Street and was soon gone.

Reaching into her purse, she took out a ten-shilling note and placed it on the table. She looked out of the window, checked to see who was in the street and then secretly reached into the embroidered purse and carefully took out a brass key and a black lettered name card. She looked at them as if she examined something of great price. 'There will be a next time, Mister Jack D'Arc, Private Detective, 5B Chalcot Crescent, Primrose Hill,' Ruby whispered smugly as she read the words and moved the key around the table with the tip of her manicured finger.

On the corner of Piccadilly, under the arch of the entrance to Fortnum and Mason with its gilt letters, Jack D'Arc searched the pockets of his jacket. With his right hand he took out the leather key fob. On the silver ring, a single brass door key swung back and forth. He looked on as if mesmerised and then he smiled. With a twist of his fingers and a turn of the wrist, the key vanished in a dramatic sleight of hand. D'Arc was the only witness to his own dexterity. He pulled up the collar of his jacket and adjusted the fedora hat in the mirrored glass of the doorway. 'I will be seeing you again, Ruby Alder,' he said to himself as he smiled and strolled away.

[5]
PRIMROSE HILL

A long line of black-painted railings edged the front of the houses in the street that led from Primrose Hill. On the corner was an old whitewashed livery yard. The stables had been newly converted to small garages for the taxicabs with their metal wheels and solid rubber tyres. Across the entrance was a low gate. It was held open by a thick twist of farm twine.

Stepping from the shadows, a solitary figure dressed in a tight-fitting jacket, dark trousers and pulled-down hat kept close to the wall. The gloved hand counted the railings, the fingers jumping the gold spear twists as if it were a childhood game. The hand stopped at the street sign that was bolted to the railings. Three houses along the street, jazz music spilled from an open first floor window.

Jack D'Arc looked out. Chalcot Crescent was misty and quiet. On the corner by the taxicab yard was a parked sedan. The ghostly outline was silhouetted against the streetlight. He had seen the car there before and it didn't seem out of place. With one hand he closed the window, stepped across the parlour and turned down the wireless. He could hear the valves humming in the large veneer box with satin-covered speakers.

On the mantelpiece above the empty fire grate was a crystal glass. It was half-filled with gin and tonic. D'Arc took the glass and drank the liquid in one long gulp. Putting the glass down on the wireless, he went back to the window and looked out again. There was still no one in the street.

Closing the curtains, he switched off the lamp and checked the bulb. He still wasn't used to electricity. D'Arc was not sure he could fully understand where the power came from. Like so many others in Chalcot Crescent, he had allowed the London electricity company to install the power line to the house. Unlike the others, he had insisted that the gas lamps remain. He had heard of the power cuts, intermittent supply and things catching fire. Electricity sparked and flashed, it was invisible, odourless and deadly. The gas lamps reminded him of the time before the war. Their glow was soft and warm without a need for any shade. Electricity did bring him the wireless. It was just a week old and every night he listened to the Ritz Orchestra. It was as if they were there with him, the music filling the upstairs room.

As he stepped from the window, the announcer spoke softly. It was a voice that D'Arc often tried to mimic. 'This is the London station of the British Broadcasting Company,' the man announced, evidently wearing a collar so tight that it made his voice rasp as the collar put pressure on his throat. 'I would like to wish you a good night from all of us here at The Ritz Ballroom in Piccadilly... goodnight...'

D'Arc smiled, switched off the set and glimpsed down at his watch. He matched the time to that of the clock on the mantelpiece. Turning off the gas lamp on the wall, he sat back in the ivory, silk-covered armchair and put his feet on the small coffee table and waited in the darkness. The house felt comfortable and safe, the darkness like a rich blanket between him and the world.

5B Chalcot Crescent had been his home for the last five years. Its white-painted walls and mahogany door had been a death gift from his grandfather. The old man was a Huguenot, who, even though born in the East End of London, still believed he was French. Theodore D'Arc had hated everything English and when Jack's father had joined the police, he never spoke to him again. Everything the old man had made from selling second-rate table goods to third-rate people had passed to Jack. That included a pair of flintlock pistols, the head of an elephant that was on the wall of the downstairs dining room and a small, but very much alive, bull terrier puppy.

Everything in Chalcot Crescent had belonged to his grandfather. On the morning Jack had received the papers from the solicitor in High Holborn, he had opened the door of the house and made it his home. A series of young housekeepers had kept the place fresh and tidy. The furniture had been recently changed and a note on the mantelpiece had said, in French, that Theodore knew he was dying and that he had decorated the house and furnished it in the manner that he hoped would be suitable.

Jack had only ever really spoken to his grandfather once. That was on the day his father had been found hanging from the rafters in the kitchen of their home in Kensal Rise. It was Jack's twelfth birthday. He had run in from school, opened the door and seen the heels of the black boots dangling before him. He had looked up. The head of his father was stretched to the side, the rope around his neck. Instinctively, he had reached out to stop him slowly spinning as the front of the neatly pressed trousers dripped with urine.

Somehow, the face that stared down didn't look like his father. There was a resemblance of familiarity. The hair was cast in the same manner, but the hanging man looked different; he was waxen with bloodshot eyes and a full tongue that hung from the mouth. Jack had waited several minutes as the scream welled up inside of him. He had tried to pull his father down but the rope would not give way. The body gurgled and sighed. It was then that Jack had screamed. His voice had echoed around the cold, tiled kitchen but no one came.

When the police took the body away, his grandfather had arrived at the house. He looked at Jack and shook his head. 'Pack your bags,' he had said in broken English. 'I have arranged for you to go to school. With your mother dead and now that *he* has done this, what else am I to do?'

The old man had turned and left the house. Later that day, Jack had been driven to a distant Dorset boarding school and never returned to the small, terraced house with its neat, white-painted windows and fire-blackened grate. There had been no talk of his father. Theodore had paid the school fees each year. Jack had stayed at the village pub when the school closed for the holidays. There was no family, no Christmas presents, nothing that could be said to be a part of a normal life.

In the parlour, the thoughts of his past life were soon stopped. In the dark stillness, Jack heard the stiff lock that held the back door turn. The tumblers jumped suddenly and then the door opened. Slowly and quietly he got to his feet and stood behind the parlour door. Footsteps made their way across the hall floor below. They were light, flighty and skipped across the tiles. D'Arc listened as they crept closer on the stair treads. A narrow beam of a dimmed lantern scanned the walls. It swept across the floor and outlined the edge of the door. Holding his breath, he pressed himself back against the wall. The footsteps came even closer. The lamplight flickered as it delved inside the parlour. A long shadow moved across the wall, so D'Arc waited in anticipation. The door opened slowly. A small, thin man stepped inside and walked towards the window. In the half-light, D'Arc could see he was dressed in work attire and a pulled-down hat. A belt wrapped tightly around his waist held a jacket in place. The man was no taller than a boy, thin and whippet-like. He picked up the gin glass from the top of the wireless, and tugged open the long drapes that covered the bay window.

'Is there anything I can help you find?' D'Arc asked.

The man hurled the gin glass. It cracked against the wall above D'Arc, the glass quickly following. D'Arc jumped forward as the man lashed out, the blow hitting him square in the chest. As D'Arc shifted back, the man lifted his foot and drove it straight out, making D'Arc stumble. The man propelled himself towards the door as he struck him again.

D'Arc managed to kick the door, forcing it shut with a slam. The man pivoted and stepped towards him. D'Arc snapped his fist through the air. It struck the man in the face. He fell back across the sofa, rolled and sprawled over on the coffee table, letting out a long groan.

Picking up the lantern that lay nearby, D'Arc shone the light directly in the face of the man.

'Interesting…' D'Arc laughed as he pulled the hat from the mop of red hair that hung over the table. 'I wondered when you would come.'

It was seven-thirty in the morning when the bedroom door was pushed open. Jack D'Arc stood in the hallway, a tray of tea in his hands. He smiled at the woman in the bed who peered back at him from over the satin duvet.

'You hit me,' Ruby Alder said in disbelief, slowly realising that she was naked.

'I thought you were a man–a man who was robbing my house.'

'That's kind,' she answered sarcastically. 'No one has ever thought I was a man.'

'You burgled my house dressed in a workman's suit and a tweed hat. What else was I to think? You looked like a man.'

'I always dress like that when I go on a job,' Ruby groaned. 'How else am I supposed to look?'

'Very convincing… is it a lifestyle choice?' D'Arc asked.

'Practical,' she replied as she screwed up her nose and scowled.

'What happened to my clothes?' she asked, feeling more and more uncomfortable that she was left lying naked in his bed.

'I didn't want to dirty the sheets, so I took them from you,' D'Arc started. 'Besides, I would have been most uncomfortable sleeping next to someone fully dressed.'

Ruby looked at the bed. The sheets were folded back where someone had stepped from the bed. The pillow was indented and ruffled.

'So, you did this?' Ruby asked. 'You took my clothes from me?'

'They have been washed and will be returned by nine this morning. I took them to the laundrette on the corner of Arlington Road.'

Ruby pulled the sheets higher around her neck as D'Arc put the tray on the bed. She was naked in a room with a man who had knocked her out, stripped off her clothes and taken them away. Now he stood at the end of the bed with a steaming cup of tea in his hand, from which he took long sips as he smiled.

'Do you do this often?' Ruby asked.

'I have to say, I have an addiction to tea,' he answered as he looked at her.

'I meant, do you take off the clothes of women you have rendered unconscious?'

'Are you offended that I saw you naked?' he asked, his voice sharp and concerned.

Ruby looked to see if there was any other way out of the room.

'It might have been nice to have been awake at the time,' she said, trying to smile as she took the cup from the tray, thinking she could throw it should all else fail. 'The last time I was naked with a man, we were both awake. That is the usual way of getting to know someone.'

D'Arc perched on the edge of the bed and smoothed his hand across the satin bedspread.

'I suppose that is at least… traditional…' he answered, counting the thin lines on her forehead.

'I was knocked out… stripped and put in *your* bed where *you* obviously slept–what else can I say? You appear to be a very strange man, Mister D'Arc.'

'You burgled my house, what am I supposed to do?'

'And that gives you a right to take away all of my clothes?'

'What is beneath the grime and dirt of an old tweed jacket and breeches is of no concern to me,' D'Arc grumbled like an old man no longer interested in women. 'I have seen many female bodies–mostly dead, may I add, and yours was no different.'

[6]
ARLINGTON ROAD

In the morning breeze of Arlington Road, the scent from the abattoir carried across the railway line. Ruby Alder walked quickly. As promised, her clothes were neatly pressed and shoes polished. The tweed cap was pulled to one side of her head and hid most of the bright red bobbed hair. Jack D'Arc kept pace. They walked close, often bumping into each other as they conversed. Ruby smiled often as he joked. Their hands touched but he said nothing and made no apology. D'Arc thought there was something about her that seemed familiar. He thought frantically, annoyed with himself that such a detail of his memory should escape him. It was then that D'Arc realised with a smile. Her boy-like grace, the narrow waist, tweed trousers and white face took him back through the years.

'Gerald Vardo,' D'Arc whispered with a fond recollection of the boy from boarding school.

'What?' Ruby asked, unsure that she had missed a vital piece of the conversation.

'Just a memory. A fond and fleeting memory that had sprung into my mind,' D'Arc answered as they walked on.

'Are you sure you want to be seen with me looking like this?' she asked as they turned the corner of the street by a row of demolished houses.

'Your offer of a proper breakfast cannot be turned down and I would like to know why you tried to burgle my house?' D'Arc answered, hoping he had done the right thing by allowing his fascination with her to overwhelm his common sense.

36

'I just had to try; that's how I got started in all of this. When I was fifteen, I met a bloke. He taught me how to break into houses. Just seemed like an easy way of making money. You looked like you had some cash to spare.'

'I am as poor as a church mouse. You would find little in my home of any value,' he declared as they touched again.

'You live in Chalcot Crescent. A very much adequate address for a church mouse, if you ask me,' Ruby laughed. 'Anyway, I just had to know what your place was like. That's why I dipped into your pocket and took the key.'

'How did you manage to take the key from the keyring? I never saw you do that,' D'Arc challenged.

'Been dipping all of my life. I love sleight of hand and magic tricks. I would sit in the back of the theatre and watch the magic acts. Got one of them to teach me.' Ruby suddenly realised that she had told more to this man about her life than to anyone else before.

'And is that how you joined the notorious Forty Elephants?'

'Notorious? Is that what they say? You been reading The Police Gazette?' Ruby laughed.

'The scourge of Oxford Street, police chases, fights, secret societies...' D'Arc joked as he raised a suspicious eyebrow.

'We drink at The Elephant and Castle. Some of the girls there were quite handy but couldn't sort themselves out. Didn't take long to get them working. We get all sorts–posh, the lot. Make a lot of money and live the life, but don't believe all you read in the papers.'

'And are there really forty of you, or is that just the reporting of the Daily Mail?' D'Arc enquired as they stopped to cross the road.

'Twenty at the last count. The Forty Elephants sounds like an army. We lost a couple who went inside,' she spoke briskly, as if she were giving too much away.

'You look too young to be the leader of such a troupe of villains. Isn't gainful employment something you have considered?'

Ruby Alder met his eyes and laughed. She could see the two razor marks on the side of his face where he had rushed his shave. She found him intriguing. There was something of the cat-and-mouse sort when it came to being with him. It was the allure of the eyes, where every sense within her told her to get away. Yet, with every word, she was pulled ever closer. After all, he was a detective, she thought to herself as they walked down the road by the railway sidings towards the tea hut that stood on the waste ground. Detectives could not be trusted–Ruby knew that well.

She was fifteen when she had first been arrested. The copper had been twice her age. His gut hung over his belt and the buttons on his shirt held in the fat. Sadly, that didn't stop him. He touched her face, moved his thick fingers down her neck and forced his face close to hers. She could smell the beer and cigarettes as the bristles of his unshaven face rubbed against her skin.

'Do me a favour and I'll do you one,' he had spat, the venom in his slurring voice evident as he pushed Ruby against the tiled wall of the cell. 'Isn't that what all this is about? Nice young thing like you shouldn't be going to prison. I could help you and all you have to do is...'

Detective Constable Perry had unbuttoned his trousers and made sure that Ruby knew what he was talking about. He forced her to her knees. All Ruby could think of was the smell of the disinfectant that had been mopped across the floor.

'I don't want to,' she had protested as Perry gripped her hair. 'Please, not like this.'

'Call it a rite of passage–a growing up–if you tell a soul, I will swear you're a liar and the Thames River Police will find you by Tower Bridge.' His fingers had twisted in her hair as he tried to force her towards him. 'Come on, girl, you know what to do.'

The door of the cell opened.

'That's enough, Perry,' the sharp voiced inspector had snapped as he stepped inside. 'They are not pressing charges. The shop has the dress and that's all they want. Leave the girl. Go back to the front desk. I'll deal with this.' Perry shook himself as he stepped away with a pig-like grin. He had left Ruby on her knees as he waddled from the room and tucked in his shirt with a grunt. 'You should think yourself lucky I came in when I did,' the inspector had uttered as he helped Ruby to her feet. 'Constable Perry has a novel way of dealing with prisoners,' the man had laughed.

Ruby had felt even more frightened. Just like Perry, he smoothed his hand across her face, bringing his thumb to her lip and slowly pulling it down as if to open her mouth. 'I, on the other hand, have more conventional methods. This isn't a place for a girl like you and I take it that you will try to keep away?'

Ruby had nodded. Her hands were shaking, she was sure the inspector could see her fear.

'Promise,' she had whispered as she stood against the wall face-to-face with the man. 'You'll never see me again.'

'Good,' he said, his face so close to her that he could feel her panted breath. 'I hear you are only fifteen. Not an age for this game, is it? I have a daughter older than you. I wouldn't want her stuck in here with the likes of Perry. You don't know what a man like that would do.'

'So, is gainful employment something you have considered?' D'Arc asked again when she didn't answer.

'What?' she answered. D'Arc smiled, realising that she had been far away. 'Sorry… employment… no… not really…'

'Then I may be able to help,' he continued as he rubbed his brow and looked across the road to the crowded, makeshift workers' café. 'You promised to pay, so I will have a fried egg sandwich and a mug of tea.'

'Do you ever treat a woman to a meal?' Ruby asked.

'It was your invitation. When I invite you, I will pay. You should keep that in mind for future reference. I will find us a seat.'

'So this will happen again?' Ruby asked.

'Hopefully,' D'Arc replied as he sat on the bench propped against the wall of the wooden hut. Ruby went inside. D'Arc sat on the bench, looking out of place; all around him were workmen in drab, oiled jackets and worn boots. They stood with folded arms and observed him with begrudged faces. D'Arc ignored them and took the pen and notepad from his pocket, allowing the silver police whistle to fall and dangle on its chain for every one of them to see.

It was enough to stop the staring, most of the men turned away after their eyes zeroed in on the whistle. They now knew who he was. It made sense. Coppers often called by to listen in on what they were saying, or pick up someone they wanted.

Ruby clutched two mugs of tea and a brown paper bag. She handed the mugs to D'Arc and then took out the sandwich, breaking it in two.

'We have to share. They have no more bread,' she said as the egg yolk ran down her fingers.

'Then share we will,' D'Arc answered, placing one cup on the bench next to him and taking his half of the bread.

They ate in silence. D'Arc took a handkerchief from his pocket and wiped his mouth and then offered it to Ruby, pointing to a trickle of yolk that ran down her chin.

'So, what did you want me for? Isn't that what you said–I could be useful?' Ruby asked as she sipped her tea.

'Our meeting yesterday was not a coincidence. I was given the case of a robbery in Fleet Street and wondered if it could be you?'

'Fleet Street? Well off the Manor,' Ruby answered. 'North of the river. Not our territory.'

'So is Oxford Street.'

'Needs must. Don't get shops like that in Streatham High Street,' Ruby answered as she watched a small dog killing a rat in the doorway of a derelict house opposite. 'Oxford Street is easy pickings and I never get involved. I leave that to the girls, I just tell them what to do and watch them do it.'

'And carry the bags they leave behind?' D'Arc pressed further.

'Sometimes I collect a few things, but the idea is not to get caught with anything on you.' Ruby knew what he was talking about. 'What was stolen?'

'It was the theft of some jewellery. A gold necklace and a diamond ring.'

'Too hard to get rid of. No one is buying that sort of thing. What's in it for you?'

'I find the jewellery and then I get rewarded by the insurance company.'

'We could run a scam. I could steal the stuff and you could get it back. I could make you even more money than you get now,' Ruby spoke quickly as if the idea would be lost if she didn't say it out loud.

'That would not be honest,' Jack D'Arc uttered sullenly.

'You were a copper. I have never found an honest copper.'

'Talk of the devil...' D'Arc murmured as a long, black sedan broke through the fog and drove slowly along the road towards the café. '... Inspector Varney from Scotland Yard,' D'Arc turned to Ruby before continuing, 'I think you better go.'

[7]
ROTHERHITHE

The door to the police car opened briskly. Inside the back, a tall, well-built man in a shabby coat peered out through a haze of cigarette smoke. He looked like a hack reporter from a Grub Street journal. His face was unshaven with eyes that were bagged due to lack of sleep.

Chief Inspector Varney was every inch a rough Yorkshireman. The collar of his shirt was torn, the cuffs unwashed. He sprawled in the back of the car and looked out. His mouth was turned up at the corner in a half-sneer as if he didn't want to speak to D'Arc, but knew he had to.

'I have been looking for you all morning. Thought you would be here,' Varney remarked begrudgingly as he lit a cigarette and blew the smoke out of the door.

'Inspector Varney, why do you seek me?' D'Arc asked sarcastically as if there would never be an ounce of respect for the man who stared at him.

'It's Chief Inspector. I was promoted. There has been a murder and I need to talk to you. Get in.' Varney moved his hulking frame away from the door to allow D'Arc into the back.

Jack D'Arc stepped into the car. He looked to the café to see Ruby peering through the shutters of the window. He shrugged his shoulders as he spun in the seat. When he looked back, she had gone.

'Why should you need my help?' D'Arc challenged as the car door was closed and the driver pulled away from the pavement. 'After all that has gone on between us, I thought I would be the last person you would wish to speak to.'

At first, Varney didn't answer. Reaching into his pocket, he took out a long envelope with a green and gold crest embedded upon it. D'Arc

41

could see that it had once been sealed with red wax. The flap hung open, the contents had obviously been read. Varney eyed him as he contemplated what to say.

'I don't want you involved in this, D'Arc–it would be better without you. I didn't want a private detective getting anywhere near this. The boss insisted. Two nights ago there was a murder in Soho.'

'There was nothing in the papers.'

'We kept it quiet. Very sensitive.'

'And why do you need my help?'

'You have been commissioned by the family and they won't take *no* for an answer. They have heard of your powers of deductive reasoning. Apparently, D'Arc, you have an almost supernatural gift of detecting crime. Pity it never showed when you were on the force.'

'I have too much work–there was a robbery in Fleet Street.'

'You have no choice,' Varney retaliated smugly as the car twisted and turned towards the East End.

'So where are we going?' D'Arc asked, counting the street signs as they approached the river.

'Rotherhithe… house for the dead, Church Street,' Varney spoke, his speech staccato and his tone dull as he stared ahead of him. 'They took her there to keep it quiet. Nobody cares about the dead in Rotherhithe; or the living, for that matter…'

D'Arc opened the letter; he could see that the seal had been crudely pulled open as if whoever did it didn't care that D'Arc knew it had been read before. The paper was crisp, expensive and foreign. There was a slight scent of gardenias.

'I take it you have read the letter?' he demanded. Varney muttered under his breath as he stared out of the window of the car. 'So you know the terms on which I am to be employed?'

'You make more in a month than I do in a year,' Varney snapped bitterly. 'Bloody nancy boy like you in your handmade suits. You go poncing around and earn that amount. It's disgusting.'

'I am a private detective. I earn what people will pay and perhaps, if they had more faith in the police, there would be no need for people like me,' D'Arc countered as the car turned into a long, deserted street.

'Then expect nothing from me. You were too soft to be a copper and you got out when you could,' Varney spoke briskly and hard, nudging D'Arc with a sharp elbow.

The car halted outside an aged building that looked like a church. An arch-top door was above three stone steps. To the side was an alleyway. At the far end was another door covered with an iron gate.

'I haven't been here for a while,' D'Arc said, trying to make conversation and knowing it would antagonise Varney even more. 'The last time was the Hoffman murder. That was the husband who drowned his wife in the bath and then threw her body in the Thames. Didn't you believe it was suicide?'

Varney shrugged. His top lip quivered in anger. He looked at D'Arc before opening the door of the car and stepping out. Taking a breath, he sighed. All he wanted to do was smash Jack D'Arc in the face. Varney crumpled his fingers into a fist and then thought better of it.

'Too much fucking paperwork...' he muttered under his breath. 'The body is in the back room. We are expected. It should all be ready,' he declared as he walked down the alleyway, not caring if D'Arc followed.

'Have they done a post-mortem?' D'Arc asked, his question blatantly ignored by Varney.

Soon they were in a clinical, echoing room. It was tiled from floor to ceiling. Under the roof was a row of frosted windows and a large gas chandelier hung over a solitary steel table in the centre of the room. On the table was the mutilated body of a woman. She was naked. A long, deep incision ran from just below her neck to her pubic bone. D'Arc seethed through his teeth. In all his time as a detective he had never gotten used to the smell of dead flesh.

'What's the matter, D'Arc? Not got the stomach for it?' Varney teased with a cocky laugh, meanwhile the body lay on the table like a butchered pig. The wound was deep. What was left of her guts were cupped in the pelvis and covered with a flap of muscle. 'This one certainly knew what he was doing. She was butchered. Found her stomach on the corner of Dean Street. The heart is missing, and so is the womb.'

The green side door opened. An older man in a bloodied white coat and surgical boots stepped into the room. He regarded Varney and then D'Arc, his eyes darting between the two of them.

'How is it they always call you when there is a lot of blood?' the man asked D'Arc in a strong Irish accent, brushing back the thick strands of grey hair.

'A coincidence, Doctor O'Brian, just a coincidence,' D'Arc stated as if he spoke to an old friend.

'Whoever did this left very little for me to look at,' O'Brian explained, knowing what D'Arc would ask him. 'The attacker was not a surgeon, but he did know where to find the heart and lungs.'

D'Arc stepped closer to the table. He looked at the girl's face. She was young and very pretty. The only mark she had was a small bruise to her lip.

'She wasn't alive when her heart was cut out,' D'Arc acknowledged out loud as he looked inside the empty chest cavity that had been cut through. 'You can tell by the blood vessels and the colour of the skin. I would say it was taken as a trophy.'

'Sick bastard!' Varney snarled as he leant forward to view the body at a closer angle. 'It was done in an alleyway off Dean Street. She was twenty feet from the road. Her body was found by a tramp. Reminds me of what happened in Whitechapel.'

'That was a long time ago. My father told me of the murders,' D'Arc mentioned as he ran his finger down the length of the wound as if he counted the abrasions. Taking a pair of tweezers from his pocket, D'Arc plucked a small piece of linen from her hair.

'He was my inspector,' Varney added as he watched D'Arc place the fragment into the palm of his hand. 'I remember your father well. Never did get over finding that woman.' He paused to think of her name. 'Polly Nichols–she was murdered on Durward Street; it was Bucks Row then. Took it to heart. I'd been in the job for two years before the murders in Whitechapel started and then they were over.'

'The Ripper was a madman,' O'Brian answered. 'I worked on three of the murders. I have to say, Jack. They are very similar.'

'He was a skilled killer who ran your father ragged. Always one step ahead and then he just disappeared.' Varney stood back from the corpse to breathe a shallow breath.

'And you think he has returned?' D'Arc asked.

'I saw one of the women he had butchered. O'Brian is right, this is very similar.'

'It was thirty-five years ago,' D'Arc said as he examined the girl's bruised lips.

'If he was in his thirties at the time of the murders, he'd be in his sixties now. Not long at all really. Not as long as I have been a copper. Not too old to be a killer…' Varney replied, trailing off as if considering the likeliness.

D'Arc seemed to ignore what Varney had said. With a span of his hand he measured a wound beneath the girl's breast–it was narrow and sliced through the skin at an angle.

'The blade was five inches long and held in the right hand. She was killed with a stab wound to the heart and then he cut her from the pelvic bone to the throat,' D'Arc pointed to a flap of skin over her stomach. 'You can see where he slashed at her. This kind of butchery would have taken at least ten minutes. She was also naked at the time of the attack.'

'And you can tell that by just looking at her?' Varney demanded.

'She is but an open book waiting to be read,' D'Arc answered.

'She's a heartless dead woman,' Varney laughed at his own joke. 'Heartless…'

'And the heart is the thing on which this case turns. Five years ago there was a murder in Paris. November 11ᵗʰ, 1918. It looked so much like this. The police never caught the man, they thought it was a foreign soldier. The body even had bite marks to the neck–just like this,' D'Arc clarified as he pointed to a set of fine teeth marks hidden behind the bobbed hair of the girl.

'Well, that's the French for you,' Varney uttered, trying to joke, as his words echoed around the mortuary.

Taking the tip of the tweezer blade, D'Arc scraped the inside of the girl's fingernail. He then looked at her hand, smoothed his fingers over hers and squeezed the flesh between each knuckle joint.

'It was a crime of passion. The murderer cut out the tongue of his victim as if to stop them speaking after death,' D'Arc commented, as he pried open her mouth.

'You knew! You bloody knew…' Varney said just above a whisper as he stared at the stump of the severed tongue.

'As soon as I saw her, I thought the similarity was too much. The cuts of the knife are identical. I have the photographs of the case if you want to see them. The murderer cleaned the blood away from her mouth, probably when he removed the tongue.'

Varney glared at O'Brian.

'I suppose you didn't think of looking in her mouth?'

'An easy mistake to make,' D'Arc answered as he nodded at the doctor. 'This victim is different. She has been well cared for and doesn't work with her hands. She is recently divorced, or has had a long engagement broken off. The marks of the ring are still on her finger. Her hair was cut at a decent salon. I believe the style is called a Dutch cut bob. Where are her clothes?'

'Taken from the scene. Probably stolen. She had no purse and no money. She was identified by the tattoo on her back; the family crest... seventh cousin of the King,' Varney sighed as he spoke. 'I've got no time for royalty.'

'She had brutal intercourse at least twice. Once before her murder, the bruises had already started to show and again later, possibly at the time of death. There are cigarette burns to both arms as if she was tortured,' O'Brian said as he shook his head.

'She was a strumpet–high class, but still a whore,' Varney scoffed.

[8]
ST MARYCHURCH STREET

It was as Varney finished speaking that the green door to the room suddenly slammed shut. The three men turned as Varney raised his hand. A woman in a fur-collared coat that trailed on the floor stood in the doorway. In every way she was identical to the girl on the steel mortuary table. She too was beautiful, her looks starting to fade, with eyes that were now lined. Perhaps thirty years older than the girl, but D'Arc could see without doubt that they were from the same family. Instantly he knew who she was. He had seen her photograph in *The Sphere*. There was no mistaking the high cheekbones, tight smile and deep blue eyes. This was his employer, Lady Elsa Gabrielle, the woman who had sent the letter that Varney had read.

She looked at Varney, the look on her face indecipherable.

'Whatever she was, Chief Inspector, she was my daughter,' Lady Gabrielle said calmly as she glanced from Varney to the body on the table.

'Lady Gabrielle... you were asked to wait,' Varney stated, walking towards her so she could come no closer.

'How can I wait knowing Alicia was in here?' Her voice changed as she spoke. 'My God, what have you done to her?!' the woman shrieked as she caught a glimpse of the cadaver.

'I think it would be best if we went outside,' D'Arc interrupted as Varney took hold of the woman and nudged her back before she could witness any more of her daughter's body.

'You have to find who did this, Mister D'Arc. I trust you more than the police,' Lady Gabrielle protested as she struggled with Varney, digging at the sleeve of his coat with her long fingers. 'She was killed for a reason. They knew she was my daughter.'

'Then I will find out who has done this,' D'Arc responded, as he took her by the hand, pulling her grip from Varney. 'Come with me, there is a room where we can talk.'

D'Arc regarded Varney. The Chief Inspector knew not to follow.

'I will speak to you later, D'Arc,' he muttered, his voice gruff and dissatisfied. 'Not too much later. This is a police investigation. Remember that, D'Arc.'

D'Arc nodded to O'Brian. The doctor gave a sympathetic smile, knowing he would rather deal with the dead than the living.

'I am here if you want me, Jack,' O'Brian spoke softly as Jack D'Arc led the woman away.

They walked close together. D'Arc slipped his slender arm around her and pulled her close. He knew it was not the right thing to do, but that didn't get in the way of him attempting to comfort the woman beside him. Lady Elsa Gabrielle was part of the royal dynasty and yet he held her as if she were just another grieving mother.

'We can talk through here,' D'Arc trailed off as he pushed the door to the doctor's office open with the toe of his boot. 'O'Brian won't mind, he keeps a small bottle of whisky in the jar on the sideboard for times like this.'

'You don't have children, do you?' Lady Gabrielle spoke in response, more as an understanding of his condition than a question. 'You can always tell a father by the way they look at another parent. They know what we all go through.'

A slightly shabby leather couch ran the length of the only window in the room. The cushions were worn with the grief of the families who had wept there many times before. The couch fronted a desk with a small coffee table between. On the table was a half dead plant in a petite china pot, its leaves hanging limply down.

'I'll get you a drink,' D'Arc offered as he let go of her aged hands as she sat down. 'It's good at times like this.'

'You never expect to outlive your children. When you see them like that... it is very hard to understand...'

D'Arc listened intently as he poured the drink and proceeded to hand her the glass. She sat for a moment and sipped the whisky as if she had drunk it countless times before.

'How did you find me?' he queried as he reached into his pocket and retrieved the letter.

Lady Gabrielle glanced up from the glass before speaking. 'You were recommended. I forget by whom. I had a call from a friend and they gave me your name. They mentioned that you were discreet.'

Her cigarette-torn voice rasped in her throat as she held back the tears.

'Varney had read the letter before he gave it to me. He is unwilling to cooperate with a private detective,' D'Arc confirmed as he listened to her sighs.

'I have friends who will help you… I know the Commissioner very well. Whatever you need to find the killer, I can get for you.'

D'Arc perched on the edge of the desk and eyed the woman, contemplating his next words. 'You are so much like your daughter,' he expressed, hoping to sound compassionate. 'It must be so hard for you.'

'She was twenty-seven years old. Alicia was my first child. I haven't seen her for two years. We argued and she was gone. Then my husband died. It seems as if I am cursed,' Lady Gabrielle answered as she placed the glass on the table and leant back on the sofa. 'She married five years ago. She was so young and it was over two years later, and now this. What kind of a life is that? All she knew was misery and pain.'

'The older I become, the less I understand life,' D'Arc answered truthfully, unable to give her a better response.

'Do you believe in God, Mister D'Arc?' Lady Gabrielle questioned as she reached forward, took the glass and slurped some more of the whisky.

'It depends what you mean by God,' D'Arc hesitated, wondering why she asked such a question. 'If, by God, you mean an old man in heaven, then perhaps not. Although I have seen many things that would indicate to a rational mind that the subject of the supernatural cannot be dismissed fully.'

'I thought I believed in God. Every Sunday I would be in the Church of Saint Magnus. The priest would drone on and on as I would continue to dream. We would sing the most dreadful hymns. I took the sacrament and asked for the forgiveness of my sins. It wasn't enough to stop my life running through my fingers like sand.' Lady Gabrielle held out her hand and snatched at the air. 'There is nothing when we die. I am sure of it. I hope Alicia was right in what she believed.'

'You say Alicia was married and divorced two years later?' D'Arc asked, changing the conversation to something that made him feel relatively more comfortable.

'At first they were never happy. It was my husband's fault. It was an arranged marriage and he thought they would be suited. Alicia never had any sense when it came to men. She made so many mistakes that when she was twenty-three, Lord Gabrielle found her a husband.' Lady Gabrielle sipped at the drink, holding onto the glass like a most precious object. 'Max Coburg was much older. He was German and very rich. When they married, they lived together in Paris. One day, Alicia walked out on him and came to see me in London. I insisted she went back. She would not tell me what was wrong, but something had frightened her. Then she vanished. Marriage is not for love, Mister D'Arc–it is for duty.'

'She took the name Alice Pringle?' D'Arc probed.

'Pringle was the name of her nanny. I often felt she loved Nanny Pringle more than she did me. I never spent as much time with her as I should,' the woman sighed. 'Hindsight is a hard master. Alicia was a very complicated child. She always fell in love, often with the wrong people.'

'Where is Nanny Pringle now?' D'Arc questioned.

'She is dead. Killed by a German shell in the raid on Scarborough. She had gone there for a Christmas holiday. It was a strange time. Miss Pringle had asked to take Alicia with her. My husband refused. He thought she was gaining a worrying attachment to Alicia. Lucky really, but then again, perhaps she would have been saved from all this.'

'Worrying attachment?' D'Arc urged.

'Yes. Miss Pringle didn't like men.'

'When Alicia went missing, did you try to find her?' D'Arc pried further.

'We took on a private detective, but he could not find her. We think that she bribed him not to say where she was. We had heard she was living in Chelsea. A friend thought she had caught a glimpse of her in Selfridges.' Lady Gabrielle studied D'Arc as she spoke. 'The police traced us through the tattoo on her back. It is our family crest entwined in her name.'

'I thought it was somewhat unusual for Alicia to have such a tattoo,' D'Arc confirmed as he sat himself next to Lady Gabrielle.

'Alicia was an unusual girl. The tattoo is something that she always wanted to have–it was the family seal. The Angel Gabriel fighting with a demon. I have to say, it is the most grotesque angel I could ever imagine; more of a monster than anything. She said it was a curse. Alicia had it done when she was eighteen. I never dared tell her father. She was his favourite child. They were so much alike.' The woman swigged the last dregs of the whisky and planted the glass clumsily on the table.

'And your other children, where are they?' D'Arc posed the question as he pushed her glass from the edge of the table.

'My son was killed in the war at Passchendaele and my daughter was killed last year in very tragic circumstances. It was in all the papers. I am surprised a man like you didn't already know.'

D'Arc did in fact already know. He had read all about the tragic death of the child in *The Times*. What intrigued him was that there had been no post-mortem. The report had said that the body had been taken for burial in line with local customs and the police had insisted it had been suicide or a tragic accident. The coroner had given an open verdict and all interest in the case had been lost. D'Arc wondered how Lady Gabrielle could speak of their deaths in the same detached manner that she had talked of Alicia.

'You must find it all very hard to cope with,' D'Arc spoke again, having difficulty in sounding concerned. 'Was Alicia always so different?'

'Different?' Lady Gabrielle answered with a scornful laugh. 'Alicia was not of this world. From the age of five, she had an invisible friend. Even gave it a name. Miss Pringle insisted it was a spirit guide, but I thought it was just her imagination. Alicia would rely on what Freya said.'

'Freya?'

'That was the name that Alicia gave to her imaginary friend. Even when she was an adult, she would talk to Freya like she was in the room,' Lady Gabrielle coughed and sat back, pulling the collar of the coat across her face. 'I am sure Miss Pringle was responsible for filling her head with that rubbish. Alicia would laugh and giggle as if they shared some great joke. We took her to the best doctors. When she was examined, they all declared there was nothing wrong with her.'

'And she still spoke to Freya?' D'Arc proceeded to ask.

'Every day, and as she got older it got worse,' Lady Gabrielle answered, fishing for a cigarette in her purse. 'Eventually, we took her to see a man named Mister Crowley. He is a clairvoyant and an expert in these matters. He said that she was very gifted and we should allow her to speak to the spirit guide whenever she wanted.'

'And it continued?' he pushed. Lady Gabrielle scanned D'Arc, wondering how much she could say without sounding stupid.

'It continued until the day that Miss Pringle was killed. I remember it well. December 16th 1914. Alicia came down for breakfast and knew something was wrong. She sat for an hour and wept. Eventually she told me that Freya had gone and would not be coming back. The strange thing was that we received a telegram that morning saying Miss Pringle was dead. Alicia didn't bat an eyelid; it was as if she already knew.'

[9]
CHALCOT CRESCENT

Jack D'Arc wandered back from Rotherhithe to Primrose Hill. The fog had cleared and for the first time that week he could see the upper floors of the dark draconian buildings of Fleet Street. London seemed quiet for that time of the afternoon. The pavements were free from the usual gaggle of children and women with perambulators and instead there was just a steady parade of people walking swiftly. As he strode through Regent's Park, he could feel the stiffening chill of autumn. The leaves were turning red and some had already started to fall. He tried to go over in his mind what Lady Gabrielle had disclosed to him. There was a nagging doubt that she had not told him everything, and that didn't sit right. D'Arc had learnt that it was not the words that fell from the lips of people that were important when solving a crime. It was what they did not say; those things kept back, almost breathed and then sucked in. It was the lies they told and how they told them, the subtle movements of the eyes. Lies came as a look away, or a half-hearted glance. D'Arc paid more attention to those things than cheap words. Everyone lied and no one was to be trusted. Those were the words that he lived by since the day his father had committed suicide.

'Trust no one until they prove otherwise,' his housemaster had spoken on the very first day at school, as the old man had wiped the tobacco ash from the front of his black gown. 'If you trust no one, you will never be let down and if you expect nothing, you will never be disappointed.'

The words had stayed with him all of these years. They had proved useful in protecting him from the complexities of relationships. D'Arc had soon discovered that being alone and living life to your own desires was preferable to sharing your heart and soul only to have it ripped out. This allowed him to stand back from the world and look at life in a distant and unengaged way. D'Arc often felt that he was an observer of the world, in the same way a child would sit for hours looking at a jar of ants.

D'Arc pondered over his thoughts as a shudder twitched his spine. He stopped, inspecting his surroundings across the park. A man in a black uniform with brass buttons sauntered back and forth, spearing the ground with a steel-tipped walking stick. D'Arc observed as the man got closer.

'You here again, Mister D'Arc?' the man remarked, acknowledging his frequent presence as if it were becoming a habit. 'Third day this week. Given up taking a taxicab?'

'They are becoming more unreliable, Mister Humble,' he answered. 'Since the demise of the horse, they cannot be trusted.'

'Exactly what I said to my wife,' Humble answered as he stabbed a paper wrapper from the ground and held it aloft as if it were a magnificent catch. 'Life is changing and not for the better.'

'She still not well?' D'Arc asked.

'Not long left,' the man sighed as he lowered his walking stick, 'but then again, it happens to us all. Penny Doctor now charges a shilling a visit.'

'Be sure to give her my fondest regards,' D'Arc returned as he shook the man by the hand, giving him a wistful smile before walking away.

Mister Humble watched the tall figure in the lengthy, black coat ignore the sign that read '*Keep Off*' and tread across the grass. As D'Arc turned towards the road, Humble unfolded the white fiver that had been slipped into the palm of his hand without a word.

Chalcot Crescent was completely devoid of people. The row of white-painted houses stretched into the distance, the facade gently bowing out of sight. It was a street in which D'Arc felt comfortable; there was no one who spied on him. Those who resided there were too preoccupied to care about the man who lived alone. They paid no attention to the occasional visitor who would come by early and leave late–that was how he liked it. The only people he knew were the servants at several of the houses. In the early morning when D'Arc could not sleep, he would often walk the street; he would meet them on the steps to the lower rooms and they would converse. Often, this was the only meaningful conversation he would have in a day.

His skills as a detective had grown less in demand that year. The cases for which he had been commissioned grew tedious. One missing person, one theft of jewellery, two of matrimonial adultery and a priest who had taken to dressing in the clothes of a cabaret artiste and ambling the streets of Hampstead. In seven months he had been required to act in only those five cases. They paid well and would keep any normal man stocked with cigarettes and gin for many years. For D'Arc, they were all over too soon. The missing person had been quickly found, the adulterers traced and confronted and the priest sent to a parish in the north of England. Now, D'Arc toyed with the stolen jewellery far longer than he should have. He stretched out the inquiries and spent more time watching the comings and goings on the street corner in Camden Town.

As he trudged towards the door of his house, he was glad and grateful to have been commissioned to find the murderer of Alicia Gabrielle. The thought had crossed his mind that Lady Elsa had never revealed who had recommended him. The letter had simply informed him that she would be willing to pay fifty pounds per day. D'Arc knew that this was an outrageous amount and yet he would never protest the generous nature of those who employed him. It was as if they believed the more they paid, the better the result.

As he mulled over the thought, D'Arc paused in his steps hastily. The door to his house was wide open, the soft jangle of music spilling into the street.. Stepping inside, he said nothing and moved swiftly so as to not alert anyone of his presence.

It was only when he was in the upstairs parlour that he knew he was not alone.

'The place was like this when I arrived. The door was open and I came upstairs,' Ruby Alder asserted as she saw D'Arc survey the trashed room. 'I haven't touched anything. I thought you would want it like that. By the way, it wasn't me.'

'I believe you...' he answered as his gaze scanned the room and noticed that every drawer had been opened, a lamp tipped on the floor and the sofa upturned. 'You would have done a far better job than this. Whoever it was did not have the time to search properly. It is just a case of knowing what they were looking for.'

'I don't think they were looking for anything. This was a warning,' Ruby answered as she stood from the chair by the fireplace and helped him put the sofa back in place.

He paused and looked at her. Ruby Alder no longer wore the tweed suit; this was a change. Her hair was now slicked back and held in place by a silver clip. She wore a black jacket over a crisp, white shirt and trousers that finished above the ankle. She appeared more masculine than ever with her style, even though her eyes were lined with mascara and her lips edged in rouge. Her feminine energy shone through with the way she held herself, and it was the stark contrast that D'Arc couldn't help but appreciate.

'I see you have changed,' he noted aloud, trying to sound warm and feeling the laryngeal prominence stick in his throat.

'Do you like it?' she posed the question as she placed her hands on her hips.

'Practical. I prefer trousers to skirts and abhor dresses of any kind,' he answered briskly, feeling a flush sweep across his face. 'Why are you here?' D'Arc interrogated, changing the subject.

'You are a detective. I need your help–I can't go to the police,' Ruby explained as if it was obvious, lowering her face to the floor as if for some reason she couldn't make eye contact with him.

'Did the police finally catch you?' he tried to joke.

Ruby looked up. Her expression had changed, and he could sense that she was frightened, or anxious.

'One of my girls has gone missing. Never went back to her apartment. Her dress was pushed through the letterbox last night. She was called Alice... Alice Pringle.'

She reached down and opened the woven bag that was at her feet. D'Arc watched as she grasped a black tasselled dress. She held it out as if he should take it. The two thin shoulder straps had been cut.

'Who found this?' he urged.

'One of the girls she lived with. Hasn't stopped crying since. Will you help me find Alice?'

'Alice Pringle is dead,' D'Arc stated coldly and matter-of-factly as he took the dress from her and let it unfurl in his hands.

'Dead? How do you know?'

'I know, because I have just examined her body. She was found in an alleyway off Dean Street. She had been murdered.'

Ruby sat down on the sofa. She scanned the room in silence as she gulped at the air. D'Arc had often seen this before. People who were told someone they knew was dead either shrieked or sat in silence. He knew Ruby Alder would not cry. She would think of what he had said and try to act as stoically as she possibly could.

'What was done to her? There's nothing in the newspapers.'

'How long has she been in the Forty Elephants?' D'Arc asked, ignoring her question.

'Two years or so...' Ruby responded, her gaze fixated on the tassels of the flapper dress as they dangled before her. 'She obviously had money. Alice mentioned that she had left her husband. Drank in the Elephant–that's how we met. We took her in. She was good at what she did and could drive a car. Best getaway driver we ever had. She gave me her wedding ring. Thing was, she never took it off until a few weeks ago. Alice said she had found another man–rich and stupid.'

'Did you ever meet him?' D'Arc pushed for more, wanting to ask a thousand more questions.

'She kept him to herself. Whoever he was, he looked after her,' Ruby answered uncomfortably as if she was breaking an oath of silence. 'They were planning on living together when his divorce came through.'

'Did she say a name?'

'All I know is that they often met at the Aurora, a gambling club in Soho Square.'

'Do you know of it?' D'Arc demanded as he sensed her voice starting to break.

'The girls went there all the time. It is too busy for me; I don't drink that often,' Ruby's voice quavered as she spoke, her body starting to shake ever so slightly.

'Then we shall start at the Aurora,' D'Arc replied as he made his way over to the window and looked out into the street.

Ruby got up from the sofa and followed; she just wanted to be close to someone. Her mind raced as she thought of how she could tell her friends that Alice was dead.

'How did she die?' she asked softly, her voice uneven and slightly shaky as tinges of desperation slipped through the cracks of the façade that she tried to keep.

'I would rather not say.'

'But I need to know. Everyone will ask. Was it quick?'

'Faster than anyone would have known.'

'Was she robbed?'

'Possibly.'

'Did they do anything else to her?'

It was an unsettling question that D'Arc did not want to answer, so he settled on throwing a question back at the seemingly delicate woman, solely to spare her from the details he was sure that she would regret pleading for.

'Do you still have the wedding ring?' he asked as he noted her shakily reaching into the pocket of her jacket.

'Thought you would want to see it. Alice told me that she didn't want to sell it and that I could keep it until she decided what to do with it.'

'Who did she live with?'

'Two friends from the gang. They are good girls, been in the Forty Elephants since they were fifteen. Live on Sloane Street.'

'Sloane Street?' D'Arc pushed for confirmation, quite surprised.

'Just because we are thieves doesn't mean we don't know what...' Ruby tried to answer, her whole body starting to shake as she came to an understanding that Alice was dead.

D'Arc took a hesitant step forward and reached out to engulf her hand in his own. Without speaking, Ruby pulled him close to her and began to sob, the raw emotion and strength of her tears taking over her. He stood uncomfortably, with her arms wrapped around him, not knowing what to do.

'All will be well, Ruby. All will be well.'

[10]
CADOGAN PLACE

The kitchen was meticulously clean. Washed tiles covered the floor on which stood a newly enamelled gas stove. A neatly folded drying towel was left on the Belfast sink, and by the door stood a mop and brush. At the end of the long pine table sat the man. His sleeves were rolled and collar detached from his white shirt. He whistled to himself along with the music that rattled from the speaker of the old wireless on the meticulously empty window ledge. Folding the pages of the *Evening Standard*, he scanned through the advertisements, peering at the miniscule text in the dim light of the single, cold bulb that lit the room. A shoeless, sock-clad foot rested on the door of the oven and absorbed the heat. Settling the paper down, he pushed back his thick, black hair and glanced up at the clock that hung on the drab, white-painted walls.

'Must be time,' he mumbled to himself as he opened the oven door and peered inside. A gust of steam and the scent of cooked meat billowed from within. The man sniffed contentedly. 'Perfect...'

Taking the cloth from the sink and using it to protect his fingers, he pulled the stone cooking pot from within. Hastily, he slipped the pot onto the table and removed the lid. There, perfectly cooked, lay a small heart and a roasted liver. Grasping the fork from the table, he lifted out the heart and put it gently on the plate. Then, picking up the knife, he sliced the liver while it was still in the pot and, with the fork, ate several pieces as he watched the steam erupt from the heart.

Several minutes later, he wiped his mouth with the cloth. Then, as if he were preparing a gift, the man took an empty brown bag and placed the heart inside. He then set the bag inside another bag. From under the table he seized the leather satchel, opened the brass clasp and, taking the paper bag, hid it within.

An hour later, he had starched the collar of his shirt, put on his Homburg and overcoat and strolled along Cadogan Place. Halting on the corner of Sloane Street, he then crossed the road, his hand gripping the Gladstone bag and his collar pulled up against the night.

The first strands of fog blew in from the Thames at Battersea. They slowly filled the street and wrapped themselves around the automobiles that chugged slowly along in lines of traffic. The man stepped into an alleyway just as a taxicab pulled against the side of the pavement. Its door swung open as Ruby Alder stepped to the street.

'I don't know why you asked the taxicab to go around the block twice,' she uttered to D'Arc as he followed her out of the taxicab.

'A habit? I always think that I am being followed and, perhaps, one day I will be,' D'Arc answered in a voice that Ruby couldn't tell was serious or not.

'Well, this is where they live. 18 Sloane Mansions,' Ruby declared as she crossed the pavement and held out her hand as if to show him the building. D'Arc looked up at and inspected the apartment block. It towered into the fog, the upper windows like the illuminated eyes of a great Leviathan. It was clothed in neat, red brick that held back the noise of the city. 'They even have a maid and an elevator.'

D'Arc looked at the large black door with a brass handle.

'There is no letterbox. How did the murderer put the dress through the letterbox?' he asked.

'It is in the door of the apartment. Third floor.'

'And they can afford to live here?' D'Arc quizzed, touching the fine door handle with his gloved hand.

'Crime pays, Mister D'Arc... crime pays...' Ruby retaliated as she pressed the bell.

'So, whoever brought the dress would have had to ring the bell to get in or they had a key,' D'Arc acknowledged as his gaze shot back to Ruby. The evening mist had caught the strands of her hair. Each one glistened below the streetlights as if covered in a garland of silver orbs. She smiled at him, about to speak.

It was then that a slight, thin woman, the size of a child, opened the door. She was dressed in a black skirt with a matching shirt and a white apron. She observed Ruby and then D'Arc, as if sizing them up.

'Are you expected?' she posed the question politely.

'Apartment 18, I am a friend of Liza,' Ruby explained.

The woman looked at her suspiciously. 'Never seen you here before,' she refuted coldly in her prickly voice.

'Tell them Ruby Alder is here, but we have to see them, it is very important,' D'Arc interrupted.

'Who are you?' she argued, refusing to move back and remaining in her place stubbornly as D'Arc stared at her.

'I am a detective,' he spat out harshly as he stepped forward.

The maid stood back, an astounded look gracing her cold features as she hesitantly allowed him inside. He seizedRuby by the hand and continued forward.

'Third floor–I know the way,' Ruby affirmed as she surveyed the tenebrous hallway.

'Is it always this dark, or are you saving the gas?' Ruby asked sarcastically as the woman regarded them with a glare without speaking.

The maid grasped her lantern and shone it towards the spiral staircase that surrounded an ornate, open elevator.

'We had a failure with the lights. Haven't had them long. I prefer gas. Never goes out. Elevator not working–we'll have to walk. Are you sure you are expected?' the maid doubted.

D'Arc disregarded the question. 'Did the residents in Apartment 18 have any callers in the last two nights?'

'None at all,' the maid rejoined as she led them up the stairs like an usherette in a fleapit picture house. 'They keep themselves to themselves. I never hear a thing.'

'Are there any other ways into the building?'

The maid's focus remained ahead, shining the lantern on the treads as if to point out the expensive brass runners that held the fine red carpet in place.

'Just the tradesmen's entrance at the rear of the building. But that is always locked; I make sure of it myself and I have the key,' the woman remarked as she rattled a keyring in her pocket. 'I only open the door when someone is expected.'

'And you are sure no one came the other night?' D'Arc pushed for confirmation again as if he recognised that she was withholding something. 'A dress was posted through the letterbox of Apartment 18, could you tell me how that could be done?'

The woman wavered as if she had been found out.

'Dress? Why would someone want to put a dress through a letterbox?' she asked, her voice suddenly breathless.

'Did you put the dress through the letterbox?' D'Arc urged indignantly, his face shadowed by the light.

'I lost the keys a week ago. They were gone for a day. When I searched my room, I found them again—must have been there all along. The only way someone could have got in is if they had a key.' The maid directed the lantern at a red door with a brass letterbox. 'This is the one you want. Ask them to ring me when you are finished and I will come and get you.'

'When will the lights be fixed?' Ruby asked simply.

'I have called the man, he should be here soon,' she responded brusquely.

Without another word, the maid turned and made her way back down the spiral staircase. Ruby and D'Arc's gazes followed the lantern going down and down into the pit of darkness.

'You think she knows more than she is saying?' Ruby asked in a whisper once she was sure they were alone.

'The woman is unmarried and lives alone. I don't think she lost the keys. She knows they were taken and then put back in her room, but is too embarrassed or frightened to say.'

'How can you be sure?' Ruby asked as she pressed the brass doorbell of the apartment.

'She looked to the floor whenever I spoke to her. It was as if she had rehearsed the answer to that very question, knowing one day someone would call upon her to testify.'

'Should we give the dress to the police?' Ruby pleaded, unknowing of what the right thing to do in this situation was.

'I fear if we do it may be the last we ever see of it.'

Ruby pressed the bell again. They heard footsteps on the other side of the door and a muffled conversation.

'Who is it?' asked a frail voice.

'Kitty... it's Ruby.'

The door opened slowly, the movement tentative and reflecting of the women inside. D'Arc heard three bolts slide and then a lock turn. The fortified door gradually swung open all the way, eliciting a gasp of surprise from the man. Standing in the doorway was a young woman wrapped in a housecoat. She had bleached blonde hair and gigantic blue eyes that reflected the candlelight on the table by the door. Her lips were ruby red and smothered in rich lipstick. The woman turned to Ruby, a soft smile gracing her lips.

'Good to see you, Ruby,' she expressed in a voice soaked in bourbon and cigarettes. 'I haven't been out since I found the dress... have you found Alice?'

Ruby was about to answer when a voice came from the darkness behind Kitty.

'Who is the man?' a woman asked warily as Kitty stepped to one side.

'Liza, it's Jack D'Arc. He's the private detective who found Alice,' Ruby returned, trying to ease the worries emanating from the women.

D'Arc could see a smaller woman standing behind Kitty. She was dressed like a man, in a black suit and white shirt. Her hair was greased back and cropped above the ears. Though not as beautiful as Kitty, he thought she had a certain attraction to her face. It was thin, elfin-like, with a small, cute nose, thin boyish lips and deep-set eyes. In her left hand she held a revolver, the firing hammer was pulled back as the woman glared at him sceptically. D'Arc glanced around the hallway of the apartment. It was finely decorated with a Queen Anne sideboard against the wall topped with a gilt mirror and a painting of a long, dead man in an Elizabethan ruff.

'Is he safe?' Liza demanded, not moving from her place by an inner door of another candlelit room.

'He was hired to find Alice. There isn't a problem,' Ruby asserted as she stepped across the threshold of the door and kissed Kitty on the cheek.

Liza pushed the safety with her finger and slipped the pistol into the pocket of her suit.

'Sorry for the welcome, Kitty has gotten a bit edgy since she received the dress. How is Alice? Did you find her? Where is she?' Liza asked, smoothing her hand across her face.

'Dead,' D'Arc stated without remorse.

'You said he'd found her,' Liza snapped back, anger detonating off of her as she stepped from the door towards him.

'I did. In the Rotherhithe Mortuary on a cold slab, with her stomach ripped open and her heart removed,' D'Arc's response was blunt as he pushed the door closed behind him and turned the key in the lock.

'What?!' Kitty spat out in disbelief as she crumbled with the shock and was caught by Liza who held onto her tightly.

'Alice Pringle was the victim of a skilled killer. Do you know the name of the man she was going to marry?' D'Arc asked, not caring for any subtleties or manners. His eyes darted to Liza and then to Kitty, hoping to gauge their reactions.

'You certainly know how to upset someone,' Liza snapped as she held Kitty close and planted a gentle kiss on her neck as she sobbed.

'The dress was pushed through your door. The killer took it from Alice and brought it here. I thought it was a reasonable question to ask,' he defended himself as he watched Liza stroke Kitty's face with her hand as if she were a pet.

Ruby stared at D'Arc, wondering what question he would ask next.

'She wouldn't tell us. She kept everything about her life a secret,' Kitty managed to murmur as she spoke through her tears. Her voice then changed to almost a whisper. 'That was Alice. She said we didn't need to know and that was it.'

'There must have been something. Alice has been living here for two years.' Ruby pushed for more, silently yearning for something that will give them some further progress.

'Do you own this apartment?' D'Arc asked before either of the women could answer her.

They didn't reply, both women looking at Ruby as if she held the secret for them.

'No,' Ruby answered, 'I do... the girls rent it from me. I bought it five years ago just after the war ended.'

He ignored her reply as if it had been noted but was irrelevant. 'Did Alice say anything about her life before she came to London?'

'She was drunk one night a few weeks ago and told me that she had run away from a man because he beat her. Then she fell asleep. I tried to speak to her about it the next morning, but she denied everything,' Kitty spoke out in a soft voice as she wiped the running mascara from her face with a handkerchief taken from her pocket. 'We knew she was married. That she did talk about,' Liza butted in as if she didn't want her friend to say anything else. Her thin lips pursed as if she was deciding how much he should know. 'Alice had her own money. She used a bank in Knightsbridge. I walked with her one day last week. She put in three hundred pounds... said it was her insurance money.'

'Did she say where the money was from?' D'Arc challenged, his eyes roaming around the hallway of the apartment.

'All she said was that her man gave it to her for being a good girl, and that he was kind and treated her well,' Liza proceeded as D'Arc tried to work out which part of Dublin her accent betrayed she was from.

'But she never mentioned a name?'

'Look, Mister D'Arc,' Liza snapped back, impatience and anger radiating off of her at what she thought were meaningless questions. 'It was good to have Alice around here. She was fun. But we kept ourselves pretty quiet. In this game it's best not to tell each other things–that way, if you get caught, you can't grass. Anyway, she was...' Liza halted suddenly and turned to Ruby as if she had said too much.

'What Liza is trying to say is that it is better for four girls to share an apartment than two. Stops the neighbours talking. They tend not to gossip,' Kitty peered over at Liza as if she would take on what she had said.

'What Kitty is trying to say is that we are not the kind of delights most people enjoy–some would say we are a 'refined taste,' Liza squeezed her hand as she spoke.

'And by that you mean?' D'Arc asked, already knowing the answer but finding a morsel of enjoyment in hearing it from their lips.

'We are sapphists, Mister D'Arc. But you're a detective and it's easy to tell,' Kitty answered matter-of-factly.

'And did Alice Pringle share in these *delights*?'

'She didn't really like it. I tried to explain but she said it wasn't right. She was brought up in a convent school. Alice could never really understand why we liked women,' Liza replied, focusing on Kitty and then glimpsing over at D'Arc.

Kitty broke into the conversation as if she was suddenly awake. 'When you saw her, was she peaceful?'

'As peaceful as she would ever be. Is that important to you?' D'Arc pushed as he watched a trickle of nervous perspiration run down her neck and into the cleavage of her breasts.

'Alice said that her passing would be quick and that all her friends would be waiting. She liked to go to séances,' Kitty spoke in a timid tone, noting to herself where the detective was looking. That coaxed a proud but shy smile from her. 'Alice did a bit herself. Took Ruthie with her one night. She always said that she could see those who had gone to the other side.'

'Are we safe here... should we go? Is it to do with *him*?' Liza whispered to Ruby before Kitty had finished speaking.

D'Arc answered for Ruby, 'Keep the door locked and your gun ready, just in case. I'll come back in the morning. I would like to have a look in her room tomorrow. Ensure that you touch nothing.'

'Why?' Kitty needled, pleased with herself that she could still get a man to look at her. What the woman didn't realise was that D'Arc didn't stare at her for what was underneath the housecoat. He stared because with each moment he built a portrait within his mind as to who she really was. With each second in her presence he formed the pattern of her life. Every detail of her hands, her face and her clothes was taken in by D'Arc and assessed.

Around her nose were the marks of nicotine stains where she had blown smoke from her mouth then snorted it back in again for a double blow. On her neck, just underneath the bobbed blonde hair, was a neat love bite. It had been done some time before but was too small to be from Liza. On her right wrist was a cord mark from where she had been tied, and just above, only visible when she reached out, were needle marks. He shot her a charming smile, knowing she would mirror his expression.

'That I will answer in the morning, Kitty,' D'Arc spoke with finality as he reached out and lay his hand on her shoulder. The woman winced, trying to mask her pain and avoid him noticing. 'We have to go. Do as Ruby says.'

They left the apartment and trudged down the flight of stairs lit only by the light coming from the doorway. It was eerily black as they descended the open spiral staircase. As they reached the second floor, Kitty leant over and shouted down to them.

'There was one thing she did say, Mister D'Arc... when she was asleep she would often shout the word '*Baphomet*' and then would wake up screaming. Does it mean anything?' Kitty disclosed, her body edged in candlelight.

'Not that I am aware of,' D'Arc answered as he looked up. Ruby caught sight of the look on his face. She realised the word meant more than he would reveal. 'But I will come back tomorrow, I would like to look in her room.'

Ruby and D'Arc continued down the stairs until they reached the hallway.

'I thought I told you to ring and I would come for you?' the maid's voice snapped as she stepped from her room with the lantern in her hand.

'We did not want to disturb you,' Ruby answered for them both.

'It's not right, I can't have strangers walking around the building,' the woman griped churlishly.

'Do you have any visitors?' D'Arc asked her innocently as he stepped closer to her, forcing her to move away from him.

'What exactly are you investigating? You said you were a detective. What kind of a detective are you?' she asked earnestly as she aimed the light of the lantern in his face.

D'Arc loomed over the woman and smiled sheepishly.

'A murder... a gruesome death of a young woman cut from her throat to her groyne and stripped of her innards,' D'Arc proclaimed as theatrically as he could, hoping she would ask nothing else.

The woman stood motionless, staring fearfully at Ruby. Then, as if she had recovered from what he had said, the maid backed away into her room. She held her lantern as if it was a weapon, her mind racing.

'Was it Miss Pringle?' she guessed.

D'Arc nodded as he turned the handle of the door and stepped into the street.

'I suggest you keep this door firmly locked. There is a killer on the loose,' he smirked before continuing, 'and he may return.'

[11]
SLOANE STREET

On the steps of Sloane Mansions, in the shadow of the gothic doorway, Ruby Alder was poised, arms folded. The street was quiet. A lone taxicab trundled along, hoping someone would flag it down. It appeared through the thickening fog. The light from the taxicab sign was like the eye of a deep sea creature. D'Arc inspected up and down the street, the sodden pavement was barren. He hated the fog; it could hide so much.

'So, did it mean anything?' Ruby broke the silence as they stood waiting a while.

'Did what?' he questioned cluelessly, knowing exactly what she meant but not wanting to let her know.

"*Baphomet*'. Does it mean something? I saw the look on your face when Kitty shouted down.'

'You are learning fast, Miss Ruby, and I shall have to take more care of what my face betrays,' D'Arc answered her with a smile. There was something about the woman that he liked. She was not just beautiful but had a life in her eyes that intrigued him, like they told a story of their own. Her skin was smooth and not sullied with makeup. Her boyish looks were best described as being uniquely pretty as opposed to conventionally attractive. However, it was the ease he felt in her company that Jack D'Arc was beginning to understand was what he liked the most. He had never felt this comfortable with anyone before, especially a woman. As he spoke to her, he found himself smiling. D'Arc wanted to laugh in her presence.

Three floors above in the bedroom of Alice Pringle, Kitty Fallance was perched on the bed, her face in her hands and tears running through her fingers. Drops of black mascara fell and dripped onto her legs and then onto the silk bedcover.

'We should have shown him. He might know what it was about,' she sputtered angrily as Liza stood over her, not knowing what to do.

'He's a copper. We have to be careful,' Liza objected, her wariness creeping off of her in waves.

'A private detective... Ruby was with him. We have to say something– Alice was murdered. Just take it to him... please,' Kitty pleaded as her lover paced up and down the room.

'It's just a key. Could be for anywhere,' Liza shrugged, her frown-lined face looking haggard in the light from the solitary candle on the dressing table.

'She wore it around her neck all the time, her man must have given it to her. Alice took it off and gave it to me to look after.'

Liza swivelled around to her, she could see the fear in Kitty's face.

'D'Arc mentioned that he was coming back tomorrow. We can wait until then.'

Kitty reached to her side and opened the top drawer of the bedside table. With one hand she reached in and retrieved a small key on a gold chain.

'Just take it to him... please...'

On the stairway of the apartments, opposite the entrance to the elevator on the first floor, the door to the tradesmen's entrance creaked open gradually. Emerging from the shadows, a dark figure in a Homburg hat and long coat waited. The man listened to the noises of the building as if to work out who was awake. Setting down the leather bag that he carried, he unclipped the fastener and reached inside. Pulling out a thin bladed knife, he ran the blade across his hand as if to test the sharpness. Then, advancing back into the door, he seized the bag and disappeared into the shadows as swiftly as he emerged.

In the apartment, Kitty rose from the bed and rushed over to the window that overlooked the street. Without speaking, she hauled open the window. Looking down, she called out in desperation into the fog.

'Ruby... wait!'

Ruby squinted up from the street but could see nothing. 'Kitty... what is it?' she yelled back.

'Liza is coming down. We found something for Mister D'Arc.'

Kitty turned from the window and pressed the key into Liza's hand.

'What are you doing?' Liza demanded, wanting to slap the woman around the face.

'Take it... quickly.'

'It could have waited,' she protested vainly, hating having to go against her own will.

'Please,' Kitty pleaded with a sweet smile, 'if you're that worried about me, leave the revolver.'

Liza gave Kitty a once-over. She reached towards her to grasp her hand, pulling her closer and slipping her hand inside the housecoat.

'You always smile at me that way when you want something,' Liza rolled her eyes as she placed a gentle kiss on her lips, her hand slipping around to the small of her back so that the coat fell open.

'And you always do it,' Kitty answered as their lips broke away for a moment. 'Ruby will be waiting–go on, please...'

Liza stepped back and admired her in the candlelight as the coat fell open around her, wholly exposing Kitty to the other woman's loving gaze. 'Stay like that until I come back,' she directed as she wrapped her fingers around the key and walked from the room. Kitty followed her to the door as Liza reached into her pocket and handed her the pistol. 'Don't answer the door to anyone.'

Slipping hurriedly into the hallway, Liza lingered until she heard the door lock behind her. Then she made her way down the stairs as swiftly as she could in the darkness. She had done this before when they had removed the gas lamps from the walls and changed them to electricity. Liza counted the steps and held onto the bannister that wrapped itself around the elevator cage. That way she was able to navigate her way, even in the dark.

Liza was soon crossing the hallway. Opening the front door, she descended down onto the pavement, leaving the door ajar. The thick London fog billowed into the hallway. Ruby and D'Arc were standing by the black, iron railings that ran the length of the building.

'Kitty said you should have this. It couldn't wait until tomorrow,' Liza disclosed to D'Arc as she held out the key with her left hand.

They couldn't hear the light tread of the man in the brightly polished, black shoes as he made his way up the stairs. In his hand, he carried the leather bag. He stepped higher and higher into the shadowy gloom, his tall frame slightly hunched over. The man counted the steps that matched his heartbeat. He stretched his fingers inside the leather glove that creased with each grasp of his hand.

On the pavement outside Sloane Mansions, D'Arc held the key in his hand, dangling the chain from his fingers.

'And she gave this to Kitty to look after?' he quizzed, never having seen a key with diamonds embedded in the thumb holder.

'Do you think it's important?' Liza pried, watching the key swirl like the device of a mesmerist.

'It could be. How long had she had it?' D'Arc responded.

At the door of Apartment 18, the man in the lengthy black coat knocked gently. He loitered by the door and listened. Footsteps came quickly and then faltered. He heard the hammer of a pistol click.

'Who is it?' Kitty called from inside, her voice broken with anxiety and hesitance.

'Miss Fallance? The maid has sent me. I am the engineer. I have to go into all the apartments to reset the lights,' the man answered in an accent that wasn't his own, hoping she would open the door.

'Who sent you?' Kitty demanded.

'The maid. She is coming up in five minutes to check they are working. You know what she is like; gave me a right roasting for being late. Having to check all the lights in every apartment now.'

His heart pounded faster as he heard the lock turn. It took his breath with excitement as the blood pulsed harder. He could feel himself slowly stiffen. The man gulped back the lump in his throat. The door of the apartment opened slightly. He stepped to one side and waited. Like a cat stalking a mouse about to come from the hole, he leant against the wall. Kitty looked out onto the empty landing. She could see no one.

'Hello... are you there?' she spoke out into what seemed like thin air.

There was no warning as the hand reached out and gripped her by the throat before pushing her back against the wall. The pistol was snatched from her and dropped to the floor. It was all so sudden, so quick, that Kitty had no time to move or react in any way. She felt like she had been picked up by a wave, shoved across the shore and dumped on the seastrand. She could smell the leather of his glove pressed against her face. The man moved her as if she was nothing but a doll. Holding her close, he pulled open the housecoat. He shut the door gently and, with one hand, turned the lock.

'Don't speak and I will let you live,' he threatened in his gruff voice as he pulled the knife from his pocket. Slipping the knife inside the housecoat, he ran the blade down her skin and cut off her briefs. Taking them with one hand, he pulled them from between her legs and stuffed them in her mouth. Then, pulling a silk cord from his pocket, he spun her around and tied her hands behind her back.

Kitty gasped, the silk in her mouth beginning to choke her.

'Do you have something for me, Kitty? Do you have something that Alice has given you? She didn't have it with her when I saw her last. She smelled just like you. I bet she stole some of your perfume before she met him, to keep the smell of the pig from her nostrils.'

The man sniffed her neck and bit at her with his teeth as he pressed himself against her.

'Please...' Kitty tried to beg through the material in her mouth.

The man eased his grip, pulling the pants from her mouth as he pushed her into the bedroom and onto the bed.

'Not one word louder than a whisper and I will let you live.'

'Liza will be back soon–please... I'll do whatever you want,' Kitty begged, tears beginning to fill her eyes and blur her vision.

'I know you will. That is what all of this is about. You will do just what I want and the first thing is you will be very quiet and not make a sound.' Stepping towards the bed, he undid the ivory buttons of his trousers. Kitty stared at the man, trying to remember everything about his face. 'Don't make a sound, that's the way I like it. It'll all be over very soon.' Putting his hand over her mouth, he got on the bed, pushing her legs open. Kitty squeezed her eyes shut as he pushed harder, his eyes rolling back as spit dropped from his mouth. 'I know you don't like men. I watched your friend go down the stairs. Thought this might cure you.'

It wasn't long before he stepped away from her. Kitty lay on the bed, the bruises already starting to show on her neck. The housecoat had been cut from her. It lay like the discarded skin of a snake on the bed beneath her. She sobbed as silently as she could as the blood came from within her and onto the silk sheets.

The man reached for another cord from the pocket of his coat, undid her hands and then tied her to the bed. Stuffing the briefs back in her mouth, he strolled from the room. It was as if he could hear someone outside the apartment. Kitty's analysing stare followed him. He seemed fearless; in control, as if this was something he did every day. The wound between her legs stung like poison ivy. She lay in the candlelight and heard him walk towards the door. There was a knock at the door.

'Kitty... let me in... Kitty...' Liza pleaded.

The door swung open suddenly. A gloved hand snapped from the darkness and grabbed Liza by the throat. It was unexpected, vicious and lightning fast. A blow followed and slammed her in the chest. Liza was pulled inside, though she was bent, doubled over in pain. She was kicked in the stomach, lifted up and then hurled against the wall. She got one look at the man and he was smiling at her as if he enjoyed every moment. The punch came at super speed, catching her in the plexus. Liza fell to the floor. The man sat himself on her shoulders, pushing his groyne in her face and keeping her pinned to the floor. He forced a pillow over her head. Liza couldn't move; her brain was screaming at her to do something but her body was rendered completely and utterly helpless. She tried to scream for Kitty, her words smothered. It was then that she felt the cold barrel of the pistol pressed against the side of her head. The last thing she ever heard was a dull click.

[12]
BUCKINGHAM GATE

In the back of the hackney taxicab that rattled along Buckingham Gate towards The Mall, Jack D'Arc's stare fixated on Ruby Alder. She had talked all the way from the apartment, her voice sounding excited, rich and warm. As the taxicab turned onto Trafalgar Square, D'Arc seized the key and chain from his pocket.

'Are you sure you have no idea where this came from?' he asked in an attempt to bring the conversation back to the case.

'I have never seen it before, Alice kept herself to herself.'

'So it's not from a crime you don't want to tell me about?'

Ruby didn't know if he was being serious. His mood had lightened the more time she spent with him, his eyes holding more of a mischievous gleam to them. He joked, often at her expense, and in return she flirted.

'Alice was a getaway driver–that's all she did. I paid her in cash. She would wait outside the stores in a stolen car and get us away faster than the coppers. She said her father was a racing driver, though we never believed her.'

'That part of her life is true. Her father was the winner of *Le Mans*. He was one of the finest drivers and one of the fastest men in the world.'

'I thought she was just a liar. Alice lived in two worlds–sometimes she could not tell the difference between them. She had a sort of sixth sense. It got her out of trouble, but she must have run out of luck.'

'I am not a firm believer in the supernatural or luck. God and the Devil are the desires of frightened men.'

Ruby realised she had struck a nerve. His mood changed like a closing moonflower as his head bowed slightly forward, his lips growing tighter as if he fought to keep in what he wanted to say.

'That is swell coming from a man like you, Mister D'Arc. The first time I saw you I thought you could be a priest,' Ruby murmured, hoping to cajole him from the grim mood that hung on his face.

He relaxed back into the seat as a laugh escaped his lips, the sound like a gentle melody in Alder's ears.

'I saw too much in Flanders to believe in a God. Man hath but a short time to live, and is full of misery. He cometh up, and is cut down, like a flower; he flees as if he were a shadow, in the midst of life we are in death.'

'Cheerful bugger...' Ruby began, fighting the urge to roll her eyes as a smirk bloomed across her lips. 'Talking like that, I take it there is no Mrs. D'Arc?' D'Arc chuckled again, it seemed to be becoming a habit. Since meeting Miss Alder he had laughed more than he had for many years.

'I don't think I could ever find a woman who would be willing to put up with my musings. It is presumptuous to think that I would need one to be successful in life.' D'Arc toyed with the idea of telling her the truth. He would have liked to see the look on her face when he told her where his desires took him. In an instant he dismissed the thought. It definitely did not go unnoticed.

'So what do you do for fun?' she asked, her voice sweet.

'Fun? That is not a word that I often think of. I have my work as a detective, but no family. My mother and father are dead. I have Edgar.'

'Never knew mine. Grew up in a children's home, left when I was fourteen. Who is Edgar?' she asked, as if the name had just come into her mind.

'My bull terrier. I got inspiration from Charles Dickens. There is a dog in Oliver Twist owned by a villain named Bill Sikes. The dog is called Bullseye; I often thought this to be unfair, so I called my dog Edgar. A fitting name for a dog, don't you think? Especially a bull terrier.'

Ruby did not think at all. She had never heard of Dickens and her life was no less rich from her ignorance.

'I've never read a book. Don't get me wrong, I can read and write, I made sure of that. But never had the time for books,' Ruby's answer was curt and to the point. 'Can't see the point of stories, but the pictures are different. I love the recent development of moving pictures.'

D'Arc breathed deeply as a broad smile came across his face.

'Then that shall be my challenge. By the age of nine, I had read a million words and you could do the same.'

'Why?' she quizzed.

'Because it expands the mind and broadens the tongue,' D'Arc answered as if he were about to start a crusade.

'Didn't see a dog at Chalcot Crescent,' Ruby changed the subject, hoping to take his mind from books.

'Edgar is currently on loan to my old Regimental Sergeant Major. He is having a problem with rats. If Edgar had been at home, I would never have been burgled and you would never have been allowed into my house. Edgar hates women.'

'Like his owner?' Ruby asked through narrow lips, a sigh of discontent flowing from her lips.

'Aurora club, Soho Square. Two shillings,' the taxicab driver interrupted before D'Arc could reply. The taxicab came to a juddering halt outside the door of the nightclub. A canopy lit by a bright, green light kept the night off the back of the burly man on the door. He stood in the entrance, his body wrapped tightly in an ill-fitting evening suit. The man smiled at Ruby as she disembarked from the taxicab.

[13]
SOHO SQUARE

The upper balcony of the Aurora Club was both decadent and sumptuous. Every gold-covered table had a view of the dance floor and the jazz band in the corner of the room downstairs. It was sweltering, the noise and smoke surging all around, with people pressed in on all sides. No one seemed to be bothered about eating; half-heard conversations were washed down with gin and Russian vodka. Ruby had been there once before a long time ago and yet the man on the door remembered her. D'Arc was impressed that he even called her by her name. The doorman got her a table upstairs, with the express instructions given to an effete waiter, dressed in tight, black trousers, stiletto shoes and a blouson shirt, that he should look after Miss Ruby and her friend. The waiter had done what he was asked and kept coming back every time D'Arc sipped on his drink to ask if he wanted any more. Ruby would nod and the man would go away, pushing through the crowds to the small bar at the back of the room.

'So you like the movies?' D'Arc asked, hoping to revive the conversation from the taxicab. 'I saw one once by Fatty Arbuckle. I can't say the acting was the best in the world.'

'That's not the point,' she shot back as her eyes lit up, fired by her imagination. 'It's called comedy. It's not supposed to be real life. If you look at Chaplin or Keaton, they are experts...'

D'Arc pushed in before she could carry on.

'I went to see Arbuckle because I had heard he had been charged with manslaughter and I was fascinated to see if he was capable of committing the crime. I think it was called *The Life of the Party*...'

'Winifred Greenwood and Roscoe Karns,' Ruby answered, her face brighter than before.

'The man obviously had no intention to kill Miss Virginia Rappe. I would suggest she died of alcohol poisoning.'

'And you could tell all that from watching the picture?' Ruby returned.

'And reading the reports in the newspaper. I found it most intriguing. You can tell if someone could do such a thing by the way they look,' D'Arc stated like it was the simplest thing in the world as he glanced at the dance floor below. It was filled with people moving to the music, too crowded to dance. They all became one, moving together in time with the beat as the lights and music turned the awkward bodies into a fluid rhythm. 'See there,' D'Arc went on, pointing to a man leaning against a pillar at the far side of the room. 'That man is a thief waiting to dip the pocket of the gentleman on the dance floor in front of him. He is working with the woman the man is dancing with.'

'How can you tell?' Ruby asked.

'I saw her pick the victim from a table at the far side of the room. She has danced him through the crowd away from his friends and any moment now...'

D'Arc was right, not that he himself had any doubts. The man leaning against the pillar stepped forward. His eyes darted over to the woman dancing. She pushed against her dance partner as she squeezed him closer. The man by the pillar dipped the pocket with his fingers and then walked away.

Ruby smiled at D'Arc as she observed as the man danced on, blissfully unaware that his wallet had been taken.

'And you can just tell by looking at someone?'

'We are like birds in a cage. We mirror the movements of each other as if life is a dance. Some of those taking part are capable of the most vile of crimes.'

'And you, Mister D'Arc, are you?' Ruby directed her question at the man in front of her, keeping her gaze glued on his.

'If you could see inside my mind, you would realise that I am a monster of depravity. Murderous, almost, but I have decided to chase the murderer rather than become one.' For a moment she could see the intense seriousness of his stare. It was as if a face was revealed from within the face and she was looking at someone completely different. 'You seem quite shocked?'

'I have never thought of that before–what people are like on the inside,' Ruby answered as the music played louder and a girl ascended the stage to dance.

'So, how do we find the man Alice Pringle was in love with?' D'Arc wondered out loud.

'He might not even be here,' Ruby shrugged, not wanting to get her hopes up.

'Then let's ask,' D'Arc tilted his head in the direction of the waiter, raising his hand to catch his eye.

The man sashayed over, his feet taking precise steps as he walked in high heels. He paused at the table, giving the pair a welcoming smile before pursing his ruby lips. They glistened in the light of the large chandelier that hung above the balcony.

'Drink?' he offered in effeminate Glaswegian, observing the glass that was still nearly full.

'I am looking for Alice Pringle. She is an old friend,' D'Arc deflected.

'Who?' the waiter answered as he slipped the cloth across the sleeve of his blouson and sank one hip lower than the other in a comfortable pose.

'Alice Pringle–my sister, she comes here all the time,' Ruby explained, looking at his tiny feet and envying the black high heels.

The waiter surveyed her up and down, a reserved smile curling on his lips. 'Alice? Do you mean Alicia?' he probed as if it was the only name near enough to Alice for him to know.

'She only used that in her family,' D'Arc corrected, leaning forward and pulling the man closer by his blouse.

'She usually comes here most nights. Haven't seen her for a while,' he rejoined as he peered back in Ruby's direction, his eyes squinting ever so slightly as he began to grow suspicious. 'She's not really your sister... not unless one of you was adopted.'

'Alicia mentioned that she would be here tonight. She is meeting a friend,' Ruby stared the waiter in the face, daring him to argue. He looked confused, probably wondering if they were the police.

'Everyone wants Alicia. Had a chap in here the other night saying he had to talk to her. Gave me ten pounds for an introduction. I pointed her out, and he said that was enough. Easiest money ever made,' he revealed as he held out the tray. 'You people want a drink or do I charge you for standing here?'

'I will give you ten to be introduced to the man she always meets,' D'Arc countered as he reached inside his pocket and grasped a small velvet bag of coins and placed them on the table.

'That's a lot of money,' the waiter's stunned gaze remained pinned on the bag.

'Is he here?' D'Arc urged further, impatience coursing through his veins.

'You are too late,' the man replied, switching hips and keeping his powdered eyes on the bag. 'Are they guinea pieces?'

'The purse is ready to slip into your hands.'

'Ten guineas?' the man pushed for confirmation as he thought, looking at the bag before his gaze darted around the crowded room.

'You have no need to count it,' D'Arc corrected as the waiter looked at him as if it were a trap.

'Are you the police?' the waiter demanded.

'She's a good friend. I need to speak to her,' Ruby pleaded, hoping he would understand.

'I heard him ask for a taxicab to 616 Eaton Square. He always signs his bill as Gerard Montague. That's all I know.'

'Is he here tonight?' Ruby's skin itched in anticipation of finally getting another step closer.

'Went about an hour ago. Alicia never came. She would always be here by nine. He paid the bill with cash and took a taxicab... I ordered it myself.'

The pair of eyes remained on the waiter before D'Arc broke the temporary silence. 'Did Alicia dine here every night?'

'That's just what the other man wanted to know. He looked like you as well, but not quite so handsome,' the waiter complimented, reaching out and caressing his shoulder.

'What was the man like?' D'Arc noticed the thin, red-lined scars that crossed the wrist of the waiter as he posed his question.

The man saw where D'Arc's gaze fell, shrugging the sleeve of his blouse so it fell lower in return.

'Many men asked for Alicia. They thought she was something they could buy from the menu. The man was tall, dark, probably in the military. He had that look about him. I would say he was about forty or fifty, a handsome face, blue eyes.'

'Took a good look at him?' Ruby's voice was sarcastic as she arched a perfectly plucked eyebrow.

'I take a good look at every man–it's my job. I am employed to keep them happy–whatever they may want,' the man gave a simple answer, looking at D'Arc as his brow furrowed. There was something about D'Arc that he found familiar. The waiter scanned his face. 'Haven't I seen you somewhere before the Miramar or the Turkish Baths at the Savoy?'

It was a question that D'Arc obviously did not want to answer. Ruby saw his face change. The benign smile fell from his lips, his eyes narrowing as he thought of what to say.

'You must be mistaken,' D'Arc chided, responding to him as if he was a child who found out something they shouldn't have. 'I have never been to such a place.'

The waiter held back his smile, internally smirking as he eyed up Ruby next to him. 'Then a mistake it must be,' he quipped as he snatched the money from where it lay and shoved it swiftly in his pocket. 'Shame really,' he ventured, 'I would quite like to meet a man like *you* in a place like *that*.'

As they departed the Aurora and stepped into the thick fog that swirled through Soho Square, it was obvious that D'Arc didn't want to talk.

'So, what now?' Ruby pressed as D'Arc traipsed ahead towards Frith Street. He pulled up the collar of his coat and shrugged his shoulders, not turning. 'Do we go to Eaton Square?'

'*We?*' he replied with a sharpened voice as he stopped outside a boarded-up tobacconist shop. 'I have things to do and I can get you a taxicab.'

'I thought we were to find who killed Alice?' Ruby implored.

'That may be the case, but some things are best done alone.'

Ruby could see that the cold, steel reserve of Jack D'Arc had been broken. His eyes gave away the turmoil of his heart and she was left wondering if it had been the parting words of the waiter that had caused his consternation. His face had changed when the man had spoken of the Miramar and the Turkish Baths. It was as if the mention of their names brought D'Arc great dismay.

Ruby knew them well. They were not talked about in polite society. In the Elephant and Castle public house, the men spoke of them with sneers and disdain.

'*Queer palaces for men with peculiar tastes*', an old lag had said of them. Ruby knew that old queens in search of rent boys used the Savoy Turkish Baths. Some of them would be robbed as they walked the nearby streets, yet they were often wealthy and fearful of calling the police in case their secret was found out. None of them wanted to be accused of pederasty. Families could be lost, names disgraced and friends shamed. Ruby mulled the thought as she watched D'Arc who brooded in anger.

When much younger, she herself had dressed as a 'Tom' and lured a fat Dulwich tea importer to Green Park. It was obvious that he thought she was a boy as he kept calling her lad and demanding she remove her vests. The man had offered her two shillings if she walked with him for an hour. In the moonlight of a summer's night she had taken the man far from the gates. With an adenoidal moan, the man had found a patch of grass and demanded Ruby lay down. As he unbuttoned her coat she had brought out a knife and took all he had. It had amounted to three pounds and a few brass coins, a thimble and a broken pipe. He had screamed for mercy, calling on the saints and the Mother of God to *'bring damnation on the bitch with the knife'*. That had been the first and last time she had pulled such a trick.

It was a chance meeting with an antique dealer in Battersea that changed her mind. Angus Kemp was middle-aged; well, he seemed that way to Ruby. He was well dressed, most polite and utterly considerate. The business he conducted from the back room of his small shop was well used. In his dealings with the thieves of South London, he was always honest. Mister Kemp was a friend of *Mrs. King*–as the women in the laundry opposite had mouthed theatrically when she told Ruby.

Whoever's friend he was, Kemp bought what he could from disreputable sources. Ruby had sold him a watch she had found in the pocket of a man on Oxford Street and they had soon become friends. Kemp invited Ruby to dinner every Sunday. In return, she ironed his vast array of shirts and fixed the green carnation in the lapel of his jacket. It had not been long before Ruby had been introduced to George. He was a young Bohemian man who visited in the late afternoons. His long hair touched the shoulders and he always complained of the walk from West Hampstead. In the large room above his shop they all took coffee together, talking of London life and finer things. Kemp was regal and proud as he sat in the baroque armchair and admired the fine paintings that hung so out of place on the walls of the room. He would serve cakes and triangular sandwiches on a three-tier plate with napkins folded to resemble swans. Then later, when he wanted to nap, he would send Ruby and George for a walk in the evening air.

It had been George who, on a saunter across the park, had confided in Ruby what he was.

'I am different,' he had disclosed as he burst into tears and sobbed in fear of losing her friendship. 'The trouble is that I am...' he could not bring himself to even give a name to the feeling he had.

Ruby had hugged him close and told him that she understood.

Yet, as she gaped at D'Arc, she didn't think that this sort of delight would interest him. Well, that was her own selfish hope.

'Taxicab?' Ruby offered as she followed a pace behind him as he pushed through the people on the pavement. 'I don't want to go home.'

'What about your friends? They need help. You can't leave them alone at Sloane Mansions,' D'Arc countered.

'I thought I could come with you, be of some help?' Her voice went up a pitch at the end of her question, nervous to what D'Arc's response would be. D'Arc ceased his walk and stepped back into a doorway of a shop to allow those on the pavement to pass. Ruby stood close to him. He seemed exasperated, as if her presence made him agitated. D'Arc pushed back his hat so it sat on the top of his forehead. He leant against the door of the shop and put his hands deep within the pockets of his coat to check the contents. 'Was it what the waiter said to you?' Ruby asked.

D'Arc's eyes were glued on the marble step beneath him. Upon it were raindrops scattered like tears. He skidded the sole of his right leather shoe back and forth anxiously, smashing each one.

'Does it make a difference to you?' he shot back.

[14]
MEARD STREET

From the doorway, they trudged in silence through the alleyway that ran behind Bateman Street. It was dingy, dirty and scattered with the snoring carcasses of the vagrants drunk by midnight. Ruby stepped over several sleeping bodies. It looked like a fog-bound morgue and stank like a charnel house full of piss and cheap beer.

D'Arc pressed on, not offering a hand to Ruby as she struggled to pick her way through the detritus of the London underworld. Leaving the alleyway after another twenty paces, they crossed Dean Street with the bright lights of the jazz clubs and bars. They hung high above the echoing doors, casting reflective lights onto the smog-bound street below. Ruby remained close to him as D'Arc pushed through the crowd of men who gathered around two girls outside the Mardi Gras Club. The girls were smoking pink cigarettes jammed into the ends of long, lacquered holders that stuck in the air like porcupine quills.

It was as if D'Arc could not see the crowd through his stubbornness and unpleasant feelings looming over him. Ruby thought he could have easily stepped into the road and walked around, but she then realised that D'Arc had chosen to push his way through, though no one seemed to mind. The men were not at the time of night where the Appaloosa cocktails made them want to fight. They all parted; some grinned at Ruby, one even asked her to drink with him. Then they were out the other side. D'Arc took the first turn to his right; it was the entrance to a narrow alleyway lit only by a meagre streetlight high above the sign for Meard Street.

'This is the place,' he confirmed to Ruby. 'I believe it was near here somewhere.'

D'Arc swivelled and took a glance around the alleyway. It had been freshly swept, the rubbish taken away, with any sign of a murder washed from the alleyway walls with its broken bricks and smashed fall pipes.

'Feels bad coming here,' Ruby mumbled with a shiver.

'I always like to revisit the crime. It is as if the place can speak. Bricks and mortar are never silent. If you can get inside the mind of the killer...' D'Arc deliberated as he cast a glance around him. Ruby could see that what the waiter had said was now forgotten. 'Interesting,' D'Arc muttered as his eyes shot to the floor and then high above him. 'Everything has been altered as if they didn't want me to find out.'

'Can't believe Alice would end up here,' Ruby answered, making her way towards D'Arc.

'So close to Dean Street. She must have been followed–someone who knows the place well. She hadn't been to the Aurora on the night she was killed. Is there anywhere else nearby she could have gone?' D'Arc contemplated as the light at the end of the alleyway flickered.

'I didn't know her that well. Alice kept everything to herself. She talked to Ruthie, treated her like a little sister.'

'Where would Ruthie be tonight?'

'Dancing, that's all she likes. Don't know where... London is a big place.'

'And the séances, did Alice mention them to you?'

'It was the one thing she would speak about. They were at the Vaudeville Theatre after the show was over. She wanted to take me along. I wouldn't go... not for me...' Ruby stopped speaking and looked into the gloom of the alleyway beyond where D'Arc was standing.

'Have you seen a ghost?' he asked.

'She not giving you what you want, Mister?' the first voice came from behind him.

'Perhaps she needs some encouragement,' another voice spoke in an accent almost echoing the first.

'The lady is far too covered up in all them coats for this kind of place. Let the dog see the rabbit, Missy. Let's see what you're hiding beneath that fancy coat.'

D'Arc turned hastily; behind him were two men wearing work clothes and flat caps. Their boots were soiled with clay and mud, hands charred with the dirt from the river. From six feet, D'Arc could smell the taint of sewage upon them. Both men came closer, and as they appeared from the shadows, D'Arc noticed that they were two hands taller than him and far wider. Their bodies were work-hardened and stocky, like hay-fed horses.

The taller, scruffier one of the men stepped forward, pushing D'Arc to one side as he moved towards Ruby.

'What you are doing is not wise,' D'Arc warned as he plunged his hand into the pocket of his coat.

'Why is that? Want to keep her for yourself?' the man snorted back, his voice deep and gruff.

'Not at all. You can have her if you so wish. She does not belong to me,' D'Arc answered as he turned and began to stroll away.

'What are you doing, Jack?' Ruby's voice rose to a clamour as she noticed that she was being left alone in the alleyway with the two mudlarks.

'Jack don't want you,' the other man snarled, his stocky frame leaning against the wall as he chewed the end of a hand-rolled cigarette.

'Two for the price of one?' the first man quipped, the look in his eyes showing no remorse as he turned to consider his companion. 'How much do you charge?'

Ruby pinned her glare to D'Arc as he began edging his way towards Dean Street.

'Jack?!' she shouted, the pitch of her voice asking the question.

The smaller man stepped across the alleyway and blocked D'Arc so he could go no further. 'Need to talk to you, Jack. You don't think you can leave without giving us a tip. After all, we are doing you a favour trying this one out. Never know what she might have that a gentleman don't want,' the man grumbled as he held out an expectant hand.

D'Arc halted in his place, looking at Ruby. She stood in the shadows of the alley, pressed against the wall.

'You want to speak to me?' his voice posed a threat, almost as if he were challenging the leering men in front of him.

'We'll see to you and then the woman.'

'It would be best if you turned away now, Ruby,' D'Arc raised his voice to reach the nearly trembling woman, pulling his hand from his pocket and hiding it behind his back.

The man guffawed, yanking down the peak of his flat cap and stepping towards him like a bear in a pit fight.

D'Arc snapped his hand from behind his coat, his fist leaping forward as the man advanced towards him. The sound of crunching bone echoed in the alleyway as the knuckleduster that fit snugly on his right hand smashed into the man's face. The mudlark fell to the ground like a shot beast, making no sound as he lay in the dirt. D'Arc turned in a haste.

'Not one more step,' the other man warned, holding Ruby by the throat and pressing a knife against her face.

D'Arc howled in laughter. 'As you are about to find out, that is the stupidest thing you could have ever said.'

'I'll cut her pretty face if you come anywhere near,' he yelled back.

It was the last thing the man said. Ruby Alder clenched her fist, each finger wrapped in a large ruby ring, as always. With all of her force, she smashed it upwards as fast as she could. The cold stones and silver clasps tore at his face, making the man stumble forward. Ruby lashed out with both hands and, jerking her elbow violently into his stomach, the man dropped to the floor. As he knelt on the ground with blood streaming from his face, she swung at him again. Then as he fell back, she kicked him in the stomach. He slumped face down in the dirt. Ruby grabbed him by the long clump of hair that hung about his ears, lifting his head in one hand and then striking him again and again until his face poured with blood.

'*Enough!*' D'Arc attempted to warn, though knowing she would not stop.

'Don't ever touch me again!' Ruby screamed at the man as she began to search through the pockets of his jacket, taking his money, an old snuff box and a hunter pocket watch.

'What are you doing?' D'Arc asked.

'He's paying tax for touching me. Old habits die hard, Jack. Old habits...' she murmured, kicking the man one last time for good measure before she crossed the alleyway to his companion and began to search him.

'Is he alive?' D'Arc queried, his eyes following the woman's movements.

'He's breathing but has nothing, not a penny,' Ruby uttered before digging her heel into the man's stomach as if it were a punishment for being poor.

'He will never forget what you did to him,' D'Arc was about to shoot back. He turned to Ruby, but the blow that came was swift and unexpected.

'And neither will you.'

'What have I done?' he protested, cradling the side of his face that ached with the stinging blow.

'You were going to leave me,' she exclaimed in disbelief. 'Leave me like a piece of meat for those two brutes!'

'It was a ruse to get their attention away from you. I was putting the knuckleduster on my fingers.'

'You were walking away. I saw you,' Ruby disputed angrily. 'Never do that again.'

On the floor by their feet, lying in the mud was something white and round. The man bent down and retrieved it from the dirt.

'What is it?' Ruby wondered, her anger abating.

D'Arc held up a small button, it looked as though it had been hewn from whalebone and engraved with minute lettering. One side was black and the other white. Rubbing it in his fingers, he smoothed away the dirt.

'Wolfe and Son, they are tailors on Sackville Street. It was ripped from the jacket. These buttons are unique and of great price. What is more, there is blood.'

D'Arc pointed to a small, dried droplet stuck in the ridge of the button. It could hardly be seen in the light.

'Are you sure?' Ruby doubted. 'Someone could have lost it.'

'That may be the case, but I have to find out. There is something about this murder that is not right. I am beginning to become suspicious that there is a motive at work that is beyond understanding.'

'What do you mean?' Ruby's swirling thoughts got cut off as he dropped the button in her hand.

'It is all too easy. A clue here and a button there. I feel as if I am a puppet and the master's hands are somewhere above me in the clouds. I dangle on a string to find a man who should hang from a rope.'

'And what do we do with these two?' she indicated to the floor with a flick of her wrist.

'I don't think they will wake for some time...' D'Arc reassured as he took the button from her hand and slipped it back into his pocket. 'I am glad you never let me down. I thought you would be able to fight, but not as well as that. In future I shall have to be on my guard in case I am attacked.'

'Why should I ever do that?' she asked with a hum as they made their way towards the street.

'You are a woman, anything is possible.'

'Where now?' Ruby motioned to their surroundings as they stepped onto the street.

'It is time for me to think and time for you to dream. I will meet you at ten in the morning at Sloane Mansions. Then we will be one day closer to discovering who killed Princess Alicia Gabrielle.' D'Arc rubbed his hands together as if with mirth. 'I will find you a taxicab,' he continued as he took her gently by the hand.

'Princess?'

[15]
REGENT'S PARK

In the growing light of a London dawn, Inspector Varney pushed open the back door of the police sedan and slipped from the leather seat. He stood in Chalcot Crescent, the electric lamp on the iron post flickering in the fading gloom. In two long strides, he had crossed the stone pavement, walked up the steps of the house and banged on the door.

'D'Arc... D'Arc...' Varney's voice boomed as his thick fingers rapped against the wood. A few moments later the door opened and Jack D'Arc's frame filled the doorway with his housecoat tied tightly around the waist. 'Get dressed,' Varney's command made no room for argument as he turned and made his way back to the car.

'Good morning, Chief Inspector, would you like breakfast?' D'Arc quipped, a smirk fighting to grace his lips as the inspector stopped suddenly and begrudgingly turned back around.

'Don't bloody "*good morning*" me, you piece of shit. The car is waiting,' Varney snarled.

'Am I being arrested?'

'You bloody should be. This time you are a witness. Ruby Alder is already at the station. Been there half the night.'

'They attacked us. We were only...' D'Arc ceased speaking his defence, thinking it unwise to continue.

'What are you talking about?' Varney's voice dripped with suspicion, the early morning dampening his mood even further.

'Nothing,' he answered as if it didn't matter. 'I will join you in the car.'

Varney waited fifteen minutes and in that time smoked four cigarettes. He flicked the carcass of each one into the street, trying to land them into the pot of a small, ornamental bay tree.

As he finished the fifth cigarette, the door to the house opened with D'Arc stepping outside soon after.

'Scotland Yard?' D'Arc posed the question simply.

'They're both dead. *You* were the last people to see them alive.'

'Who is dead? I am sure that when I saw them last they were breathing.'

'Two women, Sloane Mansions. Ruby Alder said you were both there last night,' Varney stated with a snarl as D'Arc closed the car door and slid in next to him.

'So... where are we going?' D'Arc broke the brief silence as the sedan drove towards Regent's Park.

'Sloane Mansions. The Commissioner wants you to be taken to the scene of the crime.'

'Ruby Alder–is she at the station?'

'Scotland Yard with some hooker. You'll see her soon enough. Commissioner insists you go to the murder scene.'

'Why should it matter if a private detective goes to the scene?' D'Arc fought the urge to roll his eyes.

'Apparently, you have friends in high places. Someone has insisted that the Commissioner help you as much as possible and I have become Jack–in–the–bloody–middle,' Varney released a sigh, his displeasure more than evident as he slouched back in the seat and folded his thick arms. 'How the hell did you get involved in all this?'

'I am beginning to wonder that myself,' D'Arc's voice was a mumble as the car sped around the outer circle of the park and passed the fine houses with their white-painted balconies and manicured hedges.

It was not long before the police sedan pulled up outside Sloane Mansions. The building appeared grim in daylight, free from the mantle of fog. D'Arc's gaze turned up instinctively, just as he had done the night before. It reminded him of an Edinburgh tenement with its high windows and Castilian roof. Stepping from the car followed by Varney, he adjusted the brim of his hat.

'Before you ask, it's a murder-suicide,' Varney barged into D'Arc's back as they walked up the steps.

In the expansive hall, the maid sat on the steps sobbing. A uniformed constable stood next to her, making no attempt to console the woman.

D'Arc shot her an awkward smile as they proceeded towards the lift. The hallway looked larger in daylight, with the staircase spiralling up further and further towards the fourth floor. The large art deco elevator filled the centre with its caged doors and gold leaf.

'There was a power cut last night,' D'Arc mentioned as Varney opened the door and stepped in, pressing the button for the upper floor. 'Did the maid see anything?'

'More than she will tell,' Varney muttered, not wanting to answer the question.

D'Arc counted the clicks of the steel chain that pulled them higher. The elevator cage rocked from side to side and then stopped. On the landing, a man that D'Arc thought was far too old to wear a uniform stepped forward and opened the door, feebly saluting Varney.

'All ready?' Varney's question was directed at the man, who replied with a curt nod.

D'Arc followed him inside the apartment, unprepared for the sight that lay before them. On the floor of the hallway was the body of a woman, laying in a pool of thick, rich blood. One side of her head was fragmented and there were remnants of her brain scattered all over the floor and on a discarded cushion. Her legs were pushed together as if the body had been moulded after death.

'Interesting…' D'Arc trailed off, peering down at Liza and noting the pistol in her right hand. 'She has been posed. Suicides do not pose when they are dead.'

'Wait until you see the one in here,' Varney's voice was melancholic, knowing that it would get worse.

D'Arc dubiously made his way into the bedroom, the sight rendering him silent momentarily. On the bed was Kitty, her body naked and she had been propped up in the bed and supported with pillows. Her clothes were cut from her, stomach ripped open and a peculiar carving of a five-pointed star cut into the right breast. Her eyes were wide open and face contorted in an almost welcoming smile. It was as if the murderer had pressed her face so that she looked that way. If it wasn't for the ripped-open abdomen, D'Arc thought, she looked quite happy.

'Razor cuts. Surgical knife. They are the same as those on Alicia. They didn't kill her,' D'Arc thought out loud. 'Then she was slashed with a different knife–see the wounds are jagged and thicker.' D'Arc retrieved a pencil from his pocket and motioned to the wound on her breast that he was referring to. 'The pentagram is very interesting. If this were a murder-suicide, I would never expect to see that. After all, this death took time. A lover strikes quickly,' D'Arc looked at the reddening between the legs of the body. There were scratches and abrasions as if something sharp had rubbed on each inner thigh. 'She has been raped, by a man,' he added.

'Stabbed, strangled and then her ear was cut off. Murder-suicide. That's what it is and what you will tell the Commissioner. This is not another Ripper murder.'

'Why?' D'Arc pinned his glare on Varney.

'Because I don't bloody want it, that's why,' he answered with an ounce of finality, snatching a cigarette from the packet and lighting it up, making a point of it to blow the smoke in D'Arc's direction.

D'Arc retreated from the bedroom to study the body in the hallway once more. 'And this is a supposed to be the suicide?' he asked Varney, who followed like a tweed-clad lap dog.

'The other girl that lives here has admitted that she and Kitty Fallance had a fling with each other. The one on the floor with her brains on the carpet must have found out. She killed the woman and then shot herself. Isn't that the tradition in Lesbania?'

D'Arc examined the body; the pistol lay in the palm of the right hand, the fingers curled loosely around the grip. A long and ornate pillow lay on the floor as if a platter for what had once been inside her head. His eyes switched to the wall; there, in the skirting board, was the small hole where the bullet had fragmented. It was surrounded by splashes of blood and fragments of brain.

'This was not a suicide,' D'Arc whispered, more to himself than anything.

'What?' Varney peered over the shoulder of the detective as he spoke.

'Have you ever known anyone to lay on the floor, put a pillow over their own head and then pull the trigger?' D'Arc challenged, the idea seeming even more absurd the more he let it linger in his mind.

'They were *sapphists*, you never know what they would do.'

'Kitty was raped by a man of at least fifteen stone in weight. This woman could not have done that unless there was a man here as well.' The deliberations rumbled through his head as he played out the possible scene in his mind. He got to his feet and looked around as if he projected the events around him. 'Did you find the heart?'

'It was a murder-suicide, and this one on the floor also killed Alicia Gabrielle,' Varney insisted, his words loud and abrasive.

'There is something that connects them all–Alice, Kitty and Liza, but these murders are not it.'

'The only thing they have in common is that they all were velvet sniffers who spent their days thieving from shops on Oxford Street and robbing old ladies. They were members of the Forty Elephants, but I think you know that already,' Varney's answer was contemptuous and dripping with disdain.

'A right-handed shot to the temple.'

'And?' Varney replied, as if he couldn't care less.

'I saw her before her murder, she had the gun to protect herself. The gun was in her left hand. Left hand, Chief Inspector, left hand.'

'Cut off the ear of her lover and then killed herself. The one on the floor also murdered Alicia Gabrielle,' Varney snorted the words, his excitement evident. 'That's why the Commissioner wanted me to show you. It's stumps, D'Arc, end of the game. You can tell that to Lady Gabrielle. Her daughter was killed in a lovers' tiff.

'But what about the heart?' D'Arc insisted. 'Did the killer leave it here?'

'In the kitchen, on the table,' Varney replied regretfully as if he wanted to ignore the question. He found D'Arc irritating. 'How did you know about the heart?'

'Laid out as if a meal ready to be eaten?' D'Arc questioned as he sauntered along the passageway to a small room with an open door.

He went inside. There was a narrow table, a cooker, sink and all that he expected in an apartment like this. It all looked meticulously clean, as if the occupants never used it and always ate out. On the table lay a white china plate with a cooked heart dumped on it. It had sagged as it had cooled down and now looked as if it were made of blood-soaked cabbage. Next to the plate lay a knife and fork.

'Strange what some people do. Do you think she would have eaten the heart?' Varney wondered as he stood behind D'Arc, who was on his knees with his head in the oven.

'It was cooked elsewhere. This oven has never been used. Fresh as the day it was purchased,' D'Arc stood up and glared at Varney. '*Bon appetit...*'

'The doctor said it belonged to a woman aged twenty to thirty. It has been cut roughly from the body, I think it is from the victim of the Dean Street murder. I would say that the woman in the hall murdered both Kitty Fallance and Alicia Gabrielle. Ruth Caddick returned home at two twenty-five in the morning and found them dead. Game over, D'Arc. Murderer, victims and motive.'

'Why didn't Liza wait for Caddick to return and kill her as well, if it was a crime of passion?' D'Arc retaliated.

'It's going to be just how the Commissioner wants it, D'Arc. Tell him that the crime has been solved and we can all have a happy life. It needs to be done today. Do I make myself clear?' Varney tried to sound threatening as he leant closer to D'Arc, pressing him back against the cold, painted wall of the kitchenette.

'If that is what you desire,' D'Arc answered, his face close enough to Varney to smell the cheap cologne that soaked the collar of the sweat-stained shirt that he wore.

'I am glad you understand what the Commissioner wants. Sapphists, D'Arc... you can never know what motivates such sick, deviant people.'

[16]
YORK MANSIONS

Dull light spilled in through the row of opaque windows that lined the corridor of Scotland Yard. Jack D'Arc followed Varney step by step. Taking everything in about the man that he could, D'Arc wondered why the hems of the Chief Inspector's tweed trousers were so tattered. He could see that the heels of his shoes were worn, as were the elbows of his jacket. As well as that, the collar of his shirt was torn. Immediately, D'Arc knew that Varney was a man who lived alone.

'How is your wife?' D'Arc was too intrigued to allow Varney's condition to go unnoticed. He had heard that Varney had married a shrew, a woman from Halifax with a temper to match the hostility of the town.

'Dead,' Varney replied without remorse. 'Of course, I don't mind. She left me three weeks before. Mrs. Varney said that I was too hard to live with. She went to live with her sister in Halifax.'

'I am sorry to hear that.'

'I know, Halifax is not a place I would like to live,' Varney joked, his sentence ending in a chuckle. It was the first time he had been remotely pleasant with D'Arc, if you could even call it that.

'How did she die?' D'Arc enquired, hoping it was the polite thing to do.

Varney ceased his movements. It was an uncomfortable conversation, made evident as Varney squirmed in his place slightly, squinting in his direction. A dark mood swept across his face as every sinew twitched.

'If I thought you really cared, I would answer you,' he whispered, almost nose-to-nose. 'You are so bloody hard to work out, I never know when you are taking the piss.'

Thankfully for D'Arc, a door opened at the end of the corridor. A police matron in a long, black skirt, with a silver chain to the waist, stepped through. Her face was lined and mantled by straw-like, grey hair that was pinned tightly to her head.

'This way,' her voice was curt as she directed Ruby Alder and a younger woman to follow.

'I asked them to bring you here straight away,' Ruby clarified to him as the girl at her side tried to smile. D'Arc could see that they had both been crying. The younger woman smoothed the long locks of brunette hair away from her wet face.

'They took me to Sloane Mansions,' he explained.

'Ruthie found them. They had been murdered,' Ruby trembled as she spoke, her hand gripping the one of the younger woman at her side by way of introduction.

'That's for us to decide,' Varney might as well have thrown his hand in Ruby's face, his tone and posture were that dismissive. 'From what evidence we have, it looks as though it was a murder-suicide. I don't think we'll be looking for anyone else.'

Ruby looked at D'Arc. He raised an eyebrow and slowly shook his head in disagreement.

'Do you need us for anything else?' he asked Varney.

'No, Mister D'Arc, your job is done. I will tell the Commissioner our findings and I am sure you will relay everything to Lady Gabrielle,' the man scoffed in response.

'It would be best if we left this place,' D'Arc advised Ruby and the other woman.

'I want statements from you all. You can call in at Chelsea Police Station at your leisure—well, at least by the end of the week.'

'What about Liza and Kitty?' the young woman asked softly, raising a finger to her lips.

'It's fine, Ruthie. I'll sort everything,' Ruby reassured as she wrapped her arm around her.

The woman sobbed again as if the comforting was too much. 'I can't get them out of my head,' she whispered as Ruby held her close.

'Sort of people you should have stayed away from. Totally unnatural what you all got up to,' Varney's cold tone was further poisoned by his traducing tongue as he stepped to one side. D'Arc stared, incredulous, at Varney as he spoke again. 'Don't go digging. The case is closed, D'Arc... the case is closed.'

The Chief Inspector followed them as they walked towards the doors of the building and stepped into the street. He stood on the steps as a dark red Ford, driven by a tall, black man, pulled up outside.

'Mondo,' Ruby sighed, speaking to the driver as if an old and trusted friend. 'We need to go home. Ruthie is coming with us.'

The man nodded and waited until both women had got in the back of the car.

'What about him?' Mondo questioned, his voice rich as he pointed to D'Arc.

'He's coming too,' she answered for him as Mondo slipped the car into gear.

On the steps of Scotland Yard, Varney stood, arms folded as he stared daggers at D'Arc. 'Remember what I said... murder-suicide...'

'I think you are wrong, Inspector. Whoever shot Liza was right-handed, but she used her left. The bullet was in her right temple. A left-handed person would not do that. It was murder, Inspector.'

'Is that deductive reasoning, D'Arc? Bollocks...' his answer was glib, as if him being wrong wasn't even a possibility.

'I will prove you wrong, Inspector...'

D'Arc stepped into the Ford and slammed the door shut. As the car drove away, he continued to pin his stare in Varney's direction.

'So, do you think it was a suicide?' Ruby pondered the thought as she aimed her question at D'Arc.

'That is what Varney would like you all to believe. I think they were murdered... and by the same person that killed Alicia.'

His words stopped whatever conversation may have taken place as the car drove along the side of the Thames. Turning past Battersea Bridge, they were soon outside a tall mansion block that fronted onto the park.

Mondo stopped the car and jumped out, opening the door for Ruby and helping her to the pavement. Ruthie sat in the back of the car, tears running down her face.

'Don't worry, Ruthie. I am sure things will be fine,' Mondo attempted to console the woman as he took her hand.

D'Arc followed them through the mahogany doors of the building and up a long flight of marble steps. Ruby opened the door of the apartment and trudged in. Pushing open two white, glossed double doors, she pointed to a long, cream sofa in front of the window. D'Arc sat and leant back against the cushions whilst Ruthie sat opposite, her hands clasped tightly and her face pensive and fraught.

'Did you have an affair with Kitty?' D'Arc questioned before Ruby could speak.

'Sometimes, Jack D'Arc,' she scoffed, frowning at his insensitivity.

'It's fine, Ruby,' the woman's voice was meek and almost sounded defeated. 'I don't mind. The thing is, Mister D'Arc, was that Kitty didn't love Liza. She wanted out, we were going to run away. Liza found us together and there was an argument. I hadn't been at the apartment for a week. I had been staying with friends.'

'And Alicia… Alice?' he asked.

'She told me I was stupid to get involved and that Liza was trouble. Liza may have been many things, but she wasn't a murderer,' Ruthie explained as she bit her lip. 'The night Alice was killed, Kitty and I were together. She came to see me in Hampstead. Kitty was trying to smooth things over until we could get away. We were going to leave next week.'

'And go where?' he asked abruptly.

'Brighton,' she stated, 'I have family there.'

'Did you know about this, Ruby?'

'Not until this morning. As long as the girls can do the crime, what they do in their life…' Ruby trailed off with a shrug of her shoulders as if she had seen it all before.

'And you found the bodies?'

'I opened the door and saw Liza in a pool of blood. She had the gun in her hand. I ran to the telephone and saw Kitty tied to the bed. She was staring at me.'

'Was the door locked?' D'Arc asked, the question quite unexpected.

Ruth turned to him and then to Ruby.

'It was open… I mean, it was unlocked,' she answered softly as if it were vital to be truthful.

'Did you go in the kitchen?'

'No, I telephoned the police and then Ruby. I stood in the parlour. I didn't dare move.'

Ruby retrieved the key that Kitty had given them from her pocket and showed it to Ruth.

'Have you ever seen this key before?'

'It belonged to Alice. It was in her bag. I saw it there. I was looking for some money. I needed to buy some cocaine.'

'Do you know where it came from?'

'She told me later, when she showed it to me. Alice said her man had given it to her for safekeeping and that the key would change their lives.'

'Did you ever meet the man?' he continued his questioning as he got up from the sofa and walked to the tall window that was draped in fine, silk curtains.

'I saw him once at the Manhattan.'

'The club on Greek Street?'

'That's the one,' Ruth nodded softly, hoping she could remember.

'What was the man like?'

'It was dark. I couldn't see him well. I need glasses but never wear them, and I was full of cocaine, I didn't care. Alice took him into a private room and bought me a drink. I woke up in a grubby hotel in Kilburn with a fat man who paid me thirty quid. Well, he gave me two quid and I nicked the rest when he was asleep. The man you want was tall… got dark hair, a thin face–looked like you.'

'And was that the only time you saw him?'

'It got serious. He stopped paying and they began dating. Alice wanted to marry him and he was getting a divorce. She took me to a séance after the show at the Vaudeville Theatre. *Madame Baphomet.* Alice said she wanted to know what was going to happen to her, it was something she really liked doing. Alice would say that she really believed that people who were dead could speak to you.'

'What happened at the séance?' Ruby asked before D'Arc could continue his onslaught of questions.

'We all sat round a table. Madame Baphomet closed her eyes and went into a trance. Then, she started to speak in a strange voice and tell people things. She said that I would find happiness in a place by the sea. I hadn't told anyone about Kitty then. No one knew, so she must have been telling the truth.'

'How many other people were there?' D'Arc pressed.

'About ten I think. It was candlelit and we all held hands. Alice knew the woman really well. When it was all over, she took her into a dressing room for instruction.'

'Instruction?'

'Alice was going to be a clairvoyant. Madame Baphomet was teaching her how to get in touch with those on the other side.'

'And you believed her?' D'Arc's voice was sceptical.

'A few days before she died, Alice said that she knew she was going to die. She said she had woken up in the night and seen her father standing at the end of her bed holding out his hand. She said he had come for her, to take her home.'

[17]
THE STRAND

The night had given way to heavy rain. Along the Strand, the gutters and spouts were overwhelmed. Water spilled from the high rooftops in torrents. The road outside the Vaudeville Theatre flooded to the rim of the pavement and the taxicabs were pushing through the water that ran along the street as if it were a small river searching for the Thames. D'Arc stood under the flashing canopy of the theatre, shaking the rain from his hat. Waiting in line, he studied the poster on the wall; it listed the acts that made up the cast of the review. Many were names he didn't know, and some were more famous–Gertrude Lawrence, Herbert Mundin. He searched the names until he found what he was looking for. Under the billing of a magician who used an automaton doll named Svengali to predict the future, was that of Madame Baphomet. She would close the first half with an extraordinary display of clairvoyance. Well, that is what the poster claimed.

D'Arc waited at the ticket office. The line grew longer behind him but still not in the numbers that he had expected.

'Circle... single ticket... back row?' he requested as he held out a five-pound note.

'Plenty of room, sit where you like. Not a popular revue... Betty Morris is singing at the Alhambra. We've lost a lot since they started with the wireless,' the chihuahua-like woman had answered as she gave him his change, touching his hand for an unusual length of time. 'I can bring you a drink during the interval if you want,' she attempted to flirt with a wry smile more suitable for a woman half her age.

D'Arc didn't answer. He could see that the woman had made a mental note of where he would be. Walking to the upper circle, he found a seat and settled down. It was not the one on his ticket but, like she said, the theatre was half empty. He wondered if the rain had kept the people away or if the woman was right and the wireless was to blame. Taking off his coat, he folded it neatly and laid it across the seat to his right. After placing his damp hat on top of the coat, he sat back uncomfortably and pulled his jacket collar higher. Far below, out of sight, the orchestra tuned slowly. There was the crass strumming of violins and sudden sharp notes from a trumpet and clarinet. All then fell silent as the sconces on the red, brocade walls faded. The curtain opened as limelight flooded the theatre. A troupe of performing dogs danced onto the stage accompanied by a marionette playing jazz music. The meagre crowd applauded miserably as if they had seen it all before and nothing would ever excite them again.

Jack D'Arc noticed someone slip in next to him in the darkness.

'I wasn't invited,' Ruby Alder's voice was sharp and ended on a slightly high note as if questioning why. The woman folded her arms and slumped in the seat, taking in her surroundings before paying attention to the show before her.

'I never thought to ask,' D'Arc didn't look away from the stage as he responded to Ruby.

'I was expecting a call.'

'Really? That is somewhat presumptuous,' the man sighed.

'You are a hard man to find,' she continued, paying attention to an athletic dog leaping through the air and turning somersaults.

'I didn't realise you would be looking for me.'

'Do we watch it all?' Ruby enquired expectantly.

'Everything.'

The lights flickered with the shadows of the performance. The warmth of the theatre wrapped itself around her. Ruby's gaze turned up at the high-vaulted ceiling stained with nicotine and covered in fat-faced cherubs. Slowly, she closed her eyes and savoured the night. She was soon asleep, her head resting on his shoulder and her arm draped lazily around his waist. Ruby snuggled close to D'Arc. She felt warm and safe and in her dreaming state, she didn't think of their closeness.

Uncomfortably, D'Arc watched as a thin, effete man in a frock coat took the stage. He told the future with an automaton doll, to the amazement of the crowd. By an act of Mesmer, the magician invited a man from the audience. Hypnotised, the subject of the performance had his hand pierced with a long needle and felt no pain. D'Arc was sure the man was not a stooge or conspirator. The magician seemed to be genuine as he beguiled the small crowd with acts of wonder.

Later, whilst he waited for the performance of Madame Baphomet, a goblin-like comedian in an oversized, satin waistcoat bustled onto the stage and bored D'Arc with his infantile jokes. The crowd seemed to be less than sympathetic. A man in a guinea box threw half a chicken, D'Arc's eyes darted to it as it slid across the stage, landing at the comedian's feet as a sign of discontent. The curtains closed expeditiously before the man began to sing. The compère took to the stage and the audience fell silent. In dark tones, he hushed the crowd even further. The lights dimmed and a violin began to play.

'Ladies and gentlemen,' the man spoke in utter seriousness. 'The Vaudeville Theatre brings you something not for the faint-hearted. This event will probe the depth of your soul and bring the dead back among us. Madame Baphomet, Seer and Clairvoyant.'

Ruby jerked awake from her sleep as he introduced the upcoming act. 'That's the name Alice spoke in her sleep. The woman that Ruth told us about,' she elbowed D'Arc softly.

'And why we are here,' D'Arc stated.

There was loud applause as a woman dressed as an Egyptian queen strutted slowly onto the stage. A smaller man followed her with a gold crown on his bald head. Madame Baphomet had a thin, muscular frame with a slender neck. The makeup on her face was daubed on the skin in swathes across her eyes. Thick, rouge patches highlighted each protruding cheekbone.

Madame Baphomet turned to the audience, her face expressionless as she seemed to stare into the crowd. Though her face was painted with profuse makeup, the cracks of the years could still be seen as if they were painted on the skin.

'There is a woman here with murder on her heart. I have someone calling to me from the other side. Their name is Freddy.' Her voice was cold, echoing out to the silent crowd. As the words were spoken, a woman gasped. Madame Baphomet's head darted straight in her direction. 'Does it mean something to you?'

There was a moment of silence before the voice answered.

'It was my father. He was killed… murdered in Essex last year. They never found the killer,' the woman announced from the front row of the stalls.

The assistant to Madame Baphomet applauded vehemently. The audience clapped politely in return. Madame Baphomet continued for the rest of the half hour. Ruby and Jack D'Arc watched intently as one by one the audience emptied from the theatre.

'Not what I would have turned up on a wet night for,' D'Arc commented as the final curtain fell. 'Not even Gertrude Lawrence could keep them in their seats.'

Ruby yawned more out of boredom than lack of sleep.

'I now know why I stopped going to see revues,' she pointed out blankly.

'So how do you spend your time when you are not robbing the rich?' his response came lightly with a hint of snarkiness and his gaze remained watching as the baroque lights flickered back to life.

An innocent chuckle escaped her lips in response.

'Magazines, music and the wireless,' Ruby listed, knowing it would come as a surprise to the man before her.

D'Arc raised a brow of approval.

'I would have thought it would have been the musical hall,' he answered sarcastically as he got to his feet.

'What a coincidence, I was just thinking the same about you.'

By the time they had descended down the stairs to the dressing room of Madame Baphomet, the line of people waiting to see her had stretched down the passageway. The plump man wearing the crown stood by the door. Folds of thick skin flustered under his ample chin. He eyed the crowd warily as if he looked for those who were rich and well-to-do. The man scanned each person with a beady glare. D'Arc could see that he was looking at their clothes, the make of their hats and quality of their gloves to see if any met his approval.

Ruby edged closer, pushing along the passageway to get to the door with one of her hands gripping D'Arc by the fingers. Finally, she stopped when she had jostled their way to the front of the queue. The crowned man took a look at them, again, as if he was analysing them.

'The séance is ten pounds for one seat and starts in five minutes,' he spoke with an effeminate squeak, playing with his tie.

D'Arc pushed four white five-pound notes across the shoulders of the people in front of the man.

'Two seats close to Madame Baphomet,' D'Arc requested as the man looked at him warily, as if there was something about him he didn't like.

'Sold out... sorry,' the man's answer was brisk.

It was then that the man gasped inexplicably, his face contorting as he held his breath. Ruby moved closer and closer until her face was next to his.

'What's your name?' she asked softly.

'Crowley,' the man answered in a half-groan.

'Well, Mister Crowley,' Ruby whispered, 'I will let go of your very small but perfectly formed packet when you give my friend the tickets for the séance. If not, I will grip them tighter and tighter until they fall off.'

'The séance is full,' he bleated like a stuck pig, as her grip slowly got tighter. 'Are you sure you don't have a seat for me and my friend?' Ruby asked purposefully, her voice threatening but sickly sweet as she twisted her hand.

He thought for a moment as beads of sweat trickled across his forehead.

'Sorry. I made a mistake. You have the last two seats at the table. Madame Baphomet will be speaking to the departed very soon,' Crowley's body juddered with his words.

[18]
THE VAUDEVILLE

Ruby sat on the bow-backed seat next to D'Arc. The dressing room was big enough for a table and thirteen chairs. The white-painted walls were covered in dresses and costumes hanging from a high rail and across from Ruby was a long, wooden mirror. It covered most of the wall and was edged with small, brass candleholders. Each one had a light within that shone dimly through the meshed cover. The long table was in the centre of the dressing room. It was covered in a crisp, white cloth that had been freshly starched. Around it, the mahogany chairs were pushed awkwardly together. In the centre of the table was a silver candelabrum that hung with faux crystals. Crowley remained by the door, arms folded and a permanent scowl on his face. Ruby caught his glance and he forced a smile. A woman came through the door and Crowley helped her to the last empty chair. She nodded to the thirteen people around the table. A young woman, who was obviously the partner of the older man at her side, applauded politely.

Madame Baphomet looked at each face and smiled. It was as if she searched for clues from their shadowed glares as to who each one was. D'Arc followed her glances.

'I think it would be best if we introduce ourselves to the spirits gathered around us,' Madame Baphomet placed her hands on the white cloth and spread out her fingers that resembled a wrinkly-skinned spider.

The man next to her coughed, his body language nervous.

'I am Lord Tobias Hanthorn,' he introduced as he turned to the woman next to him.

'For what it is worth, dear spirits, I am Cecilia De Vere,' the woman in the black fur coat and tight hat said, half-laughing.

'It is important, very important, that we address the spirits,' Crowley reiterated as he hovered by the door.

'Janine Goldman,' said the tousled-haired flapper in front of Crowley. 'George Huxley.'

'Sara Priestman,' answered a girl in a flapper dress as all eyes turned to her.

The man beside her halted. D'Arc smiled, knowing he was trying to hurriedly think of a name to hide his indiscretion.

'Doctor Charles Morton,' he finally drawled.

The introductions went around the table until it was left to Jack D'Arc to introduce himself.

'I am Jack D'Arc,' his voice was barely a whisper, 'and I bid the spirits welcome.'

Madame Baphomet shot him a suspicious glare as she raised a wrinkled brow that creased the thick, pasted on makeup.

'You do not believe and yet you have been close to death many times. I see war and fighting,' the woman stared at him from under dark, heavy eyelids. 'A bullet wound in the leg and a man hanging from a rope. It is your father. He has killed himself in despair and you blame yourself. Does that answer your scepticism?'

'I come here with an open mind, Madame. If there are spirits then I am eager to hear what they have to say.'

'Very well,' she uttered. 'I will speak and see what message they have for you.'

'Each of you can ask one question,' Crowley chirped as the candles flickered. 'Madame Baphomet will soon be in spirit and then we begin.'

Ruby shivered as she looked at Baphomet, whose head was slumped towards the table. The woman groaned, breathing in deeply as a shudder took over her body. One by one, the candles died in the cuplike holders. The room grew darker until only the dim flames of the candelabrum lighted it. D'Arc smiled to himself at the preciseness of the timing. He thought it was not by coincidence. Miss Goldman gasped and threw back the ringlets of her hair so they fell back over her shoulder. In the shadows, D'Arc could just make out the trace of a tattoo on the nape of her neck.

'Are they here?' she breathed, her body and posture remaining still.

Baphomet groaned as she breathed, as if she was taking in the spirits around her. It was then that she lifted her head back and, with a long finger, pointed at the young woman to her right.

'When will I be married?' the slight woman urged as she squeezed the hand of the older man with her.

The man shuffled uncomfortably, his mouth twitching benignly.

'I see a church and roses. It is a day in summer. You stand on the porch, radiant and beautiful. A tear is in your eye. But it is a funeral and not a wedding,' Madame Baphomet grinned innately. 'There is a woman here called Dolly. She says she was your nanny. Is that true?'

'Yes,' nodded the youthful woman, 'but I didn't know she was dead.'

'She wishes you well and wants to speak with you privately.'

'It shall be arranged,' Crowley butted in as if the remarks were duly noted.

'Is Dolly safe?' she proceeded to ask, her voice gentle and innocent.

'She is on a swing at the bottom of a garden. It is on an apple tree. She is holding a rag doll.'

'That's my swing... my doll,' the woman's voice was as small as she was and tearful, as if she had been taken back to a place in childhood.

The man with her took hold of her hand tightly.

'And what else?' he pressed further.

Madame Baphomet moved on. She raised her hand and pointed to Ruby.

'You, why are you here?' her voice darkened, her face contorting whilst her eyes remained on Alice.

'I want to speak to Alice.'

'There is no spirit here of that name.'

'Princess Alicia Gabrielle,' D'Arc answered for her.

He saw Baphomet shudder at the same time that Crowley stepped towards the table, but no one noticed.

'Madame Baphomet does not know anyone by that name,' Crowley insisted. 'If we can kindly go on, lots of people have questions.'

At the end of the table, Madame Baphomet gripped the starched, white cloth in her ever-tightening fingers. Her body convulsed as if shot through with electricity. She opened her eyes for a moment and moaned. Then she spoke.

'Ruby... Ruby, is that you?' said the voice of another woman from the mouth of Madame Baphomet.

Ruby immediately got to her feet and looked about the room, her stare urgent as if trying to decipher what was happening.

'Where are you, Alice?'

'I'm cold... waiting to go over,' the voice said again, Baphomet's head rolling back as she spoke. 'It's dark, Ruby, so very dark.'

'I can't see you, where are you?' Ruby begged as the others around the table sat back and stared at the changing face of Madame Baphomet.

It was as if the years fell from her face–her skin smoothed, the eyes mellowed. What had once been wrinkled skin was taut and firm. In the half-light of the room, it looked as though she was another woman.

'You have to be careful, Ruby. He's not to be trusted,' the voice of Alicia Gabrielle echoed in the room.

'Who murdered you?' D'Arc implored.

'It was dark. You were in the alley. You were in the alley,' Baphomet repeated as her body shook.

'What can I do?' Ruby asked, certain that her friend was in the room.

'I'm not alone. I can hear Kitty and Liza. They are calling for you. We'll all be together.' The voice turned silent. Madame Baphomet sat straight and looked down the table at Jack D'Arc. Her eyes were night-black and stared at him as she spoke. 'Look after Ruby. He's coming for you, Ruby... coming for you...'

'Gerard Montague?' D'Arc demanded, hoping for more as Baphomet suddenly slumped forward and sprawled across the table. The woman groaned, trying to lift her head.

'Alistair... Alistair...' she whispered.

'It is *finished*!' Crowley shouted, his voice on edge as if he had never seen anything like this before. 'Madame Baphomet is tired. It has all been too much.'

'But I haven't asked a question,' the old man tried to argue as he held the girl next to him.

'She will speak no more. It was too much for her,' his answer was sharp, daring the man to further argue. 'You must all leave.'

Jack D'Arc waited with Ruby until the dressing room had emptied. Madame Baphomet lay against the table and did not move. She grumbled to herself, as if to exorcise whatever spirits still clung to her flesh. Crowley attempted to placate those who felt cheated out of their money; he offered free seats for a matinee séance. The young woman who had spoken first clung to his hand, begging to be seen that night.

D'Arc lingered behind Ruby as they climbed the steps to the back door of the theatre and stepped onto the street.

'Interesting,' D'Arc mumbled as he looked at his reflection in an office window.

'It was her... Alice... I am sure of it,' Ruby's voice was matter-of-fact and blunt as she watched him adjust his shirt tie.

There was a voice behind them.

'I need to speak to you,' Crowley asserted as he stood in the shadow of the stage door. 'There is something you should know. Madame Baphomet would like to see you privately. Here is my card.' The man handed D'Arc a small calling card.

'Tomorrow at ten in the morning?' D'Arc suggested, reading the Hampstead address and realising that he knew the house.

Crowley nodded in agreement, slipping back into the shadows before either of them could think twice.

'She has asked to see you?' Ruby wanted to clarify as they walked down the street towards the Strand.

'It is an interesting coincidence. I am still trying to work out how she did the voice.'

'Don't you think it was Alice?' Ruby asked, convinced that Madame Baphomet had channelled the spirit.

'I fear that it was a warning to us both.'

'Am I next?' Ruby's voice was desperate, her fears eating at her. 'Is the killer coming for me?'

'According to Varney and the Commissioner of Police, the case is solved. Madame Baphomet was a very convincing act, but I would not believe all she said. I often find with mystics that they are keen observers of people rather than listeners to the dead. They are adept at the skill of cold reading, telling people what they want to know by evaluating them beforehand.'

'But the voice, it was Alice,' she insisted.

'So it seemed. It sounded to you like it was her, but we all hear things so differently.'

'She knew things about you, Alice and Kitty,' Ruby vocalised her belief of what had happened with Baphomet, as if this opened a door to a realm of possibilities within the case.

'Madame Baphomet is well informed–but not by spirits.'

'How did she know?'

'That we will wait to find out.'

'Then I'll see you tomorrow?' Ruby and D'Arc stood on the corner and watched the crowds walk along the pavement.

'Don't you have a crime to attend to?' he joked.

Ruby took a deep breath.

'Ruth is safe with Mondo. I want to find the killer. I know it wasn't Liza, I have to know who killed them.'

'Then read the papers in two days' time and all shall be revealed,' D'Arc stated without looking at Ruby.

'I want to help you find the killer,' Ruby insisted, pulling the sleeve of his coat to halt his movements.

D'Arc turned from his distraction and looked at her. Raindrops dropped from the brim of her hat and onto her shoulders. Her lips were turned up at each side in a melancholy smile. Her overall look was not unlike that of a small, abandoned child.

'Perhaps it would be best if you stayed with me at Chalcot Crescent,' D'Arc said purposefully.

'Perhaps,' Ruby agreed.

[19]
WHITECHAPEL

The rain had stopped and the fog of Whitechapel had again filled the streets. On the corner of Durward Street, Crowley stood holding a newspaper in his hand, his foot tapping incessantly against the pavement. Fuelled by his anxiety, he found himself looking up and down the dark road as he wondered what was in the mist beyond. Leaning against the sullied, red brick wall of the board school, he waited. In the distance, he could hear the humdrum sounds of midnight and the drunks in Mile End. Here was the clatter of the market stalls being made ready and yet, there in the street, the sounds hung eerily in the air. He was not a man who was frightened of the dark. Though only average in height and more rotund than he would care to be, he was still spritely. That had come about from years of dancing as a child. His mother had wanted him to become a ballet dancer, but his plumper frame had dictated a different career.

Crowley had always had a fascination for the occult; it had started out as a childhood hobby and then, as the years progressed, he had met Madame Baphomet. She had inspired him to search further and had taken him to Egypt with her.

Now, he stood on the corner of the street and remained in the darkness. It was then, in the shadow of the fading streetlight, that he heard the voice.

'You're late,' the voice said impatiently. 'I have been here for the last hour.'

'There has been a complication,' Crowley's response came out as a murmur, his teeth chattering with the cold.

'You promised me that it would all be over. What have you found out?'

'A detective called Jack D'Arc has been asking questions,' Crowley started, talking into the darkness and not turning to where the voice came from. 'Lady Gabrielle has commissioned him. He knows about the murder of Alice Pringle.'

'How did you find this?'

'He came to the séance. One of my informants in the police told me all about him. They expect to be paid,' Crowley answered with a shiver. 'I was hoping you had money for me.'

'He is an inconvenience,' whispered the voice, 'an inconvenience that has to be stopped.'

'Madame Baphomet has asked to see him privately. She believes that Alice has been speaking to her,' Crowley continued.

'What harm can she do?'

'She knows who you are. Alice came to her often. The girl was a seer, and had her own spirit guide who could see all of our hearts.'

'Then Baphomet is a problem to us both. What can you do?'

'I have ways of keeping her quiet,' Crowley explained. 'What about the police?'

'They are in my pocket and will not cause us any harm. It is in the best interest of the police that our secret is kept safe.'

'Madame Baphomet is suspicious of me. She thinks I take too many notes of what her clients say.'

'That is why you are with her. We need to know what is said in private. Her clients are of great interest to me.'

'You promised I didn't have to do it for long. It's been nearly a year,' his protest came out suddenly, almost sounding petulant.

'You are a victim of your own success. The information you have given us is most useful. If Baphomet is a problem, then she will have to be done away with,' the voice drawled as a thick envelope was stuffed into Crowley's pocket. 'Take this as a down payment.'

'I cannot harm her. I will stop her talking–warn her of what may happen.'

'Actions have consequences, Mister Crowley... consequences.'

'I do not need to be reminded of that.'

[20]
PRIMROSE HILL

Three miles from Durward Street, along the City Road and Albany Street, Jack D'Arc sat in the upstairs parlour of the white-painted terraced house and poured Ruby Alder another deep glass of claret. She held it between her finger and thumb and kept her gaze locked on him as he stood by the coal fire and sipped his drink. It was her third glass. Already, the warmth of the coals had reddened her cheeks. Ruby had slipped her shoes from her feet and wondered what would happen in the night. As they had walked back from the theatre, she had told herself that it was only fascination and purely convenience purposes that she was accompanying him back to his house. It would be easier for her to stay there and then go to Hampstead the next day, rather than travel to Battersea and then come back over the river.

Ruby knew she didn't need convincing; Jack D'Arc had something about him that was fatally attractive to her. He was the first man in a long time who had not tried to expose himself, kiss or grope her at the first instance, as often happened when she drank in the Elephant and Castle. In fact, he had remained distant even during those times when he could have easily taken advantage.

The only things she had found out about him were the snippets that had fallen in her lap by accident. Even when he spoke of himself, it was often devoid of true facts. In return, she felt as though he knew her well, not that she minded. D'Arc was gauche in his words; he was blunt to the extreme and was severely lacking in social graces. He seemed uncomfortable in her company at times, but she wanted to know him more. She mused the possibility that he did not find her or any other woman attractive. He had the slight look of a lover of Greek and a purveyor of the Turkish Baths.

When Ruby first saw him on Oxford Street, she could see that he was precise in his dress, everything about him was neat and dapper. From the carefully knotted, silk tie to the crisp turn-up of his Oxford trousers, D'Arc was incredibly immaculate; his hands were freshly manicured and shirt cuffs starched. He obviously spent more time in front of a looking glass than she ever would. It was, however, the sadness in his eyes that she found most beguiling. To her, Jack D'Arc looked like a lost dog in need of a home. They were deep and dark, set in a mantle of a man that was flawless.

Ruby looked around the meticulous apartment. 'Fine place for a detective,' she commented as she sipped the wine, placing the glass on the table.

'Pays better than crime,' he jested, his gaze lingering on hers for longer than what would be deemed typically appropriate.

'Is crime something you ever considered?' she asked in the heat of the moment.

'Knowing the inside of the criminal mind would make doing the deed very easy. Yet, it would be a step that I could never take. I often think that it is an easy option to relieve someone of their worldly goods.'

'You break the rules all the time,' she raised a curious brow in response.

'That is different, sometimes it is what has to be done. Rules are meant to be bent and twisted to one's needs.' D'Arc let out a gruff laugh as he opened another bottle of claret and topped up her glass yet again.

Ruby unbuttoned her jacket and allowed it to fall open, noticing as D'Arc promptly darted his eyes away.

'Is this what you do to everyone you meet? Get them drunk and then ask them your questions and read their inner secrets?' she teased.

'And are you sufficiently drunk to answer truthfully?' D'Arc enquired as he took a discreet glance at her petite figure.

'I will tell you nothing. I have seen the way you look at me. You try to peer inside the mind. You're like that magician with his Svengali doll.'

'So you were awake? You are so easy to read that you need not say a word, and I do not need an automaton.' The corner of D'Arc's lips turned up in a slight smirk as the words left him but he held it back, knowing this was the start of a pursuit.

'Then tell me all that you have deduced,' Ruby's response was quick, as if she hardly needed to think of what she would say. 'Read away, Mister Sleuth.'

D'Arc took a moment to admire her as if she were a painting. He sipped a mouthful of wine from the glass before placing it carefully on the mantelpiece.

'Your real name is not Ruby... it is Irene. Even though you have money now, you can remember the days when you were poor. Therefore, you buy clothes that are more quality than fashion. You are older than your years, for the burden of your life started sooner than it should. Your father abandoned your mother and you distrust men. Those large, green eyes have seen hardship and pain that you hope you have left behind. There was a man in your life called Haslem, who hurt you badly. He betrayed you; you still fear him. Haslem was the man who stole your heart–in him you saw everything you desired and all along he was using you. Your shoes are regularly repaired and you want to give up the Forty Elephants, yet you fear what may lie ahead because they are not just a den of thieves, but the only family you have... and you carry a small Derringer pistol. It was probably stolen from an American visitor.'

When he finished speaking, he took a breath and shot Alder a satisfied smile, knowing everything he said to be true.

'How did you know? Who told you? You can't just have read that from looking at me with one brow higher than the other like a drunk spaniel,' Ruby pointed out.

'It is quite simple and, as you say, a matter of deductive reasoning. You wear a locket around your neck. It is from your mother–a traditional thing for those given over to the poor house. It has your name inscribed upon it and a photograph of her within the charm. I saw it the other night when I helped you to bed. I know of Haslem from the letter in the pocket of your jacket that was sent to the laundry. I took the liberty to read it... a force of habit. In your pocket were also three repair bills from Taylor and Taylor, menders of bad soles. There was also a manifest of a small café for sale in Pimlico. The pistol was in your coat pocket. Therefore all those things were easy to deduce.' His voice was unapologetic and frank as he gave his reasoning behind his words. The woman applauded, picking up her wine glass and taking a drink.

117

'And what of you, Mister D'Arc, what secrets can be found by just looking at you?'

'I have no secrets,' his voice came as a whisper as he sat on the couch opposite her.

'Do you have any friends, Mister D'Arc? A lover, perhaps?'

Ruby noticed him visibly wince and then quickly regain his composure.

'If you would like to give up the Forty Elephants, then I would be willing to give you employment as a detective,' D'Arc expressed honestly. 'I have been wanting to take on an assistant.'

'Assistant? Me?' she responded as a gentle smile of disbelief graced her lips, the warmth of the room making her eyes heavy as she placed the glass back on the small table.

Before he spoke again, D'Arc got up from the sofa and checked the curtains. He casted a glance up and down the street as if he expected to see someone outside.

'It would be something you would be good at. A poacher turned gamekeeper. You are skilled at burglary. The salary would not match the amount you steal, but there would be very little chance of you going to prison. Hours are to suit and...'

D'Arc turned back to Ruby. She sat in the wingback chair by the fire and slept deeply. Her hands were clasped together as if praying, her mouth slightly open.

It was six in the morning when Ruby heard the chiming of the church clock somewhere in Primrose Hill. She could feel the soft pillow beneath her head and the warm breath blowing softly against her neck. She pulled the thick blankets close to her face and hoped for more sleep. As she drifted back into a long dream, she felt the tongue on her face.

'Jack D'Arc, what are you doing?' she mumbled in her sleepy daze, feeling the lips against hers. 'What have you been eating?'

A voice came from the doorway. D'Arc stepped into the bedroom carrying a tray of food. 'Eggs and toast with coffee?' he answered as he looked over at the bed.

Ruby opened her eyes. Staring at her, face to face, was a large bull terrier. 'Edgar?' Ruby's voice came out as a question even though she knew it couldn't be anyone else.

'He seems enthralled.' It was then that Ruby realised she was again naked under the bed sheets. She looked at D'Arc. There was no need to say what she thought. 'You were asleep,' he shrugged.

'*You* were awake.'

An hour later they were walking along Primrose Hill. The morning was fresh and there was the first trace of sunlight in many days. The smog had lifted, blown towards Dungeness by a fair wind. Edgar ran ahead of them, chasing whatever he could. Ruby stood with D'Arc and looked out over the city. It was as if her life was sprawled before her as she stared at the spires, knowing what streets were beneath.

'Were you serious about the job?' she asked, not wanting to be disappointed.

'I thought you were asleep,' D'Arc answered. 'You were snoring when I spoke to you.'

'I was, but I still heard you.'

'Are you serious about taking it?'

'There would be things I would have to do first. The Forty Elephants have to have a leader. It has to carry on. There are rules, I can't just leave.'

'The detective and the thief? I suppose this is the age of universal suffrage.' D'Arc wondered if it would be possible.

'Do you think you could do it?'

'What?'

'Turn me from a thief into a detective?' Ruby continued, her voice breaking as if the wind had stolen it from her.

'Ruby Alder, I will turn you into the greatest detective London has ever seen.'

[21]
HAMPSTEAD HEATH

In the large iron conservatory of Rosslyn Villa, overgrown with jungle plants, Crowley sat and sipped the steam from the cup of green tea. He was wrapped in a blue, silk gown with turned-back cuffs. On his head was an oversized fez adorned with hieroglyphs. He made no sound as he watched the small, ornamental birds fly from branch to branch. They danced on the floor before him, picking the crumbs from his discarded biscuit off the ornate tiles with their red beaks. Putting down the cup, his body stiffened as if hesitating to move from the chair. It was as if he had some inkling of what was to come. He listened intently, his jowly face aged by lack of sleep.

There was the sudden and jarring ring of the doorbell far away. It echoed coldly through the empty hallways and rooms of the vast, old house. Crowley slipped uncomfortably from his chair and treaded barefoot through the chain of rooms. In ten paces the bell rang again and in twenty, a third time.

Slipping the brass bolts from the door, he then turned the lock. The door opened, light from the morning flooding in.

'You did say nine, I am sure of it. Positive it was nine,' D'Arc proclaimed as he tried to loom over Crowley and push by him. 'I would hate to be late. You remember Ruby, she is my assistant.'

Ruby bit back a smile, noticing that the silk gown wrapped around Crowley was now open at the front. It hung across his stomach like a surgical gown on a man waiting to be cut open.

'You said ten, an hour early. Madame Baphomet is not ready,' Crowley protested as both Ruby and D'Arc helped themselves inside.

'Would you like us to go and come back? We could take tea while we wait,' D'Arc raised an eyebrow in question as he looked around the hallway decorated with the dead heads of exotic animals that were nailed to the wall.

'I suppose you could wait,' he gave in, closing the large oak door behind them and sliding the bolts back into place. 'Nice to have such a pretty visitor,' he ogled Ruby as he spoke.

'So kind of you to compliment. I try to take care of my appearance,' D'Arc's sarcastic quip filled the room before Ruby could respond herself.

Crowley shrugged his shoulders, doing nothing to close his gown and allowing what was left of his shrivelled manhood to stare at Ruby like the wizened skin of a dead snake. She tried to take no notice, but its strange appearance held a certain fascination for her. He saw her looking and smiled even more, clearly getting the wrong idea.

'We had a meeting last night. A small group of practitioners who have a liberal view on life. Perhaps Miss Ruby would like to come along?' Crowley suggested as he led the way through the house.

Ruby muttered something about being busy. She could see that D'Arc was smiling wickedly at her, making her worry where this was going.

'I think that Miss Ruby would love such an invite. Perhaps if you call me, I can make sure she attends,' D'Arc tried to bite back a smirk as he spoke.

'D'Arc,' Ruby growled, her gaze trailing as she noticed that in the room they walked through was a group of naked bodies sleeping close together. Some lay sprawled on the sofa open-legged. A girl slept on the rug by the fireside, her mouth covered in blood.

'A strange name, Baphomet... is it the name of a God, possibly a Devil?' D'Arc queried as he stepped over the girl by the fireside and followed Crowley through a small doorway.

'We follow the path of Isis and Osiris, Mister D'Arc. We are magicians, servants of the Lord of Silence,' he answered.

'Do you retrieve a rabbit from a hat?' Ruby asked innocently.

Crowley stopped and let his touch linger softly on her arm.

'No rabbits, pigeons or anything else. It is not that kind of magic. We seek to influence the path of human nature by ancient ritual,' he flashed the pair a broken toothed smile, just like the man behind the counter of Battersea Post Office. 'We are a temple of believers who have found the ultimate way of using the energy of the body at the point of climax to ensnare the human will.'

'Witches?' she asked.

'It is not that simple. Magic is a science of the mind with a power over the universe. Madame Baphomet is a channel for Isis.'

'Interesting,' Ruby trailed off, remembering how D'Arc would use the word like a full stop to end a conversation.

'Interesting indeed,' Crowley stroked her arm, the feel of it causing Ruby to hold back a shiver of agitation. 'You look like someone who has a fascination in what we do.'

'I was just thinking that as we came here in the taxicab,' D'Arc answered.

Crowley could see the look on the face of the detective. He pushed open the double iron-framed doors and stepped into the conservatory.

'This is our temple. It is vital that we perform our rituals naked under the stars. We are in a perfect alignment with Uranus and Mars,' Crowley smirked, gazing deep into Ruby's eyes as if D'Arc was not in the room.

At the far end of the conservatory was an altar table dwarfed by the size of the room in which it stood. Circling around it, inlaid in the floor was an intricate mosaic. Ruby thought that it looked like the star-shaped outline of the head of a goat. On the altar were two wax-covered candlesticks and a long knife. Next to the knife was a small silk square, stained with blood, on which were etched words and signs in charcoal.

'And what kind of rituals do you perform, Mister Crowley?' D'Arc proceeded to question.

'We seek to do the will of those within the group,' he answered plainly as if it would be enough to placate the questioner.

'Do you cast your circle for good or evil intent; widdershins or the way of the sun?' D'Arc stepped towards the altar and peered at the blade of the knife. 'I see that there is blood on the blade–chicken, perhaps?'

'Sacrifice of life brings the ultimate in power,' Crowley stared at Ruby as the words left his lips, his eyes burning holes into the woman. 'It is intoxicating, some would even say sexual.'

'But for that power something has to die,' D'Arc followed with.

'That has always been the case,' the voice of a woman came from the midst of the parlour. 'Violence, sex, fear, joy; they are just fleeting emotions that have an element of power.'

Ruby was the first to turn. There, slumped in a chair with a long cigarette in her hand was Madame Baphomet. She looked younger than the night before, Her face was painted in rouge and eyeshadow. Without the ornamental wig, her hair was short and combed back around the ears.

'Madame Baphomet,' Crowley bowed politely. 'I thought you were asleep.'

'Come here, sit down, let me see who it is before me,' she ignored his comment with a wave of her long, thin fingers as she pointed towards the velvet sofa in the alcove. 'Have I seen you before? The girl looks familiar.'

'They were at the séance last night. You asked to see the detective.'

'Séance? Was there a séance?' she asked as she sucked on the tip of the cigarette and breathed out the remnants of the black, noxious smoke.

'At the theatre, remember? You asked to see him.'

'The girl... Alicia... I remember, and the detective,' Madame Baphomet said as she pointed to Jack D'Arc. 'You are the detective. You are Jack D'Arc. Blood will be on your hands. The spirit of Alicia told me in a dream. I hear her all the time. They all talk of her. Troublesome... troublesome...'

'Blood? When was your dream?' D'Arc tilted his head in curiosity as a small finch-like bird landed on her shoulder, plucked a strand of hair and then flew away.

'For the last three nights I have thought of no one else but Alicia. At the séance she came through louder than any of the other spirits. She wants to talk to you.'

'Where do you get your information from, Madame Baphomet?' D'Arc took a seat on the sofa with Ruby at his side.

'There speaks a cynic, a doubter, and a misanthropist,' she answered briskly, her eyes sparkling as the opium took hold.

'I am a seeker of the truth,' he urged. 'That is all I need to know.'

'Truth? What is truth?' she asked him, holding out her hand as if it were to be taken by an unseen guest that stood close to her.

Ruby saw Madame Baphomet look up from her chair as if she stared into the face of someone close by that only she could see. The woman smiled.

'She is here now. Alicia wants to take you to the one who killed her and cut out her heart. You won't listen to her because you do not believe. All is not as it seems.'

'Heart? What do you mean?' D'Arc pried further.

'The murderer is not a man, but a monster. I saw him last night. He prowled in the darkness with a legion of demons at his heels.'

Crowley stepped forward as if to stop her from speaking.

'I think you should rest. You have a performance tonight,' he turned to D'Arc and Ruby. 'Madame Baphomet is like a wireless to the other world. Sometimes the tuning goes a little awry.'

'Idiot!' she screamed as she sucked harder on the reefer that hung from her lips. 'They shout in my ear so I cannot sleep, I need the opium just to rest. The killer is looking for two more girls. She is one of them,' she pointed a sharp finger at Ruby. 'Alicia is convinced of it.'

'How can you be sure? Does she know the name of the killer?' D'Arc insisted as he got to his feet and pushed Crowley away from the woman.

'If you could see inside my head then you would not ask such a question. You think this is all an act, don't you, Detective?'

'I believe in what I can see with my own eyes.'

'Then you look through frosted spectacles. In five days, it will all be over. Blood will be on your hands, Mister D'Arc. Her blood.'

Ruby shuddered at her words.

'Who has told you the details of the case?' D'Arc asked fervently. 'There was no mention of the murder in the newspapers.'

'I hear and see things that do not belong to this world. Each murder has been for a purpose. Find that and you will find the killer.'

'Is Alicia safe?' Ruby asked out of place, as the bird came again and snatched more hair.

'At last there is someone with faith,' Madame Baphomet let out a deep sigh. 'Don't worry about Alicia. She cannot be harmed. Look out for yourself. There is a shadow surrounding your aura and the darkness around you grows blacker by the minute.'

'Alicia, can you hear me?' Ruby's voice came out soft yet desperate, yearning for more.

Before Madame Baphomet could answer, the dagger on the altar slipped to the floor. It spun for a moment and then stopped, the tip of the blade pointed towards Ruby.

'She warns you, Ruby Alder. I can hear her calling your name over and over.'

Madame Baphomet sat back in the wicker chair and smoked on the joint until only the roach end hung from her lips. She sighed, as if her heart was exhausted and she could not move. The woman reached to her lips, took the butt and dropped it on the floor. She coughed, her eyes slamming shut as she muttered to herself.

'She will speak no more,' Crowley warned as he ushered them from the conservatory. 'Alicia was a strange girl.'

'When did you first meet her?'

'Just a few months ago. She was a gifted seer, a woman in touch with the other world. Perhaps that was her downfall, she knew too much...'

'And you had never met her before then?' D'Arc queried.

'No. Many people come here to be taught by Madame Baphomet. They all want to know how to influence their lives. Clairvoyance is a dying art, Mister D'Arc. Alicia was different, she had a true gift that was hampered by guilt.'

'Guilt?' Ruby piped up in question.

'She had been brought up as a devout Catholic. I heard her telling Madame Baphomet that she would come here and learn the magical arts and then go and confess her sins to the priest. He would tell her she was damned.' Crowley's answer was dramatic, as if his presence graced the stage of a theatre once again, his eyes inflamed.

'A battle for the soul?' D'Arc asked him as they got to the door of the house.

'He even came here and threw holy water on the steps of the house to get rid of the Devil. The priest had walked all the way from Saint Magnus by the river, in his cassock and frills. He claimed that we were evil and should be destroyed. Madame Baphomet said that he needed to empty his loins and offered him one of the neophytes. It enraged him more.' Crowley let out a gruff laugh, as if looking back on a fond memory.

'Saint Magnus? Are you sure?' he asked as they stepped outside.

'The priest said we had been held in the balance and found wanting. Mad... quite mad...'

'Does Madame Baphomet know who killed Alicia?' Ruby urged, looking into Crowley's bright, shining eyes that were tinged with madness.

'The spirits do not like to speak of such things. I will ask Madame Baphomet when she awakens.'

They stood on the steps of the house, the breeze blowing in from the heath.

'Who else comes to see Madame Baphomet?' D'Arc was inquisitive, and curious to dig further.

The answer came slowly like a reluctant river as Crowley finally pulled the robe tightly across his body and tied the belt.

'The Madame is the clairvoyant to royalty,' Crowley announced as if he had to be covered before being able to say the words. 'We live in strange times... everyone wants to know the future or speak to someone who has died. Since the war, talking with the dead has become a popular pastime. She sees many people, from the high to the very low, as long as they can afford to pay. Perhaps I could arrange a reading for you?'

'I leave the dead to the solitude of the dead. There is nothing after this life,' D'Arc's voice was dull, as if he believed there was no hope. 'When I was young I asked for someone to come back from the grave and speak to me, but there was only silence.'

The door to the house closed behind them as they walked down the path to Pilgrim Lane. 'Did you believe him?' Ruby wondered as they opened the gate and stepped out onto the street.

'Alicia's mother told me that they had taken her to see a Mister Crowley, when they suspected her of having an invisible friend,' D'Arc mentioned as he turned up the collar of his coat and snapped his fingers. 'She said Crowley was an expert in the paranormal, it has to be the same man. Crowley insisted he had only just met Alicia. I am intrigued as to why he should hide such a thing.'

'So we see the priest and ask what she said to him?'

'Just one day as my assistant and already you are on the case. Doubtless he will plead the secrecy of the seal of confession.'

'And Gerard Montague?'

'There is no such man and no such address. I worked in Belgravia for a year. The house does not exist. Yet, I have the key for the front door. First, we find the owner of the button and then we talk to the priest. Like every good Anglo Papalist, he hears confessions every day at four o'clock. Your first task is to find out what Alice said to him.'

[22]
DOWNING STREET

The office in Scotland Yard was filled with smoke. Varney slouched in a leather-backed chair and stared at the man opposite, both of them silent. Varney rolled another cigarette, reached forward and handed it to the man.

'It doesn't mean that he is that much of a problem, Commissioner,' Varney claimed as he sat back. 'D'Arc will run around and we will be there before him.'

The Commissioner lit the cigarette and blew out the smoke, then, lifting the glass, he took a slug of whisky from the white teacup that acted as a paperweight on his small pile of papers.

'So you have the murders detected?' the man asked.

'We can tell the newspapers that the woman did it; she fell out with her lover and killed Princess Alicia as well. Then, wracked with guilt, she shot herself,' Varney answered as he mirrored the Commissioner and took a swig from the cup nestled in his hand.

'Lady Gabrielle has been in touch with the King. He has written to me personally,' he flicked the ash into the saucer and eyed Varney suspiciously. 'Do you know something, Varney? When I left the army I was promised this job and a knighthood. Sir John Mccabe sounded like a great title. I never thought it would come to this.'

'How come she is a princess when her mother is just Lady Gabrielle?' Varney queried aloud as Mccabe gulped down more of the whisky.

'Her mother is more than a lady, she was once a Russian princess. That is why she has the King's favour. That is why we must have no more problems.'

'There won't be a problem. The murderer is dead.'

'The King is insisting that we give every help to Jack D'Arc. Only when D'Arc gives his conclusion will he be satisfied. You have to make sure that D'Arc speaks for us and that nothing is jeopardised.'

'D'Arc is a fool, just like his father,' Varney spat, reaching for the bottle of scotch and pouring another shot. 'He caused us a lot of trouble and there was only one possible outcome.'

'Thankfully, all that was before my time. It was a bad business, I read the file,' the Commissioner responded coolly as he smoked the cigarette in between sips of whisky. 'We have much to protect and you cannot forget that.' The man thought for a moment and looked even closer at Varney before continuing. 'How was the problem of D'Arc's father resolved?'

'Hanged himself in the kitchen of his house–D'Arc found him. Some of us felt it would be best to have his son where we could keep an eye on him. He was given a job; he did well and then the war came.'

'Why didn't he come back to the job?' Mccabe asked. 'Now he is on the outside, we have no control.'

'D'Arc was shot in the leg by a sniper... it strained his mind. He got war fever and wasn't fit to return.'

'Does he have any idea of why his father *died*?'

'None at all. The matter was dealt with very discreetly. The journalist was run over by a car on Cheapside before he could file the story. The integrity of the Yard was protected.'

'And now it comes back to haunt us?' asked the Commissioner in a voice just above a whisper. 'All from the murder of Alicia Gabrielle...'

'It is a coincidence; a fateful coincidence that will be swept away,' Varney stopped what he was saying and leant forward. He glanced around the room with its wood panelled walls and the portrait of the King hanging behind the desk. 'When are you going to the press?'

The Commissioner sighed and blew out a mouthful of smoke as he rubbed the whiskers of the long moustache that framed his mouth.

'I have told them that it is a matter of national security and until the murderer is found they are to print nothing. The Prime Minister had lunch with the editor of *The Times*. He has promised that they will abide by what has been said.'

'Why should it be of concern to the Prime Minister?' Varney asked.

'This matter is more than the death of a young woman. There are people who need our protection, reputations are at stake.' Mccabe smoothed an agitated hand across his face. He placed the teacup back on the saucer and stubbed out the cigarette. 'There has to be a convincing conclusion to this, with no end left untied–the Prime Minister insisted, I spent the morning at Downing Street. Make sure that D'Arc comes to the same conclusion as you. Do anything to persuade him, and if not...' The Commissioner lifted the cup and finished the scotch. His face looked anxious, lined with worry. '...you know what to do.'

'Just like his father?' Varney trailed off in question.

[23]
SACKVILLE STREET

Wolfe and Sons, tailors of Sackville Street, had occupied the same shop for two hundred years. The sign above the door had been repainted and the gold leaf on the window had been replaced twice. Inside it was just the same as the day it had opened. On three walls were racks of linen and fabric, in the centre of the room was a tall desk and upon it a thick ledger. It gave relation to every suit, shirt and tie they had ever made. No money was ever exchanged, accounts were rendered and paid from bank to bank. Each item of wear was distinctive, well made and only available to those who could afford such privileges. The window at the front of the shop showed nothing for sale, Wolfe and Sons traded not on what was visible to those passing outside, but on the reputation of those it served. The words on the window were deemed enough to keep those away who dreamed of stepping within: 'BY APPOINTMENT ONLY'.

Ruby scanned the words as they stood in the busy street with people pushing by in the early afternoon rush. 'So this is where we start?' she asked D'Arc as she nervously fingered the button in her hand.

'Wolfe and Sons are known to guard the secrecy of their clients more than the King guards his jewels,' D'Arc uttered as he looked in through the window and watched the effete assistant strut towards the desk and lift the receiver of the Bakelite telephone.

'What do we do?' Ruby thought of how they were going to proceed.

'Whatever we need to get that man to tell us who the button belongs to,' D'Arc replied with ease as he took hold of the brass door handle and stepped inside. Ruby followed eagerly and took in the first breath of Wolfe and Sons. It smelled of toffee and lavender mixed with pipe tobacco. The air was warm and stuffy, making them almost feel claustrophobic.

'Can I help you, Sir?' the assistant spoke, sneering at Ruby and dismissing her with a glare as he smiled at D'Arc.

Ruby could see the instant attraction. The man looked the same age as her, his fingers were manicured and his eyes followed D'Arc eagerly.

Retrieving the button D'Arc found in the alleyway from her pocket, she held it towards the man.

'He would like a jacket with buttons that match this,' she requested, her aura exuding confidence.

The assistant took a glance at the button and, nodding to Ruby, picked it from her palm.

'Has Sir been fitted here before?' he enquired as he slowly coiled the tape measure in his fingers.

'The button is quite distinct, do you know who could have bought such a jacket?' Ruby followed the gentleman to the desk where he inspected the button with a small jeweller's lens.

'It is very old and one we have not used for many years; out of stock. Is that all?' he answered with perfunctory indifference.

'We would like a suit exactly the same. Is that possible?' Ruby requested, knowing from the way he looked at her that the man could see it was a lie.

'I don't think that Sir would suit that style of button at all. Perhaps he would like something in a pinstripe? Do you have an account?' the assistant asked pointedly as he continued to try and ignore Ruby.

'It was a suit with buttons just like that, perhaps if you asked the owner he would sell the suit to me?' D'Arc badgered him as Ruby moved towards the ledger that sat on the desk as if it were a Bible on a lectern.

'It is impossible to tell from the button who bought the suit... it is a type we no longer use. Would you like the button back?' he stared in D'Arc's direction as he spoke, unable to resist the urge to ask. 'Where did you find it?'

'Certainly... it was found at the scene of a most hideous crime. A murder where a woman was ripped open and her heart taken from within.' D'Arc's voice was nonchalant as he acted out the stabbing with his hand.

'And the button is part of the crime?' the man shot back in question, handing it back to Ruby as if it would bring bad luck.

'Part of a crime?' D'Arc guffawed as they began to make their way from the shop. 'It was worn by the killer and ripped from his jacket with the dying grip of the victim...'

'Where do we go now?' Ruby pushed, refusing to admit defeat as they idled in the street.

'Wait,' D'Arc answered.

The assistant stood for a moment before crossing the room and opening the ledger. His finger traced the names on the pages as he flicked them back and forth. He then lifted the receiver on the telephone and began to dial.

'He's speaking to someone,' she mumbled as, without warning, D'Arc slammed open the door and ran into the shop. Shoving the man out of the way, he snatched the telephone from his hand and listened to the voice.

'Did you tell him who I was?' the voice asked.

'No,' D'Arc drawled, 'he did not, but I think I recognise the voice.'

There was silence. The telephone was cut dead before he could say another word.

'I shall call the police. This is not acceptable,' the assistant choked out as he tried to grab the handset from D'Arc.

'Neither is conspiracy to murder. Who was on the telephone?' D'Arc's raised voice thundered through the room, aimed right at the man.

The assistant calmly placed the telephone on the counter and ran his finger down the list of names on the ledger. He stopped halfway and let it rest for a moment beside one name in particular.

'Remember... I told you nothing,' he pleaded as he bit his lip to stop it quivering.

Ruby scanned the details on the page. She looked over at D'Arc, who smiled and then shut the ledger.

'You never said a word,' Ruby answered. 'Not one word.'

[24]
LONDON BRIDGE

The man slipped quietly through the large door of the empty church and closed it behind him as his eyes adjusted to the dim light inside. No one had noticed him leave the noise of the street behind and disappear from the world like a solitary ant into a dark hole. He stood for several moments and breathed the incense-filled air. It reminded him of his childhood, the days spent in Rome and Venice. Although ornate, he felt the old church in a busy street was quite bland. There were no paintings, no great works of art. All was ordinary, traditional and very English. It lacked style, taste and even the presence of God. On the altar, six tall candlesticks with false candles burned brightly, each lit with an oil lamp made to look like the wick of a candle. Above the altar was a tall cross, suspended from the high ceiling by a black chain. There was no Jesus, just the nails where his hands and feet should have been. It was as if the Saviour had broken free from the cross and escaped into the world. Light seeped in from the high window behind him. In the late afternoon, it cast weak shadows that danced on the walls. The man's lips curled into a smile as he strolled down the side aisle to a tall confessional box with two oak doors. As he reached the end of the pews, he stopped and, dipping one knee, bowed slightly. Then, turning to the confessional box, he dipped his finger into a small pot of holy water and made the sign of the cross. With a gentle tap he opened the door, placing the Gladstone bag under the wooden seat.

'Have you been here before?' the voice of the priest asked through the grill, as if he had been expectantly waiting. 'I forgot to ask when you made the appointment.'

'It has been many years since I last made a confession, Father. I have done some things that I need to clear from my soul,' the man declared as he sat on the wooden seat and turned his face towards the grill.

'Then it is good that you have come today. I do not have another appointment for another hour. Tell me what grieves you.' The priest knelt to face the grill, and the man did the same.

'Forgive me, Father, for I have sinned. It has been twelve years since my last confession,' the man announced, reading the words from the card on the wall before him.

'What troubles you?' the priest asked.

'It was a woman. I took her in an alleyway... she was a whore.'

'What did you do?'

'I cut her clothes from her and forced her to do things and then... I have sinned, Father Tyrone.'

'You are not beyond redemption.'

'Is there not an unforgivable sin?' the man reached down and unclipped the fastener on the leather bag as he spoke.

'What have you done that cannot be forgiven by God?'

'It was a girl... Alice Pringle. Did you know her?' he wondered aloud.

'Alicia? You know her?'

'Did she tell you anything about her life?'

'What is said in the confessional is most secret. Why should me knowing her have anything to do with your sin?' the priest questioned as he pressed his face to the grill to try and see the man.

'I need to know.'

'Then you are asking the wrong man and wasting my time,' Father Tyrone spoke almost dismissively. 'Do you seek absolution?'

'I have all I need to be free from sin,' the man disclosed as he slipped a long dagger from the leather bag and gripped it in his hand.

'Then you waste my time,' the priest announced with finality.

The dagger sliced through the grill, stabbing the priest in the eye. He slumped forward. The blade was pulled from the wound and then pushed back again and again. Father Tyrone didn't cry out. With the final blow, he slumped back. The door of the confessional was pulled open. The man stood there in his long coat, dagger in hand.

'Now you will know if you have preached the truth or lied for all these years,' he muttered over the blood-covered body of the priest.

D'Arc and Ruby had taken coffee on the Strand and then continued to walk over to London Bridge. Ruby found herself telling D'Arc more about her life, trusting that he was actually listening. Unlike most men, D'Arc did not interrupt, nor did he offer any advice; he just listened, straight-faced and determined. After realising that she had talked the length of Fleet Street, Cannon Street and Scotts Yard, Ruby fell silent. She hoped that she had not said too much. It was her wont and a cause of her consternation. In silence, they traipsed on until they reached St Magnus Church.

The vast oak doors of the church opened slowly. Fog spilled into the church like thick treacle. Emerging from the mist of late afternoon, D'Arc strode through the doors, Ruby trailing after. He sniffed the air as if something from his primaeval past told him what had gone on.

'Father Tyrone!' D'Arc hollered, knowing the priest was expecting them as he took off his hat.

The words echoed around the church as Ruby made her way down the aisle to the chancel and stood on the steps.

'He's not here.' Her brows furrowed in confusion, 'I thought you had telephoned to say we were coming?'

'I did. He invited us to the church and then to the vicarage. I am surprised he is not here.'

As he spoke, a single drop of blood dribbled down the side of her face. Ruby caught it with her hand before looking up to where it came from.

Above her, dangling from the cross and nailed in place was the naked body of a man. Ruby suddenly realised that she stood in a pool of blood that had soaked into the carpet of the church.

'Jack! Look…' she choked out, her voice stolen by what she could see.

D'Arc stared at the cross where Father Tyrone hung limply. There were nails through his wrists and feet. His side had been cut open and his eyes gouged from their sockets.

'Do as I say Ruby, the man is very close,' D'Arc demanded in a whisper as he pointed towards the doors of the confessional box, hidden in the side aisle of the church and out of sight behind the tall stone pillars.

Ruby slipped the small Derringer from her pocket, cocking the hammer and adjusting her hold on the gun in the palm of her hand.

'Is he there?' Ruby's voice was low, careful not to give away their presence.

D'Arc nodded and pointed to the door. Ruby aimed the gun as he slowly tiptoed towards the confessional. With one hand he took hold of the brass catch that held the door in place.

Suddenly the door burst open, smashed with such force that it fell from its hinges. D'Arc was thrown to the floor as the leather bag hit him on the head. A man appeared from the darkness, face shrouded in a silk scarf, black hat pulled down to the eyes.

'Stop!' Ruby fired the pistol as she yelled, her shout echoing through the church.

The bullet hit the bag as D'Arc got to his feet. Again the man lashed out, dropping the dagger as D'Arc stumbled from how his head struck the side of the pew. Fumbling with the pistol, she aimed again as the man darted towards the door of the church. The crack of the pistol echoed around the building as the door slammed shut.

'Ruby... come back!' D'Arc shouted as she gave chase.

'He's getting away!'

'Leave him.'

It was an hour later when they lowered the body of the priest to the chancel floor. Varney had arrived in a car within half that time and they had waited until the scene could be photographed. Father Tyrone posed for the pictures. Blood covered his face, his body hanging from the nails in his wrists.

Ruby sat at the back of the church, her face in her hands, not wanting to look up. D'Arc inspected the body as Varney moved from side to side, changing the weight from foot to foot.

'Don't look so bloody smug, D'Arc. This isn't good for you,' he whispered as they studied the body of Tyrone. 'What were you doing here anyway?'

'I had information that linked Tyrone to Alicia; she would come here for confession,' D'Arc explained as he looked at the empty eye sockets and the deep wounds that penetrated the brain. 'Do you now believe that Liza isn't the killer?' D'Arc raised an eyebrow. 'Stabbed through the eyes and his tongue has been removed. Just like the others.'

'This is totally different. What has this got to do with the other murders? Looks like some religious nutter getting their own back.'

'So it was just a coincidence that he happened to be murdered an hour before he had agreed to tell me about Alicia?' D'Arc challenged, smelling the alcohol on Varney's breath and realising he was drunk.

'They happen all the time. Just because he had his tongue cut out doesn't make him the victim of the same killer,' Varney insisted. 'What about the eyes? Alicia had hers, and so did that other girl.'

'Tyrone was alive when he was put on the cross. He cut his tongue out so he couldn't scream.'

Varney didn't answer. He narrowed his eyes, glaring as he took a look around the church as if it seemed familiar.

'If I am right in thinking, wasn't this the church your father came to?'

'How did you know that?

'I was at your baptism–I remember it well. Maypole Day 1892. Great-grandparents were Huguenots. Your father always thought that made him different… a bit special,' Varney's tone and the look on his face were smug, as if he knew that his words would rile D'Arc.

'I am here to solve a murder, not talk of my father.'

'So what do you think?' Varney pointed to the priest on the cross.

'We found him when we arrived at the church. The place was empty… not a person in sight. The priest has been dead for less than an hour–stabbed in the left eye socket as he sat in the confessional. The blood stains on the floor show he was dragged here and nailed to the cross before being winched into the air,' D'Arc announced as he pointed out the wounds on the body to Varney. 'It is the same man. A forceful blow to disable the victim and then he can do what he wishes. The man always chooses a place where he will not be disturbed and yet he likes to take chances by leaving the door to the church open. This murder was thought out, quite dramatic and for our benefit.'

'He went the way of his Saviour,' Varney wiped the spittle from his mouth as the words left his mouth.

'It had been planned that way.'

'And you saw no one?'

'The church was empty.'

'So why is the death of a priest the same as the whore and the dead sapphists?' Varney asked, pulling the hip flask from his coat pocket, opening the pewter cap and taking a lengthy swig.

'They shared one thing in common.'

'And what was that? Killed by Jack the Ripper?'

'I am yet to work it out.'

'And you never will. This isn't the same as the others and no one will ever say it is, do you understand, Jack D'Arc? It frightens the people to think *the Ripper* is back on the streets. There is a civil war in Ireland, talk of revolution and Bolsheviks. The last thing we want is people being frightened of the Ripper.' Varney swigged from the flask again. 'This is the work of a religious zealot... understand? That is what the Commissioner will tell the newspapers.'

'If that is what the Commissioner wants.'

'Exactly, D'Arc... just what he wants,' Varney spat as he lurched towards him. 'It would be best you keep away from any more investigations. Go and tell Lady Elsa Gabrielle that her daughter was murdered by a lover. You will make friends in high places.'

'I have all the friends I need, Chief Inspector... all the friends I need.'

[25]
SEVEN DIALS

The Latin American woman sang in a dark recess of the Seven Dials Café on the corner of Earlham Street. She twisted her fingers in her beautifully and tightly curled hair as she sat on the tall barstool at the back of the piano. As the man played, fingering each note precisely, she harmonised along. Her voice was soft, mellow and soothing, matching the mist surrounding the street outside. The room was quiet for that time of the evening. The tables by the window were empty and the barman had already washed all the glasses and placed them neatly on the wooden shelves at the back of the bar. At a table by the door, D'Arc sat next to Ruby, though neither had eaten. The plate of eggs was untouched and the coffee had formed a milky skin around the cup. Ruby waited for the singing to stop before she asked the question. The woman got up from the chair and sauntered over to the bar. The elegant woman crossed her long, brown legs and peered over at Ruby, her eyes deep green and set in a beautiful, rounded face. Ruby smiled back; it was a look that the woman liked.

'Why did you lie to Varney?' Ruby's question was sharp as a razor as she sipped on her cold coffee.

D'Arc beamed cheekily as if he was a child that got caught out.

'It was simply omitting the truth.'

'You said the church was empty.'

'It would not do him any good to think that we had seen the murderer. Varney would have asked too many questions,' D'Arc clarified. 'Anyway, I am not sure if he wants to find the murderer. Nor am I sure that this was the same man who killed Alicia.'

'You also concealed evidence.'

'I will eventually give him the dagger. I have often wondered as to the merits of the bags that women carry and now I know the reason,' D'Arc smiled at her even more, just relishing in the feeling of being near to her. 'I am not concealing the evidence… more delaying it falling into the hands of Scotland Yard.'

'If I was searched by a copper, how would I explain a blood-stained dagger?'

'Possibly in the same way that has kept you out of prison for so long. You are obviously an expert in dealing with the police. I saw you at the back of the church, it was a most convincing performance.'

'I was trying to stop myself from throwing up. You and Varney looked at the body as if it was a piece of meat.'

'So much can be learnt from the dead–they speak as if they are still alive. Father Tyrone told me many things. He drank too much, smoked with his left hand and had most probably fallen in love with Alicia. It was not just her soul he wished to save.'

'How do you know that?' Ruby probed as she leant forward so that no one else could hear.

'It is the fate of many a priest, especially Anglo-Catholics. They start life with high virtues of prayer and celibacy. Often they find themselves surrounded by middle-aged housewives searching for God and then they succumb.'

'Speak from experience?'

'I have dealt with two matrimonial cases where the priest was the man who had encouraged the adultery. Passion is passion and often Christ cannot stop it. I once knew a priest who, during the Mass, was so sidetracked by the face of the woman on the front pew that he thanked God for the passion of his dear Son, his mighty erection and glorious ascension. For several weeks after, every time he was in church he would walk round the vestry repeating time after time resurrection… resurrection.'

'That's a strange word to hear you say, Jack D'Arc,' Ruby answered simply, not understanding him. Alder's voice was alluring and soft, yet pointed and sharp when it needed to be, which was perhaps another thing that gravitated D'Arc towards the woman. 'I never thought you would know about passion.'

'I am a detective and passion is what drives the human heart,' D'Arc remarked as the barman came to the table with a shot glass on a small tray.

Pointing to the woman at the bar, he said, 'This is from Valentina. She wants to know if Madame will join her?'

'Thank Valentina for the drink, but Madame is taken for the evening by me,' D'Arc raised the coffee cup and nodded to the woman as the words left his mouth.

'Taken for the evening?' Ruby shot back. 'Is that all the time we shall spend together?'

She looked on as she saw his face redden. He breathed deeply and looked out of the window, his eyes flickering from the glass and back to her.

'I'm sorry. I just wanted to spend some time… it's not often I get a chance to speak to someone who…'

D'Arc paused his words as he watched as Ruby started to laugh, reaching out with her hand and letting her fingers graze his softly.

'How come I never heard of you when you were a copper?' she wondered, hoping to put an end to his visible discomfort.

'I was kept from the streets; protected by friends of my dead father. They thought that I would suit being a detective, looking at evidence rather than drinking in the grubby pubs of Mile End.'

'Why did he kill himself?'

'He never got over the Whitechapel murders. My father became obsessed that the killer was an American called Tumblety. He had fled to America and died in 1903. My father could never come to terms with him getting away. He fulfilled the sentence that should have been for the Ripper. About a week before he died, I heard him talking to another detective who had come to the house and I listened at the door. My father said he had found a link between the murdered women. He said the name of a man that I couldn't hear. My father hanged himself in the kitchen of my house. It was on my birthday–I found him.'

They didn't speak, the silence palpable as the two of them remained unspeaking, not wanting to say the wrong thing. Valentina went back to the piano and started to sing. She looked at Ruby as the words of *Down Hearted Blues* hung in the air thicker than the smoke.

'So what Madame Baphomet said was true,' Ruby eventually commented as she sipped on the Cointreau.

'I blame myself? That is what I told the police at the time of his death. I suspect that is where she got her information. Madame Baphomet employs the art of what I call cold reading. She is a skilled observer of the human condition. She looks at the person and assesses how they dress and speak, their age and background.'

'But she knew your father hanged himself,' Ruby was intrigued by what D'Arc had disclosed.

'Someone gave her the information. I am well known in London. It would not be hard for her to have heard about me, so I suspect that she was told by an old colleague.'

'A copper?'

'As you said, many of them are more criminal than any of your gang of thieves.'

'And now the Ripper is back again?' Ruby asked.

'The one we seek is not the Ripper. He is far too young.'

'Did you see his face when he ran from the church?' she asked.

'No,' D'Arc replied, his hushed voice excited, 'but that does not mean I do not know who he could be.'

'How?'

'He wore a coat made in Germany. He smelled of cheap cologne and smoked cigars. His breath had the odour of garlic and the bag he carried was made in New York. However, that will now be discarded, as the bullet you fired went through the side.'

'And you saw all that in such a short time?'

'Ruby,' D'Arc grasped her hand in his before continuing, 'every second in the presence of someone tells us more than the words we speak.'

'Do you think I shot him?'

'He didn't flinch so I suspect not. Did you want to?'

'He was going to kill you.'

'That is a hazard of this occupation. The man we are dealing with is not a criminal, he is an assassin.'

'A murderer.'

'More than that, Ruby. This man enjoys what he is doing. To him it is an art form, a statement of intent.'

'But why?'

'Did Alice ever tell you anything about her life or her lover?'

'Just what I have told you.'

'There is a connection between the murderer and the Forty Elephants. That is what makes me believe that he will strike again. He believes that Alicia has shared a secret with one of you and the only way he can keep it that way is by killing you all.'

'But what about the priest?'

'That, Ruby, is obvious. Father Tyrone was murdered because of what it was thought he knew; Alicia went to confession. The murderer must have believed she had told the secret to the priest. Even though the seal of the confessional bound him, he had to die. It is also possible that the killer knew what Father Tyrone thought of Alicia. That means you and Ruth are also in danger. He is killing all those who knew her, one by one.'

'Ruthie?'

[26]
SCOTLAND YARD

In a windowless office with drab furniture and a desk stacked with unread files, Varney sat, head in hands. He breathed deeply, his last cigarette hanging to the side of the full ashtray in front of him, the smoke rising like incense. It twisted in grey spirals to the ceiling and around the low tortoiseshell lightshade that hung above him. The bulb flickered as a lone moth beat itself against the light, singeing its wings and falling to the desk.

Varney didn't look up as the door opened, he had heard the footsteps coming along the corridor and knew the man.

'Don't worry, Varney. The Home Secretary told me. Another murder,' the Commissioner announced his presence as he slammed the door and planted himself in the chair opposite, putting his feet on the desk. 'I could do with a drink and from the look of you...'

'Half a bottle of whisky and a few pints,' Varney muttered before the Commissioner could complain he was drunk. 'You never get used to seeing them. His eyes were cut out of his head. Just two bloody holes. D'Arc said he was alive when he was nailed to the cross. Cut his tongue out so he couldn't fucking scream.'

'It turns out that Tyrone was the confessor of the Prime Minister. They had been at Trinity College together. Good friends. The Prime Minister wants answers.'

'Well, he's got a bloody problem then because it was the Ripper. I told D'Arc to keep away from now on. I told him that you would say that the murder was religiously motivated. I have already spoken to *The Standard*. They are going to print that it was a sectarian attack by Fenians; if in doubt, blame the bloody Irish.'

'Was that wise, Varney? The last thing we want is trouble with them.'

'If you'd have been around to make a fucking decision and not pissing it up the wall at your club, you could have come up with something better,' Varney snapped.

The Commissioner tried to smile, ignoring what had been said.

'There is only so much I can take, even from you,' he answered solemnly. 'Will D'Arc agree? I had the Home Secretary call me again tonight. The King has asked him for a swift outcome, Lady Elsa has been putting pressure on him. There are other matters… certain people need to be protected.'

'Surprised she could drag the King away from his stamp collection.'

'It would seem that she and the King were once "*good*" friends…'

'Didn't think he had it in him–not like his father,' Varney yawned. He had not slept for two days as the thickening, bearded growth on his chin bore testimony. 'So what do you want me to do? We could find D'Arc in the Thames by Tower Bridge–beaten by ruffians and dumped in the water? Throat cut across, his tongue torn out by its roots, and body buried in the rough sands of the sea at low-water mark, where the tide ebbs and flows. I remember teaching you the sign and Due Guard of the apprentice. How many years ago was that?'

'The last thing we want is another body. Once he has told Lady Gabrielle about the murder of her daughter, perhaps D'Arc should be out of the way for a while. He could languish in Pentonville until we find the killer.'

'From what I know of D'Arc, he would love it–all those men locked up in one place. He would think it was a fucking queer monastery.'

'The killer needs to be found and others need to be dissuaded from the action they are taking,' the Commissioner explained as he stood at the desk and drank from Varney's glass. 'O Lord, my God, is there no help for a widow's son?'

They were old words to Varney, words that should never be spoken in such a place. He laid his eyes on the Commissioner; the man held his hands high in front of him as if to ward off great evil and then quickly brought them to his side.

Varney had been a member of the Grand Lodge for thirty years and twice the master. When his wife had left him, the Masonic Order had been his comforter. He had encouraged many men to follow the way of Hiram Abif, the Commissioner was no exception. He knew the gravity of the ancient words and the sign, and only in times of mortal distress should they be given together.

'How deep is the shit you are in? If I am to help you, I need names. You tell me what you know and I will get you out of this fucking mess,' Varney murmured as he stared pointedly at Mccabe.

'You must tell no one…'

[27]
BATTERSEA PARK DRIVE

The door of the taxicab opened as it pulled up to the pavement. Mondo stood outside the entrance of York Mansions. He rubbed his hands together, fuelled by his nerves, as he watched Ruby get out of the rattling taxicab, followed by Jack D'Arc.

'I couldn't stop her, she said she felt cooped up. Ruthie said she had to go out and meet a friend,' Mondo managed to stutter out before they could close the door of the taxicab or pay the driver.

'How long ago?' D'Arc urged, slamming the taxicab door and taking two strides to cross the pavement.

'About an hour,' Mondo answered, his eyes flashing back and forth as he followed them to the door.

'Did she say where she was going?' Ruby's voice was stern as they stood on the wide stone flag under the brick arch of the building.

'She made a call. I heard her say Belgravia when she asked the operator. Then she ran out. I tried to get her to stay,' he attempted to defend himself, seeing the simmering anger in Ruby's fraught-lined face.

'Mondo, you could have stopped her,' she stated with a straight face.

'I tried, Ruby. But she said she would be safe and had to see him to get things sorted,' Mondo was gesturing with his hands as he spoke, feeling defeated but trying to explain himself.

'And you have no idea who she spoke to?'

'She called a man. I am sure she said Belgravia when she said the number. To be honest, I wasn't really listening…'

Mondo sighed and looked at them as he shrugged his shoulders.

'What did she say to him?' D'Arc butted in.

'Just asked him to come and get her and gave the address. He said five minutes and she was gone,' Mondo explained with another forlorn shrug. He stood like a mountain and his jacket was tight across his expansive chest. 'If I had tried to stop her, she still would have gone. It was too late.'

Ruby stepped towards the door and pulled on the handle.

'I can ask the operator who she spoke to. I am sure we can find out.'

'Good,' D'Arc looked at Ruby with his response. 'I will meet you in the morning at the taxicab rank, Eaton Square–ten o'clock.'

'Where are you going?' she pried as D'Arc began to walk away.

'I have to see Lady Elsa Gabrielle,' he shot back. 'It's best I go alone.'

'I could come with you.'

'No. Stay here with Mondo. Ruth may come back. If she does, find out where she has been.'

'Should we tell Varney?" Ruby proposed the question as she stepped inside the building and watched D'Arc disappear.

He didn't answer as he vanished into Battersea Park.

'What you doing getting mixed up with an enquiry agent?' Mondo asked suspiciously as he followed Ruby up the stairs.

'I'm giving up the Forty Elephants. One of the other girls can take over,' she stated, not looking back.

'You worked so long, so hard.'

'It wasn't worth it, been thinking for a while. I have to give it up... you wouldn't understand.'

'Is it to do with Haslem?' Mondo was relentless with his questioning as they got to the door of the apartment.

'Some of it,' Ruby hesitated as she spoke. 'I want a new start. I've found a café in Pimlico, with what I have got saved and working for Jack D'Arc, I should be alright.'

'What?' he clamoured. 'Working for the law?'

'He's not the law and he has offered me a job. I quite like the idea,' Ruby replied, unable to help the smile that curled on her lips.

'You like the idea of working with D'Arc, or you just like the idea of D'Arc? Do you think Haslem will let you go that easily? He is one jealous man,' Mondo's voice came out challenging as he stood by the door with his thick arms folded.

'Haslem had his chance. What did he do? The man smacked me around the face and thought I would like it.'

'And you stabbed him in the leg.' A broad smile came across Mondo's face with a half-laugh at her reply. 'Never seen the man look so pissed.'

'He got what he deserved. Haslem has no respect.'

'He was asking for you the other night at the Elephant and Castle.'

'Tell him to keep away,' Ruby ordered, trying to cover up the anxiety that began to persistently eat at her. 'It's over.'

'He won't like you hanging around with Jack D'Arc. Haslem will get it all wrong, you know what he is like. If he can cause any trouble...'

'Jack's not interested. He's not like that.'

'He's a man,' Mondo scoffed but ended his comment with a smile on his face. 'Of course he will be interested, how can he not be? You are beautiful.'

She looked at Mondo and took hold of his hand, burning to the touch as she squeezed his hand slightly.

'And you are such a kind man,' Ruby finished as she placed a gentle kiss on his cheek.

[28]
ALDFORD STREET

Standing in the empty street, D'Arc glimpsed up at the light in the highest window of the once elegant house in Mayfair. It stretched to the sky and formed part of a long terrace. The vast door, set in a stone arch, had its own lamp. It cascaded the pavement with white phosphorescence that appeared to be walled in by a thickening fog. D'Arc pulled once on the brass doorbell rod with its dull, ivory handle. He heard nothing until the door started to peel open gradually. The butler–a small, bald man with a shoddy, black coat hurriedly pulled onto his slightly rounded frame–looked out, his face half-hidden.

'Are you expected?' the man queried before D'Arc could get a word out. 'It is rather late.'

'Jack D'Arc for Lady Elsa. She told me to come as late as possible.'

The servant pouted his bottom lip as if to discourage D'Arc before hesitantly opening the door further and gesturing for him to step inside.

'I suppose you could wait in the morning room until I wake Madame,' he trailed off with a Brooklyn drawl. He waited until D'Arc stood in the hallway before he shut the front door and turned the lock. Showing him into the morning room, the butler switched on the chandelier light and paused until it had stopped flickering before pointing to a chaise lounge in front of the window. 'If you would like to sit there, I will fetch Madame.'

D'Arc listened to the footsteps of the man methodically taking each tread of the stairs one at a time. Taking a glance around the former lavish room, he noticed the outlines of picture frames that had been taken down only to leave the wall around where they had been looking faded. It was as if the house had been stripped bare an item at a time. The mantelpiece was empty of everything bar a single old photo in a silver frame. Around the edge of the room were places where furniture had once pressed into the carpet, and in the middle of the room, in front of the grand fireplace, was a threadbare, leather sofa. The stuffing sagged underneath its frame, spilling horsehair on to the equally worn carpet. The only painting left on the wall was set high above the fireplace. It was of a man in a military uniform looking out over the lawns of a country estate. In the far distance on a high scarp was a small folly; it looked like a cluster of stones built up to be the house of a hermit. The man in the painting was distinguished. His face was sallow, and a thick, black moustache girded a wide mouth. The lines around the eyes were framed in neatly cut, black hair. At the feet of the man was a Labrador dog that slept in the fading embers of a summer sun.

The door to the room opened, though D'Arc had not heard any approaching footsteps. There before him was Lady Elsa Gabrielle. Her face was cleansed of makeup, her hair held back with a headband. She wore a silk gown that trailed to the floor, with nothing beneath. As she stepped into the room she looked D'Arc up and down with inquisitive eyes. Her face remained without emotion, stern and set like steel.

'It is quite late for a house call, I never see anyone after midnight.'

'You asked me to come as soon as I knew who had killed your daughter,' D'Arc returned, trying to match her lack of emotion with his voice. 'There is something I need to know.'

'You know who killed my daughter?'

'I have all the pieces in my hand and yet I fear this is a jigsaw of jagged glass with one piece still missing.'

'I asked the King to speak to Scotland Yard. They will give you all the help you need.' Lady Elsa raised a curious eyebrow at the man as she crossed the room and took a seat on the sofa opposite the empty fireplace.

'The Commissioner wanted me to tell you that your daughter was killed by her female lover,' D'Arc shot back.

'Is that true? I never thought that Alicia could manage to be a lesbian. It would be too mechanical for her, she never liked gadgets.'

'No. A man murdered her. I believe that she knew the attacker and did not expect him to kill her.'

Lady Elsa kept her composure and D'Arc remained watching her every move. To him, she looked like a large cat that took in every sound and every sight, before they attacked. Her hand trembled slightly as if she was frightened to move. Pausing before she spoke, she stared at D'Arc with squinted eyes as if she searched his soul.

'Why did she not expect him to kill her?'

It was not the question that he had expected, nor was it usual for the mother of a murdered daughter to behave in such a way as this.

'She did not fight,' D'Arc spoke simply as he watched her play with the silk collar of her night coat just above the breast. 'There was no skin under her nails and no sign of a struggle. Whoever killed her, knew her well.'

'How can you be so sure? She was murdered in Soho, in a dark alleyway amongst the vagrants.' Lady Gabrielle got up from the sofa and moved closer. 'Chief Inspector Varney came to see me last night. He never mentioned anything about her being killed by a lover, but if you think it was someone who knew her, wouldn't that fit?'

'I am sure it was a man. It is all a matter of the force used, but these are not questions for a time such as this.'

Before he could continue speaking, she reached out and put the tip of her finger on his lip.

'I have a room upstairs… perhaps we could speak there. We would not be disturbed,' Lady Gabrielle spoke softly as she slipped her finger from his mouth and trailed it down his neck and along the line of his lapel.

'If I am to find the killer, I need to know about your daughter,' D'Arc cajoled as he took hold of her hand and allowed it to drop to her side.

'I can be of no help to you,' Lady Gabrielle dismissed as she walked to the cabinet on the far wall, opened the door and poured two long glasses of Sazerac bourbon. Turning, she walked back to D'Arc and handed him a glass. 'Alicia hardly ever spoke. Even when she was a child, she was always in another world. Alicia was always the centre of her own universe. It is hard to get to know a child who has never wanted you in her life.'

'And your other children?' he proceeded to ask as he sipped the drink and breathed in the fragrance of grain and burnt oak. 'Did you feel close to them?'

Lady Gabrielle smiled as if the question reminded her of agreeable times.

'They were so different compared to Alicia. Both of them were so much like their father and yet he loved Alicia far more,' she sighed in defeat. 'Now they are gone. Three children given over to death.'

'Did she ever mention anything about her husband? Do you know where he is?' D'Arc pushed for more information.

'Max Coburg is in New York. When Alicia left him, he sailed to America within days... he has connections in Atlantic City. Coburg works with a man called Johnson, who always wears a vulgar, raccoon coat and red carnation.'

'And he is still in America?'

'So I have heard. Is that important?'

'I would like to speak to him. Did Alicia ever say anything about her marriage to you?' D'Arc wondered as he stood by the empty fireplace and sipped on the whisky.

'It was an arranged marriage,' Lady Gabrielle's response was guarded. 'Eddie, my husband, took care of everything. Alicia didn't have a dowry and Max was a lot older, Eddie knew him through business before the war. There was no love. Are you a married man, Mister D'Arc?'

'There has not been the time; the war... my job...' he made his excuse, knowing that Lady Gabrielle did not believe him.

'Perhaps that is a good thing. I can't say I was happily married. Eddie was not the most attentive of men, he never made me feel cherished.'

'Is that what a woman wants?' D'Arc pondered the question, wanting to pursue the case to its conclusion.

'I wanted to be happy, have a family, a nice home,' she stumbled on her words, her hand raised as if to show him the lost glory of the room. 'Instead I got all of this. I have only been widowed for three weeks. I feel cursed. All my children are dead and I am on my own. It is a curse for what I have done in life.'

'I don't believe in such things, Lady Gabrielle. Life is life and has much sadness and joy along its path,' D'Arc answered slowly.

'Were you a soldier? They are words of a soldier trying to make sense of the war. My son spoke like that when he came back on leave.'

'Passchendaele; I was wounded and discharged,' he sighed. 'No longer fit to fight. I spent some time at a spa in Harrogate. My war ended very quickly.'

'It did for my son. He died in a charge on a German gunpost. I had asked Eddie to get him a job back in London and not at the front. He was a Brigadier general and could do that sort of thing. Eddie thought it would do him good to fight. How wrong he was,' her voice came out bitter and empty, as if she could see the final moments of his life play out in her mind.

'Your husband wasn't to know.'

'My husband didn't care, Mister D'Arc. The only thing Eddie cared for was himself. I have never met a more selfish man. He loved Alicia more than he did me and towards the end, that was even more obvious.'

'Have you heard of a man called Gerard Montague?' he let out the question simply as he looked around the room, trying to work out what had been most recently taken.

'Not in my particular circle,' she replied coyly, the name taking her by surprise.

'He frequents the Aurora Club.'

'That is not a place where I would go. Are there any more questions?' she remarked, going to the cabinet and filling her glass.

'Do you know anyone who lives in Eaton Square?'

'Is this relevant, Mister D'Arc? Is that what is keeping me from my bed?'

'It will help my inquiries. Someone said a name that was linked to Eaton Square. I am sure it was Gerard Montague.'

'No one comes to mind. A tardy sort has infiltrated Belgravia recently. Have you tried asking the operator?' Lady Gabrielle let out a hearty laugh and raised a brow. 'Are you sure we can't speak upstairs? I am aware that the staff eavesdrops. He's American and, like all Americans, wants to know everything.'

D'Arc, in his usual manner, ignored the question.

'One final thing, why are the police watching your house?'

'I didn't know they were. Perhaps the Commissioner thinks I need protecting,' she sparred skillfully as she stepped closer, knowing it would make D'Arc feel uncomfortable. 'Perhaps that is another job for you?'

'How much money do you owe?'

'What? What do you mean?' she snapped back, putting down her glass and pulling the lapels of her nightgown closer together, not dissimilar to some kind of defence mechanism.

'The room has been plundered of what is of value. It is obvious that, one by one, things of any worth have been sold. You have one servant who is your butler, driver and cook. And your hands show that you have taken to cleaning. I noticed them at the mortuary. The only painting you have kept is that of your husband and you serve bourbon in brandy glasses.'

'That obvious? I take it that you will join me, Mister D'Arc,' Lady Gabrielle didn't bother trying to deny it, returning to the cupboard and taking the bottle to refill her glass. 'In truth there is no money to pay you, so the least I can do is give you a drink and tell you what you want to know. I didn't know how to explain to you and knew that sooner or later you would discover the truth. I am due some money but these things take time.'

Glass in hand, she slumped on the sofa and patted the seat next to her. D'Arc sat obediently as he glanced at her face; warm eyes, soft lips, tear-stained cheeks.

'What business was your husband in?' D'Arc needled Lady Gabrielle.

'He was an arms dealer; Eddie said to me that the war was the best time in his life. He was a British soldier and yet his company sold arms to the Germans through a company in Paraguay. When the war was over, he scoured the world, selling all that was surplus to further the desires of madmen. My husband was a bastard, a complete bastard.'

She smiled and sighed as if she had wanted to say the words for a long time, and as if doing so had been a weight lifted off of her shoulders.

'So what went wrong?' D'Arc pressed, shuffling back to allow more space between them.

'My husband was dealing arms to the Irish Volunteers. He was in business with a man whom he should never have trusted. There was a ship that was seized just off Cork, it was full of weapons the company had bought from the government. Churchill had even given them a discount. Late one night, a group of Fenians climbed on board. They took the ship and all of the weapons… half a million pounds. It seems such a large amount and I shudder to say the words. Friends have been good and the King is very gracious. Sometimes, I have to sell a little something to make ends meet.' Lady Gabrielle slipped her hand from the back of the couch and touched his long fingers.

'I read that Lord Gabrielle died suddenly,' D'Arc revealed, leaving his hand in place.

'My husband committed suicide. He drank a bottle of laudanum and then jumped from the balcony. It was kept from the press. There was an accusation that they allowed the ship to be taken so that the Fenians could fight the Civil War. Now Alicia has gone. Mister Churchill has promised to keep the matter secret,' Lady Gabrielle looked up at the portrait of her husband as she explained, who stared benignly down at them both.

'So are the police protecting you?' D'Arc insisted.

'I have had death threats,' she answered calmly.

'From a man called Johnson who always wears a vulgar, raccoon coat and red carnation?' D'Arc repeated her words back to her in question.

'Is nothing a secret from you, Mister D'Arc?' she replied, caressing her glass in the palms of her hand like a cauldron that would tell her the future. 'How did you know?'

'A deduction… a guess,' he fought the urge to roll his eyes. 'Lord Gabrielle was exporting whisky. I saw the label of the bottle that you poured, but what was in the glass was not a Saserac. It must be presumed that he was distilling it in Ireland and shipping it to America?'

'You deduced correctly, Mister D'Arc. Max Coburg contacted him and said it was an easy way of making money, Eddie knew people with cargo ships. He hired the ships and filled them with illegal whisky. They were sent to the coast off Atlantic City and loaded into boats and taken ashore. Max Coburg took care of everything, but the money never came.'

'And your husband threatened them?'

'Would you believe that he sent them a letter from his lawyer?' Lady Gabrielle snickered. 'Eddie sent a letter to a mobster. He expected the man to do what he asked.'

'And?'

'The man wrote back telling him that he would have to look out for his family. The next day Eddie killed himself.'

'Are you sure it was suicide?' D'Arc urged her. 'Many murders have been disguised to look that way.'

'The police were adamant. Varney was sure,' she shrugged in nonchalance, sipping the whisky and allowing it to wash around her mouth before she swallowed hungrily. 'Half a bottle of whisky and a dose of laudanum. He went to the balcony and jumped into the street. It took him an hour to die. He never spoke… just looked at me through those doleful eyes. If he had been a dog, they would never have let him suffer that long.'

'Have you heard from Max Coburg recently?' D'Arc got up from the sofa and walked over to the window.

'Max would not come back here. He would not be welcome.'

D'Arc peered down at his watch and then finished the whisky in his glass. Lady Gabrielle knew the conversation was now over.

'I think I know who killed Alicia, but I have to be sure,' he claimed as he made his way towards the door.

'There is one more thing,' Lady Gabrielle spoke out, following him across the room. 'I lied about Eaton Square. The man who was in business with my husband is Lord Finisterre. He lives at number thirteen.'

'Thirteen? Are you sure?' D'Arc questioned, scanning her face to see if she had lied to him.

'I am very sure, as they were once good friends. Sadly, when Eddie died, they felt they could not come to the funeral. Strange how people change when hard times come upon you. He had known Alicia since she was a child. One Christmas, when she was fifteen, we had a party. Finisterre came without his wife and he and Alicia spent the evening talking together. I think that was the night she first fell in love. Understandable really, he was such a sweet man. He once took me to the opening night of *The Importance of Being Earnest* and now he doesn't speak,' Lady Gabrielle blurted out as D'Arc took hold of the ornate door handle and smiled at her, looking around the room one final time. She knew there was nothing else to say and nothing more to be gained. 'Are you sure you don't want to come upstairs and talk?' she raised the offer once again, her voice despondent and frail.

[29]
YORK MANSIONS

The dull ring of the telephone in the hallway woke Ruby from her three hour sleep. It crept into her dream like a soft and distant fire bell. She slipped from the single bed and crossed the linoleum floor. It felt cold as she traipsed unsteadily, the gin from the night before still ringing in her head. Reaching out from the room, she picked up the receiver that sat on the small, mahogany table. She worried that the sound had woken Mondo as he slept in the parlour.

'Yes, this is 2377,' Ruby answered quietly as the cold, steel voice questioned her.

'We have a call for you,' the operator answered abruptly as if her night had been disturbed.

Ruby heard the line judder as the call was connected. It crackled like static as she waited to hear a voice while she brushed the sleep from her eyes.

'Hello?' Ruby began once she heard the line open.

'Ruby Alder?' the man's questioning voice boomed through the phone, his voice dry as if he had been awake all night. 'This is Inspector Morris, of Scotland Yard. We have had a message from Mister Jack D'Arc, he is sending a taxicab in ten minutes.'

Her mind spun quickly as she tried to banish the lingering dreams and listen to what he was saying.

'Where to? What has happened?' she responded with the only questions she could think of.

'I don't have that information,' the man stated, his voice insistent. 'The message comes on the authority of Chief Inspector Varney. I believe you know him. He was most adamant.'

'In ten minutes? I'll be ready,' Ruby replied without thinking.

As the line went dead, Ruby clicked the receiver back in its cradle. Crossing the hall, she opened the parlour door where Mondo lay asleep by the dying embers of the fire. He snored gently, the embroidered blanket on his chest rising and falling with each breath. Ruby closed the door and, taking a pen from the drawer of the table, carefully wrote the message. Turning, she put the note on the table by the telephone, sure that Mondo would see it there.

Pulling on a tweed jacket and long skirt, she dressed hastily and again checked the room where Mondo was still asleep. Ruby thought of waking him, but just as she was about to speak she changed her mind. The note would explain–it was all that was needed, she thought to herself, before opening the door of the apartment and breathing in the nighttime fragrance of the newly varnished wooden floor. It reminded her of the orphanage when she was a child. It mixed with the cold air that breezed in through the door. It was a memory of the Monday mornings when breakfast would be served early and she and the other children would mop the floors with thick varnish. The doors to the house would be opened to pull in the winter air, and when the mopping was over, they would stand in a line by the far wall and wait for the polish to dry. Sometimes they would wait for an hour, unable to leave the hall for fear someone would walk across it.

Ruby wavered and looked back to the parlour. Then, without thinking, she silently closed the door. Soon, Ruby was at the entrance to the apartment and then walking along the street. It was dark, fog-filled, and the trees in the park hung with long spiderwebs of dew. The only traffic was the constant procession of neatly spaced taxicabs that processed along Battersea Park. Their lights came closer like white orbs breaking through the mist. They would pass swiftly, rattling into the night towards Chelsea.

Ruby turned back to the apartment. It was as if she hoped to see his face at the window. She couldn't decide if it was the voice of the man on the telephone that had given her the welling feeling of discontent that something was not right. It was like a dull ache in the pit of her stomach that would not leave her.

Once again, Ruby took one more hesitant look at the door. The solitary lamp hung down on the brass chain and lit the entrance. It called her back as if the light were a sanctuary. In three paces, she was at the gate. Her hand gripped the latch.

'Miss Alder?' the voice asked as she heard the engine stop behind her. 'A Mister D'Arc has sent me to collect you, to take you to the north of the river?'

[30]
EATON SQUARE

A row of freshly painted railings surrounded the tree-lined park in Eaton Square. The dying leaves of the tall platanus trees clung to the long branches. The ridged bark twisted from the stocks, as around each trunk were holly bushes that grew together thicker than gorse. Jack D'Arc hid in the gloomy shadows behind the small, creaking, iron gate that had been left unlocked. He had a perfect view of 13 Eaton Square. A tall, black streetlight lit the pavement outside and shed light onto the balcony above the door. The house ascended from the street, floor upon floor. The windows were in darkness and tightly shuttered. Five storeys high, with a deep basement, it boasted elegance. A box hedge, cut to knee height in black pots, lined the entrance. The paintwork had been washed of London grime, the door knocker polished. The door stood inviting those who passed by into the beloved home. Seizing the key from his pocket, he looked at the fob and for a moment wondered if it would fit the lock. That would be too much of a coincidence, he thought, as he stood under the cover of the trees and watched his breath rise like smoke. As he waited, he counted the windows of the house and then each pane of glass in every window. D'Arc stopped at seventy-six on five floors, not counting the basement.

A black taxicab stopped outside the house, its tyres cutting through the large pool of water in the road. The driver waited before the doors opened, and from his hiding place, D'Arc could see the burning embers of a cigarette in the back of the taxicab. A man stepped out and pulled the fur collar of his coat higher against the night. He stood like a soldier, straight-backed and broad-shouldered. Plucking the cigarette from his mouth, he flicked it to the ground. As he moved, he tugged at the cuffs of his shirt with a gloved hand. D'Arc remained swallowed by the shadows as the taxicab pulled away. On the pavement was a young woman, wearing a long dress with black bobbed hair to her shoulders. The man was older than D'Arc had imagined, at least in his late fifties. He wore a hat that covered his brow and with one hand he took the woman and pulled her close, planting lengthy kisses down and nibbling down her neck.

'No, Monty,' the woman groaned as she couldn't help but giggle at the feeling. 'Not here in the street.'

The man ignored her and squeezed her tightly, lifting her from the ground in the long embrace. D'Arc wandered across the road and stood behind them.

'Lord Finisterre?' he called out, his brusque voice sounding from the walls of the house.

'Depends who is asking,' the man hurled back as he dropped the woman to the pavement and pushed her away. 'I don't like to be disturbed, who are you?'

'Jack D'Arc, I am a detective. I am investigating the death of Alicia Gabrielle.'

Finisterre tensed, his shock evident as his mouth dropped. He stared at the woman and then to D'Arc.

'What does he want, Monty? Who's the girl he's asking about?'

She seemed chided, angered that there could be someone else. It was as if she instinctively knew it was another lover.

'I have questions about the murder of Alicia Gabrielle. The daughter of Lord Gabrielle.'

Finisterre shrugged and took a crumpled banknote from the pocket of his coat and nudged it into the open hand of the girl.

'You better go. I will see you tomorrow,' Finisterre dismissed her.

'That's not enough. What about the money you promised me?' she implored, not wanting to move until she had been paid.

'It will have to do,' his voice turned cold as he turned from her and walked to the door of the house before looking back. 'D'Arc. You better come inside.'

The house was colder than the street, the windows shuttered and draped as if to give no sign of life. In the hallway a piano and table were covered in white sheets, the high chandelier wrapped in cloth.

'We are closing up the house, my wife wants to go to Nice–the Hotel Negresco–it has a Baccarat chandelier that she wants to buy. They say that they will sell anything for the right price.'

Finisterre tried to sound affable and warm. His hands moved in pleasing circles with each word, smiling at D'Arc as they made their way up the staircase together.

In an upstairs room overlooking the square, Finisterre poured himself a gin from a small decanter on the sideboard. Offering up an empty glass to D'Arc, he asked if he wanted a drink. D'Arc raised his hand, shaking his head.

The room was bright, the furniture was all covered, the pictures turned to the wall and mirrors embalmed in a calico cloth. It looked as though Finisterre and his wife would be leaving for a long time.

'You said Alicia Gabrielle had been murdered. What happened?'

'It has been kept from the press. Did you know her?' D'Arc's voice was thoughtful as he began his personal interrogation.

'I watched her grow up, I have known the family for many years,' he answered as he sipped the gin through his teeth and then held the glass up to the light. 'Do the police have any idea?'

'I was hoping you would be able to help,' D'Arc responded. 'Lady Elsa said you were in business with her husband.'

Finisterre thoughtfully rubbed the rim of the glass along his lips, pondering his next response.

'Sadly, it failed and we both lost a lot of money. What happened to Alicia?' he was seemingly growing impatient as he repeated his question.

'How well did you know her?'

'Since she was a child.'

'I take it that you were the man she was having the affair with,' D'Arc assumed simply, without remorse, his tone as blunt.

Finisterre paused and placed the glass on a small table next to the fireplace. He darted his eyes around the room as if he searched for an explanation.

'That is a question that takes so many liberties,' Finisterre answered, his voice edged with anger.

'Yet true,' D'Arc replied. 'You even told her that you would marry her and divorce your wife.'

'I didn't kill her.'

'It was the button from your coat that was found at the scene of the murder, and when I spoke to you today.'

Finisterre laughed in response.

'That was you? You had traced my tailor? Frightened the man to death so he wouldn't tell me who you were. I thought you were a madman. My God, what in the world?' Finisterre looked at D'Arc as if the true realisation of what was before him had become clear in his mind. 'Do you think I am the murderer?'

'So how do you explain the button from your coat being found in the alleyway?'

'My coat was stolen. Well, that is what I presume,' Finisterre stepped towards D'Arc as he seethed. 'I didn't kill her.'

'That is very convenient… a stolen coat. I have heard better excuses.'

'It was taken from the Manhattan Club on the night that I last saw Alicia. I was drunk.'

'So were you having an affair and going to leave your wife?' D'Arc retaliated.

'I was not going to leave my wife,' Finisterre fisted his hands as he snarled the words through clenched teeth.

'But Alicia was adamant.'

'She was quite mad. She said she could speak to the dead. All Alicia was…'

Before he could finish speaking, the door slammed open. A tall, elegant woman peered into the room from the hallway. She was hesitant as she tried to make sense of what she had heard. Like a ruffled swan, she shivered. With one hand the woman twirled the loose curls of her long, dark hair into a tight bun. On her feet were Indian slippers and beneath the brocade robe were red, silk pyjamas. She was younger than D'Arc had expected, but it was the stern look on her face that let him know that this beautiful woman was Lady Elizabeth Finisterre. The woman stared daggers at D'Arc, analysing him as she stood before him.

'Alicia Gabrielle was a muse. My husband has certain desires that I cannot fulfil,' she responded to D'Arc before he could question her. 'From time to time he partakes of that which he should not. For the benefits of a quiet life, I do not get in his way.' Lady Finisterre kept her gaze fixed on D'Arc, eyeing him like a scorpion protecting her brood.

'And you met her?' he asked.

'Several times,' Lady Finisterre shrugged, her posture still as elegant as ever. 'She was a pleasant girl. We knew the family well,' she gulped her breath and squeezed the long nails of her right hand into her palm as she spoke. 'I would prefer my husband to have a mistress that I can tolerate rather than a gutter slut from Mile End.'

'Even if he planned to marry the mistress?' D'Arc probed further.

The woman tried to keep herself composed by breathing deeply.

'Alicia was a fantasist. I would never leave my wife,' Lord Finisterre spat, stepping towards the woman and taking hold of her hand.

'And you were prepared to put up with all this, Lady Finisterre?'

'Some things in life are worth fighting for. A house in Eaton Square, seven thousand a year and whatever I want; it's all worth turning many a blind eye,' she countered as she plastered a doting smile on her face up at her husband. 'Besides, isn't it the modern way? Devoted wife, hard working husband and a loyal family.'

'Did you know that on the 29th of March last year *The Princess Matilda*, a munitions barge, was pirated off the coast of Cork? The guns fell into the hands of the Fenians.'

'So what of it?' Lord Finisterre urged him to continue.

'The surplus weapons had been bought by your company from the British government,' D'Arc explained as Lady Finisterre took the gin glass from her husband and drank from it.

'It was a great loss to us, the company went bankrupt,' Lady Finisterre answered for her husband in an irritated and frosty voice.

'I have heard that the Fenians paid you to leave the ship unguarded,' D'Arc shot back, casting Lord Finisterre a stony and calculated glance.

'Ridiculous!' she protested. 'My husband would never do such a thing.'

'Your husband allowed the Fenians to take the ship and defrauded Lord Gabrielle of the money. There was such a rumour of the deceit that Lloyd refused to pay out on the loss,' D'Arc stepped closer with each word.

'That was just a rumour, it was untrue. We agreed with Lloyd that we would not make a claim as it was an act of war,' Lord Finisterre contested as he put his arm around his wife and pulled her close to his side.

D'Arc watched the thoughts of the man play through his eyes, it was as if he tried to relive the events in his mind.

'We both know that it was sanctioned by the British government. They wanted the weapons to get into the hands of the Fenians so they could fight the forces opposed to the treaty.' D'Arc took a sharp breath as if he found the words hard to say. 'You were a part of that conspiracy and that is why Lord Gabrielle killed himself.'

'That is a lie!' Finisterre snapped. 'The ship was owned by Toby Hanthorn, he had shares in the business.'

'What has that got to do with the death of a trivial whore?' the Lord's wife bellowed, her face expressing her displeasure.

'The taking of the ship had nothing to do with me. That, you have to understand, is the truth. I was just as shocked as Eddie Gabrielle. He rang me the morning he found out... we were both in London,' Finisterre spoke quickly, his eyes darting back and forth from D'Arc to his wife, as if they pleaded for the truth to be seen.

'Lord Tobias Hanthorn, of County Clare?' D'Arc's heart quickened as he questioned Finisterre further.

'There is no conspiracy,' his wife insisted.

'You would be in disgrace if it were ever proved to be true,' D'Arc shot back, raising a brow as he looked the pair before him up and down. 'That day you also argued with Gabrielle over something else.'

'It is a *lie*!' Lady Finisterre shrieked.

'You told your lover the truth and she died because of it. Alicia Gabrielle was murdered because she kept your secret. She fell in love with you when she was just a child and you abused her trust.'

'Enough... *Enough*!' the woman shouted frantically as she pulled away from her husband and lunged at D'Arc, trying to slap him around the face. 'Get out of this house, I will call the police! This is a disgrace.'

'She was fifteen years old when you both fell in love. It was at a Christmas party at her house in Mayfair. Isn't that right?'

'How did you know?' Finisterre's voice faltered as he questioned D'Arc.

'And did you once love her mother?' D'Arc replied, giving life to the words.

'She was a good friend,' Finisterre defended as he touched his lips with the tips of his fingers. His face was drawn to pallor as he repeated the words.

'I believe you took Elsa Gabrielle to see *The Importance of Being Earnest* on its opening night. A very public place to display your *friendship* with a married woman, is it not?'

Lady Finisterre bristled with anger. Again, D'Arc could see her dig the nails of her long fingers into each palm as if the pain would ease her torment.

'That is a question my husband does not have to answer,' his wife's angry response butted in.

D'Arc continued to speak as he watched Lord Finisterre closely.

'Wilde is a great favourite of mine,' D'Arc continued. 'When I walked here from Alford Street, I had time to think. I could not understand why Lady Gabrielle has given me that one anecdote over everything else. If I am correct, that would have been the 14th of February 1895, St James's Theatre?'

'It is of no consequence and does not matter–now leave,' she insisted.

'In the November of that year, Alicia was born,' D'Arc disclosed as he stepped towards the door of the room, pulling the cuff of his shirt.

Lord Finisterre shuddered as if in the words a sudden and secret realisation came to life.

'What are you trying to say?' Lady Finisterre demanded as she stabbed at his shoulder with her long fingers.

'Perhaps your husband can explain,' D'Arc scoffed, his voice calm as he tried to hold his nerve.

'Monty... Monty... what does he mean?' she begged, her voice breaking into tears. 'What is he accusing you of?'

Finisterre looked at her as he tried to hold back his emotions. He slumped back against the wall, the gin glass trembling in his fingers. Groaning like a child, he slowly slipped to the floor and sat on the cold boards that circled the room. Like Tamburlaine, his head sank between his knees as he sobbed. In the stark light of the ornate room, D'Arc and Lady Finisterre just watched him crying. The man sobbed into the hands that covered his face.

Lady Finisterre didn't move. She looked at him, not knowing what to do. It was as if she did not know consolation or solace. Clasping her hands together, she held them as if to pray while she waited for him to speak unwanted words.

'There is a time for everything, Monty,' D'Arc spoke softly as he stood in the doorway of the room and watched the tragedy unravel before him. 'I think she should know the truth.'

The man sobbed even more, tears taking his breath as he gulped the air.

'I loved Alicia, more than you would ever know,' Finisterre coughed between each word. 'She was such a sweet girl and different to the rest of them. I told her everything about the deal–Hanthorn found out. I never knew, never realised until Eddie told me his suspicions.'

'On the day Lord Gabrielle killed himself, what did he ask you?' D'Arc urged.

'It was not what he asked me, but what he told me,' he mumbled.

'Yet you still continued to see her?' D'Arc pushed.

'It was for love,' he answered, looking up as he wiped away the tears from his face and glanced over at his wife, hoping she would understand.

'What did he tell you?' D'Arc insisted.

Lady Finisterre turned. She stared at D'Arc as he stood in the doorway of the room. 'That I don't need to know, Mister D'Arc. You have brought misery to my life and I would like you to leave.'

[31]
BASEMENT

The thick, black tape cut into her face and held her lips together so she couldn't speak. It was wrapped under her chin and across one side of her mouth. Her jaws were pushed together, forcing her teeth to grind. Around her wrists were tied thick, twine bindings that held her to the wooden chair. The room was filled with long shadows and a candle flickered nearby. Ruby could see the dim light from under the piece of cloth pulled across her eyes.

'Want a cigarette?' the soft voice of a man asked from the shadows behind her. 'I know at a time like this, if I were you, that is what I would want.'

Ruby nodded.

Suddenly, the tape muting across her mouth was viciously pulled from her. It tore the skin as it came away, eliciting a painful moan from her as the man laughed.

'Who are you?' she demanded, her breathing hard and jagged as she attempted to keep her composure.

'That doesn't matter,' the man spat. 'I prefer not to be on first name terms.'

'You the one who killed Alice?' she urged, needing to know.

The man cackled again as he took a drag of the cigarette and then slipped his hand around her to carefully put the reefer to her lips.

'Take some, it will help. I smoke them all the time. I guess you know why you are here?' he questioned aloud, allowing her to draw the smoke into her lungs, hold it and then blow it out. 'You scared?'

Ruby coughed as she gave a hesitant nod.

'What do you think?' she asked as she felt the reefer take effect. 'Why me?'

'I have to be certain that you can't tell anyone,' he answered, trying not to laugh. 'One of you knows the secret and because of that every one of you has to die.'

'What secret? We don't know anything.'

'But that's what you would say. It has been decided, no stone unturned and you are a stone.'

Ruby felt a hand smooth across the back of her shoulders. She tried not to move as she felt the cold, sinister touch.

'Let me see you,' Ruby muttered, trying not to shiver as the hand slipped under the collar of her blouse and towards her breast. 'If I'm going to die I at least want to know what you look like.'

He didn't answer as his hand explored her. His fingers cupped her breast and then circled the nipple, squeezing it hard until he felt it stiffen. Ruby gasped.

'Did you like that?' his voice held a teasing edge as Ruby felt the blindfold slip from her face and fall like a noose around her neck.

'It's not how I would have wanted to get to know you,' she spoke as calmly as she could, trying to rid the gasped breath from her voice. 'But if it's what you want.'

She could sense his agitation.

'When I killed Alice, she begged and begged, and then the other girl in the apartment just wept like a child. She pissed herself before I took her, it went over the bed,' the man bragged, speaking to Ruby as if she were an old friend with whom he shared the news of his life.

'She was just a girl,' Ruby snarled, her eyes darting around the room.

Somehow, it seemed familiar. In the gloom, she could see the white, tiled walls of the dingy and chilly basement. It smelled of empty wine bottles and old cauliflower. The walls were covered in faded, white paint that flaked away from the ceiling. By the far wall was a long butcher's table. The once thick base had been wire scrubbed until it undulated like a rolling meadow of wooden splinters. Behind it was a shelf of neatly stacked bottles strewn with laced cobwebs. The floor was covered in dirt and a pile of discarded sacks lay in the corner by a small, wooden door with a crack that the light seeped through from another room. The long shadow ran across the cold, stone floor to her feet. Ruby fought the desire to turn around and stare at the man.

In her head, she imagined what he would be like. Ruby thought him to be small, gratingly thin and with a wizened, ugly face. His voice sounded as if he was a man that hated life and only gave time to the shilling whores that hung around the Bermondsey Docks. He stank of expensive cologne, the fragrance that Jack D'Arc always wore. It mingled with his sweat and hung in the air around her like a cowl. She could smell it on his hand as he placed the reefer between her lips again.

'I was hoping you would be the same,' he continued as he squeezed her neck and undid the buttons on the front of her blouse with one hand. 'I just love the look on their faces when they see what I am going to do to them.' The man pulled open the blouse so it fell across her breasts. 'Beautiful,' he whispered, so close to her face that their skin brushed against each other's. 'What's it going to be then, Ruby?' the man deliberately called her by her name when addressing her, as if he was a thief taking what he desired with no remorse.

'You know my name,' she fought the need to roll her eyes at his provocation, though the words made her shudder with fear.

'I thought that would do it,' he deliberated slowly and purposefully, before licking a stripe along her face, allowing the bristles of his tongue to catch on her skin. 'I know all about you and your new friend, Jack D'Arc. I watched you as you both walked down the stairs from the apartment on Sloane Street. The girl told me that you were outside, I even saw you go into York Mansions together. That is how you were caught.'

'They'll find you,' Ruby fought back, willing herself not to cry in front of him. 'You will hang for what you have done.'

'Do you believe I came from Hell, Ruby? Do you believe that is where I will be?' he asked honestly. 'I once met a man who did the same as I. He killed and killed but was never found. When he had finished, he just took a steamer to America and was never seen again.'

'Is that what you will do?' she needled.

'The ticket is already booked. I leave in two days and Jack D'Arc will never find me. Catch me when you can, Mister D'Arc...' the man let out a breathy laugh as he began to feel up her breasts again, as if he staked some kind of twisted, violent claim on her. 'From your trembling, I take it you have been with very few men.'

'You're a sick bastard,' Ruby spat.

'One? Perhaps two? Was D'Arc to be your third?'

'Just let me go,' she began to sob, the truth discovered as her mask finally broke.

'Ruby… oh, Ruby… do you know what you are doing to me?' the man enunciated the words at a slow pace and deliberately so, as if he recited an old poem.

'I'll do anything, but let me go, please…'

'Could it be that you're joking with me?' he quizzed, followed by a yawn.

'Don't kill me… please…'

'What would you do to persuade me of that?'

'Anything you want.' Ruby regretted the words as they left her, but they fell from her lips like iron nails.

'Is that really true?' he pressed. 'Are you sure you would do anything?'

It was a question she did not want to pursue. From behind she heard the unscrewing of a bottle top; this was followed by a faint, sweet smell that reminded her of the candy shop on Arbuthnot Road. Ruby felt the hand grip the back of her head, twisting the hair in its fingers. She forced her head back so she could stare up at the ceiling. Then she saw him. Suddenly, her face was covered in a linen mask, his hand holding it tightly in place. Without time to move her head, Ruby could feel the vapours as she tried with every bone in her body not to breathe it in. Unable to hold it any longer, she gasped desperately for air as her lungs burst. The fumes from the linen filled her body and the world around her spun rapidly. She could see the blurred face of the man as his laughter faded. The darkness swept in like a flood current. Slowly, with each second, the world dimmed. Her sight grew dull until all the light faded. She could hear the man speaking, his words muffled.

'No…' she muttered, her voice dampened by the cloth that covered her face. Ruby dropped her head to the side. Her fingers loosened their grip on the chair.

'Sleep… sleep, my pretty girl,' the man coaxed as he undid her wrists and dragged her from the chair.

In one swift move, he dumped Ruby onto the table, her arms sprawled like a dead rag doll. Taking hold of the collar of her coat, he pulled her up the butcher's bench roughly until just her legs hung over the wooden edge. Holding the knife between a finger and his thumb, he began to methodically cut the coat from her. With great precision, he sliced the arms from cuffs to shoulder. As if a skilled tailor, he cut the front from the back of the coat, following the line of the seam.

Ruby breathed hard as the air rattled in her throat, feeling as if she was dying very slowly. The man pressed the linen to her mouth again until the groaning subsided. With one hand, he pushed up the long, tweed skirt and smoothed his fingers over her stocking-covered legs. His hand trembled as he cut the straps of the suspenders that held the stockings in place and then, like before, ripped the sides of her briefs and pulled them from her.

In her dream, Ruby was aware of him and how close he was to her. She could hear him moan as he stepped closer, pushing her legs apart as he undid the buttons on his trousers. He gulped like a fumbling pig.

'No… please…' she heard herself plead as she felt him pushing as hard as he could against her.

'Nicely… nicely…' the man gloated as he slowly forced himself onto her, her body unable to defend herself as he held her apart with brutal fingers.

Ruby curled her back instinctively as every muscle spasmed painfully. What he did felt distant, as if she were an onlooker. She endured each of his juddered movements as a stranger. They were laboured, savoured as he breathed hard. Her eyes opened as the chloroform ebbed away from her. She could see his face, he was grimacing as he moaned, moving back and forth with long strands of spit falling from his lips. In her half-dream she thought it was Jack D'Arc; the face was much the same, a dark brow covering blue eyes, thin lips, firm jaw. The man pushed harder, grunting each time whilst his hands moved clumsily across her body. He pulled at her clothes like a blind man until his fingers found her breasts.

Ruby reached back with her hand searching the wall until she found what she looked for with her fingers.

'Not here… not like this,' she pleaded. 'Let's wait.'

The man didn't speak. His head arched back as he looked up with a guttural moan in his throat and violently gripped her breasts.

Ruby grabbed the neck of the bottle on the shelf behind her. Pulling her arm forward, she smashed it into his face. The blow was swift and hard. The man stepped back as Ruby fell from the table. He held his face to stop the blood that oozed through his fingers and stood like a bleeding elephant. His trousers hung open, dangling on the red braces that crossed his wide shoulders. The flaps of his open shirt hung down. Getting to her feet, she whacked him again. The bottle smashed and splintered on the side of his head and it took a mere couple of seconds before the man fell to the floor. Ruby dropped the broken neck of the bottle.

At her feet was the knife, the long blade glinting in the light. Ruby bent down and picked it up from the floor. She stepped towards him, knowing what she must do. The man lay in a crumpled mess against the wall. He did not move.

'You deserve this, you bastard,' she enunciated her words as she began to make her way towards him, anxiety and adrenaline coursing through her. 'You didn't give the girls a chance. I'll make sure you won't do it again.'

Ruby stabbed at his plugtail. The blade cut through the skin as frenzied blows went deep. The man screamed long and loud. Lost in the echo, it sounded like he shouted her name. A hand suddenly grabbed her ankle and pulled her back as the man leapt for her. His hand squeezed her throat tightly, the fingers of his large hand gripped fully around her neck. He pressed her to the ground, his weight holding her down. Ruby could feel the warm, moist blood emanating from him. It seeped through her skirt and down her thigh as if it were her own. Another hand smothered her face. The soft, workless fingers grasped her lip, pulling hard.

'You feckin' bitch!' the man's voice boomed, his voice coarse as he dug his nails into her face. 'I'll feck you with that knife.'

Before the strength left her entirely, she stabbed the blade deep within his shoulder.

'Don't waste your breath,' Ruby spat in response as he groaned, puke escaping from him and dripping down onto her.

He sighed deep and sore as he slumped down and vomited again. Ruby pushed hard, letting the man slip from her and onto the cold stone floor. His eyes rolled to the back of his head as he tried to take a last look at Ruby.

Getting to her feet, she fell back against the table. Her eyes darted around the room as she attempted to grasp onto her surroundings. The man clutched the knife as he tried to pull it from his arm. Ruby could feel the fear rise in her chest as her heart beat, feeling as if it would burst. Trying to speak, the words left her mouth in frightened gasps. The man on the floor slowly pulled the knife from within him and began to push himself to his knees.

For the first time, Ruby noticed the fine suit and polished shoes. The man peered up at her.

'There's no way I will let you go.'

Ruby grabbed the chair. As he tried to stand, she smashed it down on him repeatedly. Again and again. Time and time, she hit him with all her fading strength. Standing like an ape with hunched shoulders, he pulled the chair from her. With one hand, he threw it against the wall.

Ruby stared at the man in disbelief. The blood dripped from his face and hands. He shivered, his posture and movements simian-like, as he tried to keep his grip on the knife.

'Keep away!' Ruby warned as she strived to think if she could push him from her path to the door.

'I'm going to kill you slowly,' the man murmured as he wiped the blood from his mouth. 'Then I will cut out your tongue from your mouth and fry it to eat.'

The man smirked, his swollen lip twitched as if he ached to release his laughter. Ruby saw his fingers tremble out of control. It was then that, without warning, he dropped the knife and looked down as if it was beyond what he could understand. He reached toward her with one hand like a frightened child who suddenly realised that life ended in death. Before she could step away, like a brute beast that had been fatally shot, he slumped to the floor.

[32]
HALF MOON STREET

Every taxicab that D'Arc tried to hail drove on; it was the time of night when the drivers in their hats and scarves seemed more interested in the hard beds of Clapham than picking up another fare to take them back north of Regent's Park. Continuing on hastily, he was soon away from Eaton Square. D'Arc followed the road beyond Buckingham Palace and along Piccadilly. The streets were empty, the night cold with a moonless, black sky. He thought this was how London would have been long before he was born. It echoed its emptiness like a cavern. The streetlights were out and stood like sentinels along the road. The only light was that which erupted from the doorways of the large houses that lined the roads. They cast long shadows into the street like the teeth of a gigantic whale. As he turned on to Half Moon Street, he noticed a girl on the corner. She wore a tasselled dress with no coat. When he drew nearer, she pulled the dress up higher to show more of her legs. Her face was cocaine-thin with mouth sores covered in powder. He thought that she looked as if she hadn't eaten in days.

'Business, Mister?' she asked, her voice like that of an innocent woman.

D'Arc reached into his pocket and felt the rim of a half crown.

'On a night like this, I don't think you could satisfy my desires,' he responded, his voice urgent as he pressed the coin into her open hand, eager to proceed onwards. 'Take it, eat...'

'Something wrong with me?' the girl shouted indignantly as he walked away. 'Not good enough for you? I'm clean, no pox.'

'Too busy,' D'Arc didn't bother turning before he yelled out his response, reassured to know that if he had felt so inclined to do her against an alley wall, she would at least be clean. 'The pursuit is on.'

As he walked on, a car passed by. D'Arc could see it was the police; the driver stared down at him as he rode the engine on the clutch. It carried on up the street, rattling over the sewer caps and then turning right onto Curzon Street. It didn't seem like a regular patrol. He knew the constables preferred to walk at night as they could hear and see far more as they hid in the shadows. It was what he had been taught, not that D'Arc had spent long on the streets. He had been allowed the occasional night shift away from the piles of crime reports and intelligence papers. These had filled the trays in his office to the point of overflowing. Names, places and overheard conversations all neatly sorted, were put into order. Mostly, they were concerned with Fenians and Communists. Even before the war there had been an Irish problem. Home rule had been something that they had wanted for a long time, and it was something that D'Arc found hard to disagree with. He had once spoken to a Fenian prisoner, who had been arrested for planning to blow up Paddington Station. The man had been well-spoken, articulate and proud. D'Arc had found his arguments compelling, well thought out and hard to disagree with.

'We are a proud people,' the man had exclaimed as he sipped the mug of tea that D'Arc had made for him. 'The British have been an army of occupation in a land that does not belong to them. One day they will realise that we are just a piece of rock in the Atlantic they want to get rid of.'

He thought the words just came to him from another time, but as he walked the empty pavement, they began to fire his thoughts. With each step he picked the pieces of the jigsaw until it all became suddenly and frighteningly very clear.

'Good grief...' he muttered. 'It can't be...' D'Arc stopped on the pavement and looked around in panic, his heartbeat picking up a pace. 'How stupid of me–why didn't I think of it?' he proclaimed to himself. From the corner of the next street, the long, black sedan crept along the pavement. D'Arc pinned his gaze on it as it got closer and closer before stopping completely. 'Good evening, Officers,' D'Arc greeted as two men in uniform stepped from the car and stood either side of him.

'You Jack D'Arc?' the smaller one said as he unclipped the flap of the holster on his belt.

'Is it commonplace for His Majesty's Constabulary to carry firearms?' D'Arc scrutinised, knowing the answer for himself anyway.

'Sometimes,' the other one replied. 'Chief Inspector Varney is looking for you.'

'Varney sent us to find you,' the smaller man added, his pride, albeit pointless, shining through. 'Get in the car.'

'Do I have a choice?' D'Arc wondered before turning to the smaller man, who began to slide the revolver from the holster. 'I take it that I do not,' D'Arc quipped as he stepped into the backseat of the car.

'Varney is waiting. He's had us looking all over town for you.'

'How was I found?' D'Arc queried innocently.

'Seems like you know how to upset the ladies,' the taller man chortled as he spoke. 'Some woman on Eaton Square rang Scotland Yard and we just had to search for you. A man was arrested at your house about half an hour ago,' the driver informed the man as he looked back at D'Arc.

'He was a wanted man going by the name of Mondo,' the other man replied, clipping the strap of the holster smugly.

'Do you know why he was arrested?'

'Varney wants to tell you himself,' the man answered as he continued to drive the car through the empty streets.

'Scotland Yard?' D'Arc asked as the car headed north away from the river.

The driver shook his head.

'Not too far... Varney said we had to take you to Hanover Square– thought you would like the joke.'

The car smelled of licorice and wood polish. With every movement the leather seats crunched uncomfortably, the solitary sound the only thing breaking the silence that the three men continued in for the rest of the way. Turning right and then left, the car silently slid on as if it would melt into the night. The driver would occasionally look back in his mirror, probably thinking he was being inconspicuous, but D'Arc knew that he was being looked at. It was as if the man wondered what it was about him that had caused such consternation.

'You famous?' the man finally broke the silence with his curiosity.

'Not particularly,' D'Arc shot back. 'I did your job once. Then I went to war.'

'This is Jack D'Arc, the famous private detective,' the other man's smug tone rattled D'Arc. 'I knew his father.'

It wasn't long before the car pulled into the tree-covered square. D'Arc could see Varney on the steps of a house in the corner. He leant against the white, stone door pillar and stared as the car approached. Varney turned up his collar and smoked a cigarette.

'Thought you might like this place. Jog the memory?' Varney prodded as he blew out a lungful of smoke. 'Do you remember the house?'

'It was once owned by my grandfather,' D'Arc nodded, remembering the day as a child when he had been taken through the door and into a small office upstairs to meet the man for the very first time.

'And you are here again. How strange the passage of time can be,' Varney answered as he put his hand on D'Arc and rubbed his shoulder. 'It's time for all this to end, Jack.'

'What?' D'Arc shot back in confusion. 'I didn't know anything had begun.'

'You are getting too close for comfort. Sometimes the truth has to stay hidden.'

'I thought you were a copper?' D'Arc pried. 'Without fear or favour?'

'That is a question of who you fear and where the favours come from,' Varney snorted out a laugh, almost coughing. 'You are certainly keeping me busy. I have orders from the Commissioner to arrest you.'

'For what?'

'Anything I like. Lady Finisterre is his close friend.'

'What have I done to her?'

'The Commissioner insists that you spend some time on remand until all this blows over. Class it as a holiday.'

'So why did you bring me here to tell me that?' D'Arc retaliated.

'I wanted to remind you of where you came from. You were one of us… your father was one of us. That must count for something,' Varney explained as he smoked the last of the cigarette, then threw it to the floor and stubbed it out with his foot.

'I know who the killer is,' D'Arc's stare was pinning Varney to his place as he spoke with precision and determination.

'So do I. Liza Rowe. I told you before.'

'The man has killed before and will kill again. Then where will your evidence be?'

'It's political, D'Arc. You don't know what is behind this.'

'The murder of four people and a ship full of munitions?' he answered.

'It's more than that, Jack. There are powers and principalities that run this town. The police are just a part of that. Sometimes we have to answer to people who ask us to do some difficult things.'

Varney nodded to the driver of the car and the man opened the window to hand Varney his revolver.

'This pistol was found at the scene of a murder last year. It can never be traced. It comes in handy when we have a problem to deal with.'

'Am I your problem?' D'Arc riposted as he looked for a way of escape.

'To some people you have become more than a problem. You are an annoyance that I have been asked to deal with. So, what's it going to be?'

Varney clicked the hammer of the pistol and watched the chamber turn slowly.

'Would you let the death of all those people go unsolved? Alice... the girls... the priest?' D'Arc trailed, thinking of grabbing the gun from Varney and running down the street.

'Don't make it difficult, Jack,' Varney's lips tightened in annoyance as he gritted his words out. 'Three days inside and all this will be over. In that time, I can sort out the mess. You owe it to the memory of your father.'

'I owe him nothing. He was a coward who took his own life and left me alone. In all these years I can never see anything else when I close my eyes but his bloated face, choked by the rope.'

'I brought you here because your grandfather was a thief. He made his money from crime. Took cash that had been stolen and washed it clean through his business. Your father found out and didn't have the guts to lock him up. Hookers, pimps and druggists paid for your pretty-boy education. Quite ironic, isn't it?'

'That's a lie!' D'Arc snapped. 'He was an honest man.'

'On the contrary... there is proof, all nicely locked away,' Varney countered. 'Your grandfather had many friends in the police who he helped along the way. Why do you think your life was made so easy?'

'What's to stop me going to the press with all of this?' D'Arc managed to argue back, yearning to snatch the gun from Varney and shoot him dead. 'Corruption is against the law.'

'Your pride... family honour... guilt?'

They were words that D'Arc knew to be true.

'What's your involvement with my grandfather?' he wondered.

'I protected him from those who would do him harm, and in return he helped me progress in ways that you would not understand,'

Varney's voice was proud and cocky as if what he had done had been a great privilege. 'Your grandfather was a good man.'

'I was taught to be cautious like an arrow from a bow, as it were. I now understand what you mean,' D'Arc started, 'but I know that he would have wanted you to honour the deaths and find the killer.'

'Perhaps he would, but these are muddy waters and right and wrong no longer exist.'

'But what is in your heart, is it not stirring to fight for the truth?' D'Arc referenced the Masonic oath. 'You will not speak evil of a companion, behind his back nor before his face, but will appraise him of all approaching danger, if in your power.'

They were words that Varney knew well. He clicked the hammer of the pistol and made it safe and then hid the weapon in his pocket.

'Do you joke with me, Jack D'Arc?' Varney spoke eerily. 'Who told you that truth?'

'A brother of ours in a place of light,' D'Arc shrugged, trying to remember the oaths in the book found by the bed of his grandfather.

'By what degree do you speak?' Varney's obvious shock on his face was as clear as day.

'The thirty-third, handed down with blood and fire,' D'Arc claimed, hoping his words sounded true. 'You owe me your honour and your help.'

Varney turned towards the man by the car and then to D'Arc. There was a change on his face. He stepped toward D'Arc and pushed back the fedora hat from his forehead.

'Say nothing of this,' he answered D'Arc through gritted teeth. 'Johnson... you drive... Portland Place.'

'Lord Tobias Hanthorn, of County Clare?' D'Arc raised an eyebrow. 'How did you know?'

'Deductive reasoning and meticulous investigation...'

[33]
PORTLAND PLACE

The cellar door opened with ease. Outside, the stairs were steep and overlaid with green carpet that was worn and tattered. Ruby walked painfully as the bruises ached on her thighs. The skin had been rubbed away and burnt like fire, and her coat was in tatters. What was left of the sleeves hung down like long dreads of matted hair. For some reason she held it taut across her chest, her blouse tied tightly to cover her breasts. They ached from where he had touched her, but she did not care. All she could think of was getting upstairs and finding a telephone. She knew she would call the police, tell them what had happened and wait for them. They would find the man in the cellar–perhaps he would be dead, she did not know. Ruby had left him in the darkness, his hands and feet bound in thick, medical tape. She had resisted the voices in her head that urged her to stab him again and cut from him that which had defiled her.

Taking hold of the brass handle, she pushed the door that led into the kitchen. Ruby halted, unsure if someone might be hiding from her. All she could think of was that this was the house of the killer. There could be an accomplice, someone else involved in the murders. If D'Arc were there he would know, Ruby thought. Her mind raced as she tried to picture him again. In those short passing days, she had come to know a man that had changed her life. She thought of his wry smile, and the way in which his thoughts leapt beyond her own as if he could read her soul.

As she stepped into the kitchen, Ruby paused and listened. The room was dark, with shadows of the window frames cast across the floor. The only light was that which came in from outside. The kitchen was below the height of the road, with the cellar deep below that, and in the corner was a dumbwaiter. A long rope hung down to pull the tray to the rooms above. On the wall was a row of brass service bells that hung silently. Ruby could feel the warmth from the stove on the outer wall. It crackled softly as the wood burned and gave the room a scent that reminded her of Christmas. A solitary apple lay on the edge of the table in the middle of the room. Instinctively, Ruby snatched it and slipped it into her pocket.

It was then that she touched the tip of the forgotten Derringer. There, deep within the folds of her coat, it lay undiscovered. She wrapped her fingers around the grip and squeezed it into her palm. It was warm, safe and calmed her breath.

Listening at the far door, she waited. There was no sound, no servants, nothing. Ruby wondered if she should shake the servant bells to see who would come. It was a frightening thought for her, so she proceeded to click the handle of the door. Outside was a short staircase clad in the same type of carpet. Ruby counted the treads as she slowly climbed, her hand gripping the small pistol.

Pushing open the door, she peered down the long hallway. It was tiled in marble and lit by a solitary lamp on a stone plinth by the large front door. She sensed the staircase going up to her right, hidden behind the wood panels. Hanging from the ornate ceiling was a vast chandelier. The droplet crystals hung like a thousand diamond chiroptera and sparkled in the light. Ruby slowly and cautiously made her way towards the door. A large brass key with a velvet cord was half turned in the brass lock.

'Am I being burgled?' the man's voice came as he stepped from the doorway of a room to her right, taking Ruby by surprise. 'I gave the staff the night off.'

Ruby froze and gripped the pistol even tighter. The man was dressed in a black evening suit with long tails. His dark hair was styled with macassar oil away from his face. A slight moustache etched the line of his lip. He towered over Ruby and smiled at her benignly.

'This ain't a burglary,' she answered, calmly trying to still her erratic breathing. 'Who are you?'

'Surely I should be the one who asks that?' the man answered as he took a cigarette from a silver box, put it to his lips and lit the end with a Lucifer.

'And this is your house?'

'It has belonged to my family for over a hundred years. I am just the beneficiary as long as I have blood in my veins,' he stared her down as he explained himself. 'You look as if you have been beaten. Perhaps I should make you some hot chocolate?'

His voice was soft and affectionate as if he were flirting with her.

Ruby pinned her eyes on him–he was obviously rich. The man seemed familiar, a fragrance that only a woman would notice hung around him like a shroud.

'It was you, wasn't it? You're the man from the séance,' Ruby pieced together, trying to make her voice sound stronger than her heart.

'I wondered if you would recognise me. What gave me away?' he sounded surprised.

'You killed the priest.'

'I am amazed by your deduction. How can you be sure?' he asked calmly as he regarded her up and down like a chameleon about to strike.

'Your cologne, it is ochre and lemongrass. Strange a man should wear such a fragrance. I smelled it the night of the séance and then in the church when I chased after you.'

'My goodness. You are just like Jack D'Arc,' he said as he leant against the doorframe. 'What have you done with my companion?'

'He's downstairs. I think he is dead,' she answered without hesitation.

'He should have killed you,' the man snickered. 'That was what he was supposed to do. I helped him tie you to the chair before I went for my walk. I didn't want to hear you scream as he cut you to pieces, so I went to take some air. You and Ruth were the only ones left.'

'You know who I am?' she failed to hide her surprise.

'Ruby Alder, the leader of the Forty Elephants.'

'Why do you want to kill us? What have we done to you?'

'You stupid woman, you have no idea. This isn't about your gang of thieves. It is not revenge for a long forgotten crime. Alicia confided in you a great secret. I have to make sure that secret dies with you,' he answered scornfully, as if he were a schoolmaster chiding a student.

'She never said a thing, Alicia wasn't like that. She never mentioned you,' Ruby stuttered out as she looked to the door and wondered if she could get there before him.

'Sadly, I can't take any chances, and you will not make it to the door before I kill you.'

'How did you know?' she pressed further.

'I am a hunter and I know my prey. From elephants and tigers to the smallest rat. They all look for the way of escape when they know they are cornered. All you have to do is watch the eyes.'

'And you kill people?' Ruby asked, feeling the trigger of the gun and getting ready to pull the Derringer from her pocket, aim it at his head and fire the bullet into his mouth.

'It is not for enjoyment and I have to say that I only killed the priest because my companion refused. He is very superstitious and thought that God would not look kindly on him for what he did,' the man replied excitedly, as if he didn't care telling Ruby what she wanted to know. 'My companion had his own reasons that I am sure Jack D'Arc would be able to explain. I paid him well and never thought a woman would undo him. Shame, really. He told me how he was looking forward to taking you and then cutting your throat.' The man looked at her expectantly as he retrieved the cigarette from his lips and threw it to the floor before squashing it with the toe of his shoe. 'Did he?'

Ruby knew what he meant. She could see it was important for him to know. It was written across his face as clear as the grimace that held his lips in place and creased his brow.

'He never got that far. Anyway, by the time I was done with him, it would have been impossible.'

Ruby lied. The man sounded like Haslem, her old beau. He always wanted to make her feel small and rob her of every ounce of self-esteem. She had learnt to lie to him, to challenge everything he said and turn back his wrath. This man was no different. She could see the disdain for her in his face and could sense his anger.

'Interesting. Out of them all, I reckoned you would be the easiest to kill,' the man answered casually. 'I should have realised that a gang such as the Forty Elephants must need a strong woman to lead them.'

'You seem annoyed that I am alive,' Ruby sassed.

'I will have to finish what he started,' the man gritted his teeth as he spoke, reaching into the jacket and pulling out a Bowie knife. He held it towards her, the blade pointing at her face. 'I suggest you go back down the stairs to the basement so we can start all this again.'

'Why should I do that?' Ruby countered, her fingers curling harder around the Derringer in her pocket.

'Because I don't want people to hear your screams and, besides, you may leave blood on the carpet.'

The man chuckled as he stepped towards her. Ruby pulled the gun from her pocket and pointed it at his head.

'I think not,' she answered as she clicked the hammer of the gun. 'You will let me walk from this place or I will shoot you.'

Ruby could hear her voice start to break. As she aimed the gun, she could see her hand tremble as she fought to keep it as still as possible.

'A Derringer, how pretty. I doubt you have the courage,' he scoffed, not moving. 'It is a hard thing to kill a man. I should know.'

'One step and I'll shoot you dead,' she threatened, her words spoken with each shaky breath.

'With that?' the man groaned out a half-laugh, half-sigh. 'I could kill you before you pull the trigger.'

Ruby could feel her finger close in on the small trigger.

'Don't tempt me.'

The sound of a car pulling up outside the house stopped the man in his tracks before he could reply. He turned to the door and then back to Ruby.

'It would appear I only have a limited time to achieve my ambitions,' he acknowledged simply as the pair of them heard the slamming of car doors. 'Put down the gun, it is of no use.'

'*Police! Open the door!*' the voice of Varney bellowed from outside, reinforced with the banging of his fist.

The man lunged at Ruby. She pulled the trigger, the hammer clicked… and then nothing. As she tried to fire again, the man slashed the trench knife across the back of her hand, causing the pistol to fall to the floor. With one hand, he grabbed her hair. 'You won't do that again!' he boomed as he took her by the throat and slammed her against the wall.

It was then that the front door burst open.

'Stay where you are, Hanthorn!' Varney warned as he raised his revolver and aimed it at the man.

'Get out or I will kill Miss Alder,' Hanthorn exclaimed, his tone dangerously vicious and lacking any hesitance as he held the dagger to her throat.

'We have you Hanthorn, whatever you do,' D'Arc alerted the man as he stepped into the house. 'You are under arrest for murder.'

'What makes you think it was me, Jack D'Arc? Powers of deduction?' he hollered, squeezing Ruby even tighter as he used her body as a shield.

'It was Lady Gabrielle, she told me about the death of her husband.'

'He was a weak man who killed himself. What has that got to do with me?'

'He was shamed into suicide because of what you did to him. They have all died because of your secret. Alicia Gabrielle and the priest.'

'I have no secrets,' Hanthorn defended himself. 'What secrets could kill a man?'

Varney stepped forward, pushing D'Arc out of the way. Behind him was the driver of the car.

'Put down the knife and let the girl go,' Varney demanded. 'It ends here.'

'Go away, you stupid man. Do you think that your superiors will convict me? I was protecting my house from an armed woman who broke in and killed my friend. That is what I will tell the court,' Hanthorn squeezed Ruby closer to him. 'Tell me what you have against me and I will let her go.'

'You tried to frame Lord Finisterre for murder. You stole his coat and ripped a button from it. Then you left it where it would be found by me,' D'Arc proceeded. 'You murdered a priest in cold blood.'

'That is for you to prove and me to deny. A rather elaborate way of indicting, my friend.'

'You went back to the alleyway and placed the button where you knew I would find it. The priest was murdered because you thought he would give away your secret.'

'It's true–he just told me...' Ruby exclaimed before he could slam his hand across her mouth.

'If you say so, D'Arc. Lord Finisterre will not testify against me and Ruby Alder will be dead before any of you can take a step.'

'Alicia was pregnant when she was murdered, did you know that?' D'Arc interrogated further. 'That is the real reason why she was killed. Would you have your friend go to the gallows?'

'You were set up, Mister D'Arc. Finisterre knew what would be asked of him. It was a matter of honour. Did he tell you it was me?'

D'Arc moved slowly inch by inch from the doorway. He thought before he answered as he stared at Hanthorn.

'It was Elizabeth Finisterre, the woman you love. I could see the jealousy on her face. Monty Finisterre was the father of the child that

Alicia carried and he would have been the grandfather, isn't that right? Lord Gabrielle killed himself, not because of being bankrupt or the shame of helping the enemy. It was because he could no longer live with the guilt that Alicia was pregnant by her real father.'

'The first rule of crime; don't have an affair with the wife of the man you have cheated. He was a fool and thought he could get away with it. Eddie Gabrielle couldn't father a child, but he never knew it. Elsa Gabrielle shopped around. None of her children were his. She picked the youngest, fittest of those who looked like her husband, and got them to sire a child.'

'When Alicia Gabrielle turned up, you even slept with her. You couldn't allow Finisterre to have her to himself. Everything he had you wanted: his money… his lover… his wife. You met Alicia at the séance of Madame Baphomet and then you seduced her, knowing she carried his child, because he told you. You went to the séance again and I saw you there.'

'I paid Alicia three hundred pounds, the price she asked for. She told me she could tell me my future. I got her drunk and she told me more than the future,' Hanthorn cackled as he held Ruby closer to him.

'And you gave her the key to this house?' D'Arc wondered aloud.

'My first mistake. Passion clouds the mind. Finisterre would meet her here so Elizabeth wouldn't find out. It suited me; I knew I could be alone with Elizabeth. Of course, I told her everything and it made her want me more. That, Mister D'Arc, is what passion does to you.'

'Thankfully, passion is not something that I have to endure,' D'Arc answered as he watched Hanthorn intently, looking for some weakness in the man.

'And you stabbed Alicia to death and cut out her heart?' Varney urged.

'No, Inspector. Not Hanthorn,' D'Arc corrected, his voice soft as he went on to explain. 'He paid an accomplice to kill Alicia and the others. The only one that Hanthorn murdered was Father Tyrone.'

'Right again, Mister D'Arc, but my accomplice killed because he wanted to and not because he was being paid.'

'Max Coburg killed her, didn't he?' D'Arc searched for confirmation as he held Varney back with his hand.

Hanthorn let out a gruff laugh again, pulling Ruby against the wall and pressing the dagger into her throat.

'Miss Alder was to be killed tonight and by a quirk of fate, she has turned the tables on me. I am beginning to believe there is a God of justice who conspires against me. Max is in the cellar. I think she may have killed him.'

'He tried to kill me,' Ruby gasped.

'So it really was Max Coburg?' D'Arc pressed.

'How ever do you do it, D'Arc? You amaze me.'

'You met him in Atlantic City and I presume that is where you told him of your problem.'

'A chance meeting. Coburg was only too happy to oblige. He said he had learnt his craft from a madman. You can imagine his surprise when I told him the name of the victim.'

'Whatever you say will be held against you. There are witnesses,' Varney aimed the pistol at Hanthorn as he informed the man in front of him.

'I care not, Chief Inspector. The fates have been predicted this time and I have nothing to lose. We are taught how life will begin, but never how it will end,' Hanthorn spoke regretfully, his voice dulled with anguish as he gripped Ruby tightly. 'I consider this my penance and believe you should know the truth. Friends have been deceived and boundaries crossed. I work for the government, Room Forty; I report directly to Churchill, we are beyond the law.'

'But there is more than the death of a child and its mother. Alicia also knew that you allowed a ship full of munitions to be seized by the Republicans.'

'Every army needs weapons,' Hanthorn answered.

'You did it on the instructions of someone in the government,' D'Arc insisted.

'We were supporting the balance of power in a civil war. Sometimes you have to help the underdog even if it is your enemy,' Hanthorn answered reluctantly. 'There is no such thing as right and wrong when you are at war.'

'If only that were true,' D'Arc replied with a shrug of his shoulders.

Varney moved closer, holding the gun towards Hanthorn.

'Stay back, Chief Inspector. I will kill her.' Hanthorn pushed the knife so that the blade pressed deep against her skin.

'Just put the knife down and let her go,' Varney insisted.

'I will not hang for this. It is beyond the power of the police. Such a scandal would bring down the government; they would not allow it to happen,' Hanthorn pulled Ruby with him towards the door of a room as he fought back insistently.

'Can you live with the shame of the world knowing that you are a murderer?' D'Arc pressed with a raised eyebrow as he stared at Ruby, willing her to fight.

'It is a question of what is the greater good. You were not born for such things. Honour and pride mean nothing to men like you. Finisterre and I were at the same school, our families were friends. We were born for this.'

'To murder?' D'Arc shot back as he noticed Ruby smile at him momentarily.

'If need be,' he said with a sombre voice.

'Then we shall leave you and you can go your own way,' D'Arc replied.

'What?!' Varney butted in, his voice astonished.

'Put down the gun, Chief Inspector. We cannot prove this case. Hanthorn will go free, we only have his confession and that is worthless.'

'What about the girl?' Varney asked him.

'I take it you will let her go free?' D'Arc posed the question as if it were an order. 'You have no use for her now and, if the government is on your side, then who are we to argue with that?'

'At last you understand,' Hanthorn hummed.

His words were cut short. Without warning, Ruby struck Hanthorn in the groyne with her jewelled fist. Biting his hand, she then stamped down on his foot. The man dropped the knife, though Ruby wasted no time before slamming him back against the parlour door. D'Arc leapt towards him, grabbing onto the sleeve of his jacket. Hanthorn pushed Ruby against Varney and the constables. Together they fell back against the wall. Without hesitation, Hanthorn dived through the parlour door. D'Arc got to his feet just as the door was slammed in his face. He heard the lock turn.

'Quickly,' Varney exclaimed, 'put the door in!'

His men slammed their shoulders against the wooden panels and then kicked at it with their dull, leather boots.

'He will not get away!' Varney screamed as the sound of shattering glass came from the street.

'The window,' D'Arc mumbled as he gave chase. 'He's jumped to the street!'

[34]
OXFORD CIRCUS

As D'Arc stumbled down the steps to the pavement outside, he could see Hanthorn running south towards the Langham Hotel. Even at that hour of the morning its lights shone into the square. Giving chase, D'Arc ran hurriedly through the empty streets. Ahead of him, Hanthorn paced on faster than D'Arc thought a man of that age could sprint. Soon they were running towards Oxford Circus and ahead, D'Arc could see that Hanthorn was gaining distance. When D'Arc looked again, he was gone–the street was empty, and the gates to the underground station were open.

'There!' shouted the old paper vendor setting up his stall for the morning on the corner of Regent Street. 'The man ran into the station.'

D'Arc was soon running down the long stairways and through the tiled halls towards the lower platforms in the half-light of the underground station. Ahead he could hear clattering footsteps; Hanthorn was running hard. As D'Arc crossed the bridge across the line, he looked down–the man ran along the platform. D'Arc pushed through the gap in the wall and jumped to the station below.

The platform was empty and eerily black as a late winter afternoon. The only light was from a far corridor, and it shone bright onto the southbound platform. Hanthorn stopped by the entrance to the tunnel. Far in the distance, the sound of the first morning train rattled towards the station. Looking back, he glared at Jack D'Arc, his vicious stare fixated on him. Both men panted, their breath short, their lungs burning.

'It's not worth it. You were right in thinking I would never be convicted. I am a Government Agent – a protected man. Don't

191

think you can take me,' Hanthorn spat each word as he tried to regain his breath.

'Give yourself up. If you are as you say, then nothing will come from it.'

'There is always that chance my masters could betray me. I will not hang from a rope, never.'

'Tell me one thing that I have to know,' D'Arc asked impatiently. 'How did you think you would ever get away with this?'

'It was planned that Coburg would kill you. The police would have been waiting for him. After he had committed the murder, Coburg would have been shot dead. It was all arranged. There are powers at work that you will never understand.'

'Why did you want me dead?' D'Arc asked.

'You still don't understand, do you?' Hanthorn burst out. 'You were set up for this. Everything was planned from the start. We needed you to investigate the crime. The police would have swept the matter under the carpet. It took a man like you to find Coburg, but I never thought you would find me. Coburg was to take the blame for everything. Where did I go wrong?'

Hanthorn laughed as he leant against the tiled wall below a large poster with torn edges advertising baking powder.

'Lady Elsa Gabrielle,' he answered slowly, as if her name would mean everything to Hanthorn and give the reason for his failure.

'As simple as that?' he answered. 'And you know the reason?'

'Money and love,' D'Arc replied simply.

'So you know everything?'

'Yes.'

'And you won't let me go?'

'No.'

'Walk away, Mister D'Arc. Walk away and forget about all of this.'

'Never.'

D'Arc slowly put his right hand into the pocket of his jacket and slipped his fingers into the cool fit of the steel knuckleduster. He squeezed his hand tight on the metal as he pulled it from his pocket.

'Don't be stupid. I am a trained soldier and what are you?' Hanthorn taunted him.

'You may never stand before a court, but I will ensure justice is served,' D'Arc answered as he strode towards him.

Hanthorn hesitated, eyeing up D'Arc and then switching his gaze to the platform opposite. The train rattled closer as the air rushed through the station. It blew the debris of discarded paper into spirals of dirt as it sped closer.

'This is not the time or the place for such things as this,' Hanthorn shook his head before taking a sudden leap from the platform to the track.

'Don't be so—' D'Arc shouted as he followed after, landing on the man and knocking him to the gravel track.

Hanthorn kicked back, hitting D'Arc square in the face. He fell to the ground, narrowly missing the middle rail. The ground trembled as the train approached. The wind blew like a tornado, swirling the stones at his feet. Hanthorn stood quickly, towering over D'Arc.

'This could have been so different,' Hanthorn tutted as he turned to see the white light from the train engulf the tunnel. As it sped towards him, he laughed and held out his arms as if he awaited his fate. 'Alicia said this would be the way,' he taunted. 'I didn't believe her.'

The roaring of the train drowned his words. All around the ground continued to shake. A stark, white light blinded them. There was the sudden squeal of the brakes. The train snatched Hanthorn from his feet as D'Arc pressed himself to the ground. The last thing he heard was the dull thud and the cracking of glass. All was black. The oil fumes and smoke that billowed from the carriages as they passed above him were overwhelming.

Jack D'Arc didn't hear Ruby scream as Chief Inspector Varney held her back from the platform. The body of Tobias Hanthorn, embedded in the front of the train stopped before them. It slid from its place and for a moment dangled from the broken glass then, as the train juddered, dropped to the track.

'It's Hanthorn,' Varney said to reassure her that D'Arc could still be alive.

Ruby stood in the swirling mist and smoke. The cavernous platform echoed with her screaming.

[35]
JACK D'ARC

Jack D'Arc had slept fitfully. His face was swollen and bruised. In the darkness of his dreaming, he could still smell the smoke and oil that filled his nostrils and choked the back of his throat. Far away he could hear the noises of life, they seemed humdrum and mundane. Cars, children and the occasional cart and horses all mellowed into one long, low, never-the-matter sound. D'Arc gripped to the final moments of sleep and felt them fading quickly. Opening one eye, he looked out from where he lay. The familiarity of his bedroom in Chalcot Crescent pleased him. Everything appeared just as it should be. One by one he counted the books on the shelf. Not one was out of place. The Etruscan ornament of the head of a God was on the fireplace. So too was the small statuette of a galloping horse. The curtains were drawn and yet he could see daylight. The sun touched the outside of the back window and, from the way in which it crept into the room, he could tell it was the afternoon. D'Arc moved slowly, feeling the pain in every sinew. He slipped his arm beneath the blankets and checked the bones of his legs, relieved nothing was broken. He lay back and tried to breathe, though the pain in his chest suggested to him that at least one rib had been fractured. He was naked. Someone had carefully undressed him and washed his body. D'Arc could smell the soap on his skin. It was not his usual Lux and was obviously French, but this, he did not mind. As he turned in the bed, the door to the room opened.

'It's three o'clock. I brought you breakfast,' Ruby said as she placed a tray of tea and toast on the bed next to him and took the folded newspaper from under her arm.

194

'Did you–' he trailed off in question as he lifted the sheet and looked within.

'Yes. You didn't complain and were no different to any other man. Varney brought you back here. He said it would be the best place. They didn't want you to go to hospital–said there would be too many questions. You made *The Evening Standard*. Front page.'

Ruby handed him the folded newspaper and then poured the tea.

D'Arc analysed the front page and then read it out loud in a sardonic, theatrical voice.

'Lord Tobias Hanthorn was tragically killed when he fell from the underground platform at Oxford Circus this morning. Despite the brave efforts of Private Detective Jack D'Arc, he could not be revived. The police have said this was a tragic accident and thanked Mister D'Arc for his brave efforts.' D'Arc placed the paper down and took a glimpse at Ruby. 'Is this the kind of life you want?'

'Varney telephoned. He said that was how it was to be. He told me to tell you that they would deny everything and make you look a fool.' Ruby didn't seem to be disappointed.

'And you have no problem with that? Hanthorn got away with the crime and his reputation is intact?' D'Arc flinched as the first sudden throb of pain creased his forehead.

'He's dead. Can't get more punished than that. The Final Judgment.'

'What of Max Coburg?'

'He is alive. They took him to the hospital at Pentonville Prison. Varney said they had enough to charge him for the murders of Alicia and the others. Varney also apologised–he said you were right all along and that you were a smug bastard.'

'Just a smug bastard?' D'Arc asked mockingly as he pushed himself up the bed and felt the pain shoot through his spine.

'He actually said you were a *fucking smug bastard* who was lucky to be alive and if you ever get in his way again he is going to kill you himself,' Ruby recited as she handed him a teacup that rested precariously on a china saucer. There were heavy footsteps and then a sharp knock at the bedroom door. 'You have a visitor–the Commissioner. Said he didn't want to wait.'

'Good to see you are still alive, D'Arc,' the Commissioner greeted as he stepped into the room in full dress uniform, his hat pinned tightly under his left arm.

'According to Hanthorn, I was next to be murdered and you would have covered it up.'

The Commissioner looked at Ruby before studying D'Arc further.

'I hoped this would be a private conversation?' he asked not wanting her in the room.

'Miss Alder is now my assistant. You can speak in front of her. She is most confidential, especially in the presence of the police. It comes from her former occupation,' D'Arc answered.

'I am not used to discussing matters of national importance in front of the criminal classes,' he replied curtly.

'I would suspect Miss Alder is far more honest than anyone involved in this sordid business. Tell me what you have to say and then you can find your own way out.'

'It is an important matter,' the man's fist and jaw clenched as he spoke the words slowly.

'You have come to tell me what I am to say and what evidence I shall give.'

'I am glad you are already ahead of me. Now that Lord Hanthorn is dead, his name is of no importance in this matter.'

'And if I said it was?' D'Arc asked.

'Then you would become an enemy of the state and we would have to take action,' the Commissioner answered, devoid of emotion, his eyes cold as steel. 'The official story will obviously differ from the truth. You will be seen as a sleuth and a hero. When Coburg is convicted, there could even be a job for you in Room Forty.'

'A place full of liars and murderers like Tobias Hanthorn?'

'The heart of our secret service. Hanthorn was my close friend. The man was serving his country; Varney should have arrested you as I asked and this would never have happened.'

'Did you know it was Hanthorn who was behind the killer?' Ruby asked, opening the curtains and allowing the fading sun to fill the room.

'That is of no consequence.'

'And Elsa Gabrielle, will she be arrested?' D'Arc asked.

'No. Lady Gabrielle will move to Nice once the trial is over. Alicia was a very rich girl and Lady Gabrielle is the beneficiary of her estate.'

'The money left to her by Lord Gabrielle? I thought he was bankrupt?' D'Arc's tone showcased his discomfort.

196

'The Prime Minister decided that it would only be right to pay the family what they had lost in the tragic incident of *The Princess Matilda*. Lady Gabrielle knew of this some weeks ago.' The Commissioner looked at Ruby and then again to D'Arc. 'You won't let me down, will you, Jack?'

[36]
OLD BAILEY

It had rained for most of October. The mornings were as drab and darkened as night and a northern gale had stripped the leaves from the trees along Primrose Hill. The grass of Regent's Park had been frosted for three mornings that week. Frozen diamonds of hail lined the sides of the road and lay on the ice-covered puddles of dirty rainwater. There had been no fog for all of that month. London had been cleansed of the dirt and smog, and it made a change for Jack D'Arc to see the swirling clouds that blew across the sky. As he stood on the steps of the Old Bailey, D'Arc wondered if it would snow. The air smelled of Christmas and had a chill that crisped the dew at the tip of his nose. Stepping inside, he walked the long, ornate corridor with its paintings of angels and stood outside the courtroom. His timing was perfect. It was as if somehow he had heard the calling of the Honourable Sir Marcus Sheridan through the thick oak doors of Court One.

'Calling Jack Henry D'Arc,' the usher shouted down the empty corridor that was more like the anteroom of an Italian cathedral than a court of law. As he spoke, he swished the long, black robe around his arm as if a Roman pontiff.

D'Arc stiffened himself and walked through the open door and into the courtroom. He had been there many times before but the sombre wood that lined the walls and starkness of the white-painted ceiling gave it the appearance of the crematorium in Golders Green. Making his way through the sullen faces that packed the court, D'Arc stepped into the witness box. He paused before he swore the oath, the words coming from his lips as if he recited a well-known portion of

Shakespeare. D'Arc had often wondered if he should affirm his oath rather than swear. No one had ever asked if he believed in God and he wondered if he could be held to account for the lies he knew he was about to disclose. Something nagged in his mind, a still, small voice urging him to tell the truth. He looked around the court. All were before him, staring hopefully and with curious eyes. He looked at each one in the long pause as the prosecuting barrister leafed through the papers, to the obvious annoyance of the Honourable Marcus Sheridan. The judge sat regally in the chair above D'Arc. He looked meagre-framed and lost within the folds of the red robes and full wig. He sniffed his nose like an oversized spaniel as he eyed D'Arc with a wary glance.

D'Arc looked at the faces: Ruby Alder, Varney, Madame Baphomet, Crowley, Lady Gabrielle, Lord Finisterre and finally, wrists strapped in iron, Max Coburg. They all looked expectant as if he were the last one to perform. Ruby tried to smile at him as their eyes met. He could see she looked worried, intimidated and anxious.

It was the sight of Max Coburg standing on his feet and gripping the rail that sent a slight shudder down his spine. D'Arc thought the man looked like a frightened animal. He could see he was panting his breath, his face still scarred from the beating that Ruby had given to him in the cellar of the house. Ruby had been vague on the details as to what had happened to her. She had dismissed it as if it were a Saturday night scuffle in the backroom of the Elephant and Castle. Chief Inspector Varney had managed to keep her from giving but the slightest morsel of evidence to the court. D'Arc had read the account on the way to court in the back of the taxicab, and what had been reported in the *Evening Standard* was certainly not the truth. Whatever had happened to her, she wanted to keep it from him and that, he had to respect.

D'Arc glanced towards Judge Sheridan. The man smiled at him as if he too was aware as to what was to be said. It was as if he were just an actor about to give his lines that would fall on the ears of the deaf.

'When did you first realise it was Coburg who was the killer?' the barrister asked, his lips tightly pursed as if to keep in his teeth.

'When I saw the body of Alicia Gabrielle. She had been murdered in a style that was familiar to me. In 1919, a woman in Paris had been killed in exactly the same way. And there were reports of similar murders in America that have gone undetected.'

'And you think Coburg is responsible?' the man asked without looking at D'Arc, as he read from the mass of papers on the desk before him.

'Max Coburg was in Paris and Atlantic City. He slaughtered his ex-wife and her friends because he thought they would go to the police and accuse him of the Paris murder,' D'Arc answered, looking eye-to-eye with the judge. 'He had a motive and the opportunity.'

'Liar! Tell them the truth!' Coburg barked. 'It was not me. Hanthorn killed the priest.'

'Are you telling us the truth?' asked Judge Sheridan as he poised his quill pen, ready to write the answer.

'All I am certain of is that Max Coburg is the murderer. He killed Alicia Gabrielle and her companions–she knew that Coburg was back in London. They had seen each other once at a club in Soho. Coburg knew the only person who could send him to the gallows was Alicia. He wrongly thought she had told her friends about the murder in Paris, so they had to die to cover the deceit.'

'Tell them everything, D'Arc, tell them everything!' Coburg yelled as the defending counsel got to his feet. 'Tell them about Hanthorn.'

'My client is adamant that a conspiracy has taken place against him. What do you say to that?' the man shouted in a voice that carried theatrically to the back of the courtroom.

'*Order!*' snarled Sheridan as he slammed the pen on the desk and banged his fist. 'Do you forget where you are?'

The man bowed as if a scolded dog at the feet of its master.

'The law conspires to defeat wickedness and has to be upheld at all costs. The facts are plain to see. Max Coburg murdered Alicia Gabrielle to cover the truth. That is all I know.' D'Arc lowered his head and looked at the old, ragged Bible that lay on the sloping shelf of the witness box. He slowly read the word '*Holy*'… it was a word etched in gold leaf and stood out from the faded black leather cover. He could feel the knot twist in his stomach. D'Arc knew what it meant, a word said by his father night after night in the prayers he would say over him in the small room at the top of the house before he went to sleep.

'*Holy… Holy… Holy Lord… Defend us from all the perils and dangers of this night…*'

He thought of his father, he could see his face and hear his words. It was as if they were together again. D'Arc steadied his hand against the witness box.

200

'I have a question,' the defending counsel said in a chastened voice. 'Are you an honest man?'

The words took D'Arc by surprise.

'Pardon?' he asked the man directly.

'Are you honest?' the man repeated himself, as if he knew something to the contrary that had been hidden from the light.

D'Arc struggled to think. It was not a question that he did not expect to be asked. Yet the words of the answer that he had so meticulously rehearsed were now forgotten. Somehow the answer had been lost, spoken over by the voice of another. He heard his father speaking in his head. He said one word over and over: *Holy.*

'I am so sorry, what was the question?' D'Arc shook the melancholy from his head as the apology fled him.

'I question your honesty, Mister D'Arc,' the advocate gritted out impatiently as his gown opened to reveal a gold fob chain that hung across a fine, silk waistcoat.

D'Arc looked stunned. He stared at the judge and then at Ruby. Lifting a hand, he wiped his lips as he thought of what to say.

'Honestly? You would like me to speak honestly?' D'Arc pressed and then went on. 'You ask about conspiracy as if it would lessen the guilt of the man before us. I will tell you the truth and the jury will then decide.'

Varney leant forward as if he would leap to his feet and stop D'Arc from speaking just as Coburg stepped back and sat on the bench, his hands clasped in tight fists. The courtroom waited as D'Arc observed his surroundings, the silence broken by the sounds of the street.

Judge Sheridan eased slowly forward and spoke to him quietly. As he spoke, he pulled back the cuffs of his red coat and then pushed back the frame of the spectacles onto his nose.

'What you are about to say could alter the course of legal history and trust in the government,' he said in a voice that only D'Arc could hear.

'You cannot prompt a witness,' the advocate objected.

'I asked him to continue, and that will be for your benefit, Mister Ross,' Sheridan snarled as he pointed the quill at the man, swiftly turning back towards D'Arc. 'Think, Mister D'Arc...' The judge again whispered.

D'Arc paused in his reply.

'There is no conspiracy. I am satisfied that I know who killed Alicia Pringle and all the reasons for it. They may never be known in this courtroom,' D'Arc pointed to Max Coburg before continuing, 'but that man cut out her heart and the child she carried.'

It was as if everyone in the room gasped together.

'My God...' muttered the foreman of the jury. 'How could you?'

'He cooked the heart and left it in the apartment where he had killed Kitty Fallance and Lisa Rowe, after he had raped his victims.'

'*Enough!*' screamed the advocate as he held up his hand to silence D'Arc. 'No further questions.'

'Is the truth too much?' D'Arc shouted back with a confident and sharp voice. 'He will not be convicted by my words but by his actions.'

Ruby Alder stood and looked at him. Chief Inspector Varney grabbed her hand and pulled her to her seat. 'This is not the place,' his voice was gruff as he squeezed her hand tightly. 'That is enough to see him hang.'

On the flight of stone steps outside the court, D'Arc and Ruby Alder stood together. The clouds had cleared and a late afternoon sun tried in vain to reach the street below the leaded roofs above. Ruby paced up and down as they waited and pulled the fur collar of the long camel coat around her tightly.

'Are you going to wait for the jury to give its verdict?' she asked D'Arc, as he stood under the arched entrance and admired the plasterwork on the ceiling above.

'There is no point,' he answered without shifting his gaze. 'Coburg is guilty and Judge Sheridan will order him to be hanged.'

'Does that bother you?' she urged.

'Intently, but what was I to do?' D'Arc shrugged. 'If we had not agreed to say what they wanted, we would have ended up dead, I am sure of it. I have long suspected that Room Forty has been responsible for many things.'

'We could have gone to the press.'

'They have the newspapers in their pockets and the police. We could have done nothing. Hanthorn is dead and will not trouble us again.'

'But why did they really die?' Ruby asked him, knowing there was more to the truth than he had ever disclosed to her.

D'Arc didn't have to answer. Walking towards the doorway was Lady Gabrielle. She crossed the marble floor like a swan reflected in the cold water of a vast lake. Her long skirts, overlaid with a hunting coat, swirled as she walked. Around her neck draped the pelt of a dead fox.

It hung its shameful head across her laced shoulders in a fixed scowl. A silver, raven clip held it to the collar of her tweed coat. The woman was dressed for winter, her matching fur hat pulled tightly to her head. By her side was Lord Finisterre. D'Arc could see he had lost weight. His face was pinch-thin, the skin of his jowls sagging across his jaw. The man looked tired, with dark rings that circled his eyes.

'I have the money I owe you, Mister D'Arc,' she began as she unlinked her arm from Finisterre and searched for an envelope within her pocket.

'It is not needed,' he answered as he stepped into her path, making sure she could go no further.

'I insist. It was I who got you involved in this sad saga and you need to be paid for your troubles,' Lady Gabrielle answered with a wry smile as she looked at Finisterre. 'One thousand pounds, I think you will find that is what I owe you.'

'But the case was not solved to my satisfaction,' he answered as he pulled the cuff of his shirt from the sleeve of his jacket.

'The jury have agreed, I have just come from the court. Max Coburg will hang,' she answered, her words heavy as if they were no reward.

'I have to say that at first I didn't realise who had killed your daughter,' D'Arc started as Lady Gabrielle handed him a thick, wad-filled manila envelope.

'Max Coburg... just as you said,' she answered.

'If only that were really the case,' he stared into her eyes as he spoke his truth.

'What do you mean?' Lady Gabrielle asked as Finisterre tried to pull her away without his intentions being seen.

'Your daughter was murdered by many people and for many different reasons,' D'Arc replied, not moving his glare from her.

'I have just spent three days listening to the evidence, Mister D'Arc, and I heard no other names mentioned,' interrupted Lord Finisterre.

D'Arc turned his head like an automaton.

'Lord Finisterre, I am sorry to hear that your wife left you and moved back to the country. I hope it was nothing to do with what I said that night.'

'You are a bastard, D'Arc,' Finisterre muttered.

'And the woman you are with is a murderer,' he answered as he drew his breath. 'Not only did she murder your lover, but also the child she carried. Has Lady Gabrielle confessed to you that she and Max Coburg were lovers? Isn't that why Alicia left him?'

'They argued,' Lady Gabrielle said, her voice weak as if taken by surprise.

'We don't have to listen to this,' Finisterre cut in as he again tried to pull her away.

'I want to know what he has to say. I have paid him well,' Lady Gabrielle swallowed hard and squeezed the gloves she carried in her hand.

'I ask you this, Lord Finisterre. Did Lady Gabrielle not encourage you in seeing Alicia when you told her she was back in London?' D'Arc asked.

Finisterre looked at Elsa Gabrielle and then to D'Arc.

'How did you know?' she asked.

'Coburg, Hanthorn and you each had a motive to kill Alicia. I soon realised that you, Montague Finisterre, told Lady Elsa where Alicia was living. But, you did not know that Lady Elsa was having an affair with Max Coburg. At a chance meeting with Tobias Hanthorn, it was Lady Elsa who told him of the concerns she had over her daughter. She was the one who informed him that Coburg would be willing to solve the problem. Lady Gabrielle knew that Hanthorn had a weakness and that, if found out, he would be disgraced. It was Hanthorn who, after the death of Lord Gabrielle, persuaded the Prime Minister to pay the money for the loss of the arms shipment. Suddenly Alicia was a wealthy woman and she didn't even realise. That was kept from her and if Alicia was dead, then Lady Gabrielle would inherit the money... isn't that correct?'

Lady Elsa Gabrielle took a deep breath and raised her head.

'Speculation, Mister D'Arc. You have no proof.'

'I have all the proof I need to see you hang. Your daughter was murdered so you would inherit the money. Your husband had cut you from the will when he realised you had been unfaithful to him so many times. Even though Alicia was not his child, she was all he ever had.'

'But that is just a fanciful thought,' she answered. 'It was Max Coburg who killed her and not me.'

'Coburg was an instrument of her death. He acted out of malice and fear. He wanted her dead so that she could not tell anyone about what happened in Paris. He was only too willing to do the job for you,' D'Arc replied. 'Murder often satisfies the desires of more than one person. You all have what you want.'

'And what of Tobias Hanthorn, what reason did he have?' she asked.

'Simple,' D'Arc quipped. 'Hanthorn was a spy for the government. It had been him who had arranged the stealing of the munitions from *The Princess Matilda*. He had to keep that a secret and would do anything to stop her speaking of it.'

'Hanthorn was an honourable man,' Finisterre sneered.

'He was so honourable that he also had a dalliance with Alicia behind your back. He gave her the key to his house so that not only she could meet you, but him also.'

'You liar. He was my friend.'

'A friend who also slept with your wife.'

'So what will you do with your speculation?' Monty Finisterre asked cockily. 'Elsa and I were about to start a life together in Nice. Is there a fee to keep your silence?'

D'Arc looked at Ruby Alder for a brief moment. She stood behind him as if he would protect her from them.

'My silence is free, but you will live with the curse of this crime until you are both dead.'

'And then we shall be judged,' answered Lady Gabrielle solemnly as she again pushed the envelope towards D'Arc. 'Take it, Mister D'Arc. I insist.'

D'Arc held the envelope in his hand and then passed it to Ruby. Ripping open the top, she looked inside at the crisp, white bank notes.

'So is this the end of the matter for us?' Finisterre asked. 'Or will it become the reason for some future blackmail?' he eyed Ruby as he spoke.

'We are detectives, Lord Finisterre, not criminals...' Ruby trailed off in a sombre yet soft voice as she hooked her arm into that of Jack D'Arc and together they began to walk away. 'You will never see us again.'